W9-BZN-850

3/17

The Sisters of Blue Mountain

Also by Karen Katchur

The Secrets of Lake Road

The Sisters of Blue Mountain

KAREN KATCHUR

THOMAS DUNNE BOOKS

NEW YORK ☙ ST. MARTIN'S PRESS

THOMAS DUNNE BOOKS.
An imprint of St. Martin's Press.

THE SISTERS OF BLUE MOUNTAIN. Copyright © 2017 Karen Katchur. All rights reserved. Printed in the United States of America. For information, address St. Martin's Press, 175 Fifth Avenue, New York, N.Y. 10010.

www.thomasdunnebooks.com
www.stmartins.com

The Library of Congress Cataloging-in-Publication Data
is available upon request.

ISBN 978-1-250-06682-4 (hardcover)
ISBN 978-1-4668-7471-8 (e-book)

Our books may be purchased in bulk for promotional, educational, or business use. Please contact your local bookseller or the Macmillan Corporate and Premium Sales Department at 1-800-221-7945, extension 5442, or by e-mail at MacmillanSpecialMarkets@macmillan.com.

First Edition: April 2017

10 9 8 7 6 5 4 3 2 1

For Natasha and Annika

ACKNOWLEDGMENTS

Mountain Springs is a fictional town built around a real dam located in the Slate Belt of eastern Pennsylvania. Thank you to the members of the Facebook page You Knew You Grew Up in the Slate Belt If . . . for answering all of my questions pertaining to the mountains, dam, and the surrounding area. For creative purposes, a few changes have been made with regard to the geography and history of the location. Any and all errors are my own.

I spent many hours researching several topics that were essential to the plot—snow geese migration, winterkill, and dredging of dams and lakes. If there are any errors in the science behind any of the phenomena, once again, please accept they are my own.

Thank you to Renee Drago of the Northampton County Archives and Ann Binotto of the Northampton County Coroner's Office for answering questions with regard to procedures for obtaining autopsy and coroner's reports.

A huge thank-you to Super Agent Carly Watters for her guidance, patience, and collaborative nature. A special thanks to Anne Brewer, for her early help on fleshing out the idea for this novel, to Kat Brzozowski, for her keen eye and to Melanie Fried, for bringing it home. Thank you to my publicist, Katie Bassel, and the staff at Thomas Dunne Books for all their hard work. Thank you to my flat-coated retriever, Tucker, for humoring me with countless walks while I struggled to get the words down. He's probably the only dog that runs and hides when he sees the leash. And to my mother, Johanna Houck, for babysitting him always.

Deep gratitude for my new author friend and beta reader extraordinaire, Kate Moretti. I will forever read whatever you write—you're that good.

My girlfriends, in no particular order: Tracey Golden, Kate Weeks, Jenene McGonigal, Mindy Strouse Bailey, Tina Mantel, and Karin Wagner. Thank you for the laughter, the tears, the therapy sessions. I wouldn't be the person I am today without you.

And again, last but not least, my husband, Philip, and our two daughters, my everything. Philip, the next one is dedicated to you.

The Sisters of Blue Mountain

CHAPTER ONE

Spring came early the year the birds fell from the sky.

Linnet was standing at the kitchen sink with a cup of coffee, looking out the garden window, when a bird dropped. She was so startled that she'd jumped, splashing hot coffee onto her hand and staining the sleeve of her white oxford shirt.

What in the world? She leaned over the sink, first looking up and then down, but she couldn't see where it had gone. It had to have been a snow goose. She clearly saw the white down, the black-tipped feathers of its wings.

They were everywhere, the light geese that migrated late winter and early spring, flying over Pennsylvania en route to Canada. Tourists traveled from as far away as Virginia to see the snow geese making their trip north, swimming in the dam, resting in the fields. Linnet's sister, Myna, had often compared the experience of watching the thousands, sometimes tens of thousands, of migrating white birds to standing inside a snow globe after someone had given it a good shake. "And who wouldn't love that," Myna had said.

It *was* something to see, making the experience of the snow-globe effect Linnet's busiest time of year, filling all four rooms in The Snow Goose—the B&B she and Ian operated. But she'd never seen a goose drop to the ground as this one had, as though its wings were made of lead rather than feathers, its bones solid steel rather than hollow tubes.

She leaned farther over the sink, hoisting herself onto the counter's ledge, her feet dangling above the wooden floor.

"What are you doing?" Ian asked.

She lowered herself down, banging her knee on the bottom cabinet. He was buttoning the cuffs on his shirtsleeves. His tie was thrown over his shoulder so he wouldn't accidently dunk it into his coffee like he often did, holding the coffee she'd brought him earlier.

"I was looking out the window."

"I could tell. What's so interesting out there?"

Before she could answer, their twelve-year-old son, Hank, walked into the room.

"Let's go, Dad," Hank said. He'd eaten two bowls of cereal, and now he was dressed and ready for school, wearing his jacket and backpack. His hair was damp and parted to the side. She could still see where the comb separated the strands. In another hour his bangs would fall into his eyes, the white-blond wisps loose and shiny. He was a mini-version of Ian, fair and freckled, their eyelashes light and long to match their hair and eyebrows. When Hank had been a toddler, she'd had to explain to strangers on numerous occasions that no, she wasn't the babysitter, she was his mother. Yes, he looked like his father, obviously. Linnet's hair was as dark as night, and her eyes a deep brown.

She handed Hank his lunch and kissed his cheek. "Have a good day," she said.

"Yeah, I don't mind you kissing me at home, but can you not do it in front of my friends?" he asked.

He was referring to the day before when she'd picked him up

from baseball practice. She'd leaned over and kissed his cheek when he'd gotten into the car. He'd pulled away from her, sinking into the passenger's seat, mumbling about his friends watching.

"Sorry," she said now, wondering when the heck he'd gotten so big, feeling as though it was just yesterday that she'd brought him home from the hospital, her baby boy swaddled in a blue blanket, his skin wrinkly, his face pink and puckered.

Ian picked up his briefcase and grabbed a granola bar. He taught tenth-grade math at the high school. He'd drop Hank off at the middle school on his way.

"Tell me later what you were doing in the window," Ian said, and kissed her softly on the lips. His breath smelled like coffee and toothpaste.

"Dad, let's go!" Hank called one more time as he headed for the door.

When they'd gone and the house was quiet, she looked out the window again. She decided it was odd the way the bird had dropped, unusual enough to warrant a better look.

She stepped outside through the side door. Everything was wet from the thunderstorm the night before. The air was tinged with the scent of worms and bird dirt, the aroma unpleasant to some but not to her—to her it smelled like home. She walked around to the back of their three-story colonial. The daffodils were showing signs of life. The tulips that their groundskeeper, Al, had planted were starting to open. The maple and oak trees were sprouting shiny new leaves. The cherry blossoms were not quite in full bloom.

She could just about glimpse the dam between the branches. She made a mental note to talk with Al about trimming the trees to thin out the view. She charged more money for the rooms that had a view of the water, and she'd better make sure her guests got what they paid for.

When she reached the far side of the house by the kitchen's garden window, she spotted the goose on the ground. Slowly, she walked to where it lay, thinking it might be injured. It didn't move or try to get away as she approached. It still didn't move when she stood over it and then crouched for a closer look.

Dead, she thought. This snow goose dropped from the sky, *dead*.

She looked up to the sound of honking overhead. The geese had arrived during the late winter months and then had moved on. But fortunately, more geese were coming, although the flocks had thinned. There had to be a couple hundred of them on the dam at this very minute. At least, that was how many had been there yesterday. The numbers could change as soon as overnight from hundreds to thousands of snow geese, the sound of their wings, their cries, deafening. And just as fast as they'd arrive, they'd disappear, leaving only the screaming silence in their wake.

She touched her neck where the skin peeked through the collar of her oxford. She was dressed in khakis and loafers, expecting the first guests of the weekend to arrive late that afternoon. She couldn't have a dead goose in the yard, especially not when the guests she was expecting were coming specifically for the birds.

She stood and headed back toward the house to grab a pair of latex gloves. Pop had taught her never to touch a dead bird, or any dead animal for that matter, without first putting on gloves. Birds carried diseases. Pop was an expert on all things birds, a professor of ornithology at the university over the mountain, although he was retired now and spent most of his time locked in his study or sitting in his rowboat on the dam, a pair of binoculars in his hands.

She was about to pull open the side door to reenter the house when she heard the cracking of branches and the whoosh of something falling through the trees. She rushed around back again, jogging across the lawn to the entrance to the path that led through the woods and to the water. On the ground not far from where she stopped was another goose. This one was dead, too. Fear was building inside her chest. It felt a little like panic. But Linnet wasn't an alarmist, not by nature anyway.

She hurried back to the house and thought about showing Pop the birds. He'd have some rational explanation for why these two geese had fallen from the sky. He was getting up there in age at seventy-three, and his mind wasn't what it once was. But she had to believe he could make some sense of this. She wanted him to put *her* mind at ease.

She grabbed latex gloves and a large garbage bag, then went back outside and picked up the two birds, placing them inside the plastic bag with care. She was struck with a memory of her sister, Myna, when they'd been kids and their mother had been running the B&B. One of the guests, an elderly man who'd walked with a cane, had inadvertently struck one of the geese with his car when he'd pulled into their driveway.

Pop had been at the university teaching classes, and it had been left to their mother to handle it. He'd been absent more and more during that time. His research had often kept him away from home. Although Linnet hadn't known the specifics of his ventures, whenever he'd come bursting through the door with news about some man named *Grant*, their mother would retreat farther and farther inside herself, the distance palpable. It hadn't been until Linnet was older that she'd understood *Grant* hadn't been a person at all, but the monies Pop had received for his never-ending projects.

Their mother had stepped outside with gloves and a garbage bag to dispose of the dead goose like Linnet had done now.

"I didn't see it there," the elderly man had said, clearly shaken.

Myna had cried, hanging on to their mother's arm, begging her to let them bury it, to give it a proper funeral.

"You're being ridiculous," their mother had said. "It's one bird. There are thousands more where this one came from."

"No." Myna had stood her ground, crying hysterically, blocking their mother from picking it up, pleading with her to leave it alone.

Linnet could do nothing but join her sister. "She's right. Let us bury it. Let us give it a proper good-bye," she'd said.

Their mother's shoulders had slumped as she looked them over. Something sad had moved across her face, a kind of hopelessness. The light in her eyes had all but faded. She hadn't always been this way when Linnet and Myna had been very young. And there had been one time in their mother's short life that she'd been happy, ridiculously so. But Linnet had promised herself she'd never think about that time ever again.

"Fine," their mother had said. She'd dropped the garbage bag and gloves to the ground by her feet. "Bury it somewhere by the trees at the edge of the yard. And make sure you dig deep enough so some other animal doesn't come along and drag its carcass out on the lawn."

Linnet hadn't thought to ask her to join them in the burial. Myna must not have thought of it either because neither one had asked. Linnet had done most of the digging. She had been the older of the two and considered stronger. Myna had been in charge of the ceremony, lighting the candles for each of them to hold, reciting a poem she'd made up about birds and ashes and flying in heaven.

"Pop," Linnet called, and stepped into his study. After her mother had died, he'd moved into the guesthouse permanently. It was located about thirty yards from the main house. He'd spent more hours in what he'd considered his study, more time there than any time he'd ever spent in the main house. He had set up a small laboratory for his work so he wouldn't have to stay at the university sometimes until all hours of the night. He'd never liked driving over the mountain in the dark. He'd said it was dangerous enough in daylight, the road narrow and windy and isolated. Who knew what could happen to a person when it was black as pitch? Besides, his happiest days were spent in his study or on the dam, always, even when Linnet and Myna had been young, even when their mother had been alive.

"Pop," she called again, and set the garbage bag with the dead geese on the floor inside the door. She was here just yesterday and already the place was littered with coffee cups, some empty, some half full, the coffee long cold. She'd picked up the few mugs she passed and placed them in the kitchen sink to wash later. Then she straightened a pile of papers on the countertop, information about the geese and their latest migration patterns. Next, she bent over and retrieved the slippers he'd left in the middle of the floor, knowing that when he would dress for bed later that evening, he'd call and ask where they were, and she'd have to come and find them for him.

"Pop." She pushed open the bedroom door. He wasn't there. Tentatively, she crossed the room and stopped outside the master bathroom door, knocking lightly. "Are you in there?" When she didn't get an answer, she pushed the door open and found it empty. She exhaled, not realizing she'd been holding her breath, afraid of what she might find, the state he'd be in.

She laid the slippers on the floor on the left side of the bed so they'd be right where he could find them. The bed itself was in shambles. The blankets were in a pile on the floor, the sheets twisted and knotted as though he'd had another rough night's sleep.

She quickly made up the bed, positioned his slippers back in place after kicking one of them when she'd reached across the mattress for the sheets. Satisfied with straightening up, she returned to the worrying she'd found herself in earlier. It was too early for him to be out on the rowboat, bird watching. More and more lately he'd rise in the late morning, and it wouldn't be until early afternoon that he'd make his way to the dam.

Panic rose in her chest again, the same kind of anxiousness she'd felt when the second bird had dropped. She raced out of the guesthouse calling, "Pop!"

She ran through the yard and rushed down the path that led to the dock. She knew where every rock was located, where every root jutted from the ground, where the uneven terrain turned ankles. She could run on the path in the dark if she had to, but this morning the sun was rising over the mountain, lighting the way, drying the puddles from the earlier thunderstorm. It had been a fierce storm, the force of which had bent the branches of trees, rattled the shutters, wakened her in the middle of the night.

Heart racing, she broke free of the trees and stopped short when she saw him wading in the water up to his knees. But it wasn't the sight of her father in the dam that had stopped her cold. Something like a gasp escaped from her lips.

There were dead geese everywhere, hundreds of them in the water and more dotting the shoreline. Hundreds more soared in the blue sky above, a cacophony of honking she just now heard, was so accustomed to the sounds after living here all her life.

"Pop," she hollered, and rushed into the water, not caring if her shoes and pants got wet. "What are you doing?" she asked. "You need to come out of the water." She slipped her hand under his arm. He turned to her, his face contorted. His spectacles were perched on the tip of his nose. In his gloved hand he held a dead goose by its feet.

"I know," she said about the geese. "I know. Come on, let's get you out of the water. You're freezing. Look at you. Your lips are blue."

She helped him to the shore and guided him to one of the benches near the dock. His khakis were rolled to his knees, and his feet were bare. He wore the usual button-down sweater over a collared shirt, the same clothes he'd always worn when he'd been teaching classes. She'd always thought of his khakis, sweaters, and loafers as his professor's uniform. Of course now his loafers and socks were left on the dock, and his rolled-up pants were wet and caked with mud.

"Put that down for now," she said about the goose. At least he'd remembered to put on gloves before he'd foolishly gone into the water and scooped it up.

Her phone went off. She reached into her back pocket. *Ian.* "Hey," she said.

"Have you been to the dam? Have you seen them?" he asked, but he didn't wait for her to respond before he continued in a rush to tell her everything he knew. "I saw a couple of them dead in the road, but I just figured a truck or something ran them over in the night." He took a breath. "Everyone is talking about it. Does Pop know? What does he think happened to them?"

"I'm sitting with him right now on the bench," she said. Ian would know the exact spot she was talking about. He'd proposed to her on this bench. How many nights had they sat here together, how many years? It had to be at least fifteen or more. She couldn't remember and not because she forgot important dates like their anniversary, but more because she couldn't stop staring at the water, at the birds, their wings spread wide, their heads submerged with no chance of coming up for air. She couldn't process anymore than what she was seeing in front of her, the horror of it.

"Well, what does he think happened?" Ian asked.

"I don't know." She looked at Pop. He didn't seem capable of processing the scene either.

"Let me dry him off and get him warm. I'll call you back when I find something out."

"What do you mean dry him off? What's going on?"

"I found him in the dam picking up one of the birds," she said. Although by definition it wasn't a dam at all, but a lake created by several unnamed tributaries. The name "the dam" was just one of the peculiarities of the town of Mountain Springs. "But he's okay. He'll be okay." She patted Pop's leg to reassure him, to reassure *her*.

Ian didn't say anything right away. "Let me know when you find out what happened." He was being careful with her, knowing she wouldn't want to push her father into answering the questions they both had about what might've caused this phenomenon.

"I'll call you as soon as I know something." She hung up the phone and turned toward Pop. "Why don't we go back to the house? I'll fix you a cup of coffee and get you some dry clothes."

"Am I having another nightmare?" he asked. He looked so frightened all of a sudden, like a scared child, and not a grown man with a Ph.D.

"No," she said, and wiped her eye. "I'm afraid this one is real."

CHAPTER TWO

Myna stretched out on the bed, her naked body slick with sweat. Her dark curly hair stuck to the sides of her face and neck. A warm breeze blew the curtains into the room, another sunny day in Florida. She smiled, her body relaxed. Content. Her life couldn't get any better than it was right now, this minute.

She stared at the ceiling, listening to the sound of the waves, smelling the salty sea air, thinking how much she loved living near the coast. It was so different from anywhere she'd ever lived before, different from the mountains and the long cold winters of home, different from the congested cities where she'd run off to after she'd graduated from college almost fifteen years ago.

She even loved her job in the small beach town, teaching at the community college. There was something special about being in front of a classroom, seeing the eager faces of the young men and women staring back at her, sharing her knowledge and experience. She finally understood why her father had spent so much time at the university. When you loved what you did, well, you wanted to spend all of your time doing it. You didn't want to stop.

Of course, she loved Ben, too. After all, she'd rushed home

on her lunch break to join him in their condo on the bay. If she could, she would stay in bed all day, like this, by his side. And yet, she couldn't help but wonder why, moments ago when she'd thought of her life here, she hadn't thought of him first. Why was he the one thing she thought of after everything else?

But she reminded herself that wasn't always true. Five minutes ago she'd had her hands on his back, his buttocks, pressing him to her with an urgency she'd only ever experienced with him. If ever there was a man for her, he was it. Surely, she knew that by now.

She turned to look at him. His arm was slung over his face, covering his eyes. His breathing had slowed, returning to normal after the physical exertion.

He must have felt her watching him. He reached for her hand and held it, squeezing lightly. "So that was fun."

She slipped her hand away and rolled to her side, placing her palm on his chest, running her fingers through the soft patch of hair she could never seem to stop touching. "Yes, it was." She smiled. "But we should get up, or we're both going to be late."

He gazed at her. The tips of his brown hair were bleached blond from the sun. "What's the rest of your day like?" he asked.

"I've got two more classes this afternoon," she said. "And then I'm officially on spring break." She taught computer classes at the college, the job that had brought her to Florida over three years ago. She'd met Ben on her second day in the computer lab. He'd walked in looking for help designing a Web site for his charter fishing boat business. He was tan and fit, and when he smiled, his whole face lit up. There was something relaxed about him, a kind of self-assuredness that came off as confident and, at the same time, sincere. But it was his utter willingness to put himself in her hands, to admit he hadn't a clue about the first steps in creating an online presence for his business—

he'd seemed so vulnerable, trusting, and yet she'd sensed an underlying strength that had made her skin tingle and her pulse race.

Who would have thought the feeling would've lasted this long?

Three years in one state was a record for Myna if she didn't count Pennsylvania, where she'd grown up. Before landing the job at the college, she'd hopped from one IT position to the next, leaving whenever another relationship with whatever guy she'd been dating at the office had failed. It was just too awkward to keep showing up for a job and bumping into an ex-boyfriend day after day. She could still feel her sister Linnet's disapproving stare through the phone line. She could still hear the judgmental tone of her sister's voice whenever Myna had called to say she was moving on. Eventually, she'd stopped calling Linnet altogether, avoiding her sister's criticisms, resorting to e-mails and text messages during the last five years. It was an impersonal way to stay connected to someone you loved, someone who'd meant more to you at one time in your life than anyone else ever had.

But Ben was different from the other guys Myna had dated. She'd understood that straightaway. She could never seem to get enough of him. She was always left with a feeling of wanting more. And it was this very idea, her desire to be with him always, that she found so frightening.

To her, Ben was like chocolate. She'd eat piece after piece, not wanting to stop because it tasted so good. And because it tasted so good, she became unable to stop even though it had the potential to hurt her or make her sick. It was like an addiction—not the bad kind, but rather it was too much of a good thing.

Ben rolled to his side, holding her gaze, his expression dreamy. He moved her hair away from her brow. "We should get married," he said.

She blinked, stunned. He must've seen the shock in her

eyes, the confusion, because he immediately said, "What? You can't tell me you've never thought about it."

"No, I haven't," she said, wondering where the heck this was coming from all of a sudden.

"You've never thought about marrying me. Not even once?"

"No," she said with certainty.

He sat up, his posture no longer languid, but now stiff and rigid. She sat up, too, pulling the sheets and covering her bare chest.

"Well, why not?" he asked, clearly hurt.

"I don't know. It's just not something I think about."

"But why?"

"Because. I don't know," she stammered. "I just thought you knew."

"Knew what?"

"That I don't believe in marriage."

"What? Who doesn't believe in marriage?"

"I don't."

"What does that even mean? You don't believe in marriage?"

"I just don't think people should get married. I don't think it works." She paused. "It ruins things."

"You think marrying me would ruin things?"

"Yes."

He swung his legs to the floor, putting his back to her. "I can't believe I'm hearing this."

She reached out and touched his arm and then rubbed his strong shoulder, trying not to make too much of this if she could. "I love our life the way it is. Why mess with perfection?"

"You should've told me." He jerked his shoulder away. Her hand dropped to the bed.

"I'm telling you now," she said.

"You should've told me sooner."

"Why? What does it matter?" *Why was he turning this into a fight?*

"It matters to me." He stood.

"Well, I'm sorry," she said, hugging the sheets to her cooling skin, knowing she didn't sound sorry. "I just figured you knew."

"How could I have known?" He yanked on his boxers and shorts. "What kind of person doesn't believe in marriage?" He pulled on his polo shirt, the one with *Captain* stitched on the left side over his chest, his biceps bulging underneath the short sleeves.

"My kind of person," she snapped, thinking, *Fine, let's fight then.*

He stared at her, his eyes wounded.

She glared back, but it was hard to stay mad at him, not when he looked at her that way. She held out her hand, urging him to take it. "Come here," she said. Maybe it didn't have to turn into something ugly and mean. Maybe she could smooth things over before they both said something they'd regret. "Let's not make this into a big deal."

"But it is a big deal."

"It doesn't have to be." He still didn't take her hand, so she patted the mattress by her side. "Sit."

"I'm going to be late." He plucked his sneakers from the floor. "It is a big deal. It's a very big deal," he said before storming from the room.

"Ben, wait!" she called after him. "We're fighting over a piece of paper."

"It's not just a piece of paper!" he shouted, and the next thing she heard was the front door slamming shut. She leaned back against the pillow. *What the hell just happened?* He'd never talked about marriage before. She'd just assumed he'd felt about it the same way she had. Why couldn't they continue as they were, happy, easy, rolling with the tides? She folded her arms. Their life was perfect the way it was. Why was he trying to ruin it? She wanted to holler after him, "Take it back! Take that stupid word, *marriage*, back!"

She checked her phone for the time. *Shit.*

She scrambled from the sheets and hurried into her skirt. She didn't have time for even a quick shower. She rolled deodorant under her arms. It would have to do, and she slipped into her blouse. It was only two classes, she consoled herself. She could get through two classes smelling of sex. Her students wouldn't know if she didn't let them get too close.

She rushed out the door. It wasn't until she was behind the wheel and speeding down the road that some of the anger peeled away and what was left was the first stab of fear. Was it possible she could lose him over this?

If ever there was a time she wished she could talk with Linnet, the one person who knew everything about her, the one person who might've at least understood this, the time was now. But somewhere along the way she'd forgotten how to talk with her sister. They'd forgotten how to talk with each other. It wasn't always that way. They were close once, as close as two sisters could be.

She eased off the gas and pressed the brake, stopping at a traffic light. Two boys carrying a bucket and fishing poles caught her attention. They bumped arms as they walked, smiling, talking as they headed in the direction of the bay and pier. She imagined them as brothers, swapping tall fish tales. Something about the way they moved, the lightness to their steps, reminded her of when she'd been young and carefree, when the days with her sister had been as simple as fishing, catching bullfrogs, playing games to fill up the hours.

One game in particular crossed her mind: Spynow. She and Linnet had invented it when they'd been bored on the weekends when their mother had been preoccupied with guests and their father had been locked away in his study.

"S.P.Y.N.O.W.," Myna had called to Linnet, stating each letter clearly. She'd thought by spelling out the word she was being clever.

Their mother had been standing in front of the kitchen sink with a knife and cutting board, fruits and vegetables spread on the counter around her. The morning sunlight was shining brightly through the garden window. It was late spring, and three of the guest rooms in the B&B were occupied with couples who came for the tranquility of the mountains, the trails, the snow geese on the dam. Although most of the birds had gone, leaving their small-town rest stop on their way north to Canada where they'd nest to breed in the colder climate.

The sisters had a lot of free time on their hands outside of school, more than their peers who were busy with activities— soccer, dance, girl scouts, softball. They could've joined the same teams and participated in the same activities if they'd wanted, but they'd always preferred to spend their time together with only each other for company.

Myna motioned to Linnet to start the game. Linnet pushed past her to take the lead as big sister. Myna tried to hide her giggles behind her sister's shoulder.

"Shh," Linnet said, putting her finger to her lips.

If their mother had heard them at this point, she pretended she hadn't. Linnet got down on her hands and knees and crawled toward the kitchen table. Myna got down and crawled after her.

She was careful not to put a hand or knee on the creakier wooden boards.

They made it to the table safely without being noticed. Linnet slipped between two of the chairs. Myna did the same. They huddled together on the floor, trying to stifle the giggles that always erupted whenever they played the spying game. Their mother continued to ignore them, because of course she had to have heard them. Linnet started tickling Myna, and she lost it, laughing uncontrollably, pushing her sister's wriggling fingers away.

"That's enough," their mother said.

Myna jumped and banged her head on the bottom of the table, which only made them laugh harder.

Their mother pulled one of the chairs out. "Both of you," she said. "Outside. I've had enough of your silliness for one day."

Linnet and Myna crawled out from underneath the table, Myna still holding the top of her head, Linnet still giggling.

"Get going." Their mother shooed them toward the door. "It's a nice day. Out you go. Leave me be."

They ran across the yard. Linnet called, "Last one there is a rotten egg."

Linnet made it to the dock first. Myna caught up to her a second later. They lay down on the wooden planks so their shoulders and hips touched, their bodies fitting perfectly together like two pieces of a puzzle. They were the same size, the same lanky build. Their dark curly hair cascaded down their backs. They were often mistaken for twins, but they were born fifteen months apart.

The warm sun heated their faces. Their feet dangled over the side, and their toes touched the water.

"Was Mom crying?" Myna asked, noticing their mother's watery eyes before she'd chased them out the door.

"No," Linnet said. "I think she was cutting onions."

Myna had believed her then. There wasn't anyone in the world Myna had believed more than her sister.

Myna pulled into the parking lot of the square brick building that housed the computer lab and her classroom, her thoughts lingering on Linnet, their mother and, ultimately, Ben. She parked in the first space she could find, flipped the visor down, and looked in the mirror. Her cheeks were flushed. She reached into her oversize purse and pulled out lip gloss and mascara. When she finished with her face, she searched for a hair tie and quickly fixed her tangles into a messy bun.

She got out of the car and smoothed her skirt. She stared at the ground as she walked, not making eye contact with anyone as she made her way into the building, feeling self-conscious about the dried layer of sweat on her skin. When she entered her classroom, most of her students were already seated, tapping away on their keyboards.

"Sorry I'm late." She glanced at the clock over the door and put her bag and case with her laptop on the desk. The boy in the back, Dylan, raised his hand. He'd started asking more and more questions lately, ever since she'd given him a ride home one night when she'd found him walking alongside the road, hunched from the weight of his backpack. There had been something about the way he'd looked under the glow of the streetlamps on the deserted street that had made her think he'd needed help. She'd ended up driving him to a party. It hadn't been what she had in mind when she'd asked if he'd needed a lift, and then later, she'd had to refuse his repeated offers that she join him for a drink.

"Always picking up strays," Ben had said when she'd arrived

home later that night. She hadn't responded because what he'd said had been true. She couldn't pass by someone, anyone, in need of help. She wouldn't make the same mistake twice.

Her cell phone started ringing. *Ben.*

"Give me a second, Dylan," she said, and snatched her phone from her purse. Linnet's name appeared on the screen.

Myna stared at her sister's name for a long second. "So," she said to Dylan, turning her phone off and tossing it on the desk. "What can I do for you?"

CHAPTER THREE

Linnet shoved her cell phone in her pocket. She hung up before leaving Myna a message. What would she have said anyway? Hundreds of Pop's beloved birds are dead, and you need to come home. But what exactly was the emergency? She didn't know. All she knew was that she wanted her sister here.

She was standing next to Pop by their private dock. They were joined by a couple dozen people who had gathered along the shoreline, forming a ring around the dam, staring at the water. To an outsider the scene might've looked like some kind of cult, some kind of ceremony amid a bizarre sacrifice. But of course, it was the farthest thing from the truth. The townspeople cherished the snow geese, relied on the birds to bring the tourists and money into town.

Linnet recognized some of the spectators who had congregated along the bank—Susan from Jesse's Market, Brenda, their mail carrier, Terry, the husband of one of the teachers who worked with Ian, parents from Hank's school. The others she didn't recognize at all, possibly vacationers staying at the Mountain Springs Inn in the center of town. It wasn't long before Hugh Huntley, the reporter from the local news station, appeared.

He was followed by his cameraman. She wondered how long it would take before Hugh knocked on her father's door.

The sun climbed the mountaintop, casting its rays far and wide. If ever she wished for a colder spring day, it was today. If it reached seventy degrees like the weatherman had forecasted, it wouldn't take long for the birds to cook in the hot sun. And start to smell.

She pulled her phone out again, checking the time. She needed to get back to the house. She had chores to tend to. And yet, she couldn't move. She couldn't tear herself away from the scene. She touched Pop's arm.

"We need to get a couple geese out of the water," he said. "Before they start to decompose. They need to be double bagged and stuck in a freezer. We need to preserve them as best we can."

"We can do that," she said, thinking he'd read her thoughts earlier about the temperature rising even though the water remained cold. They hadn't had enough warm days this spring to heat up the dam. The icy water would slow the decaying process at least for a little while. The fresher the kill, the more conclusive the test results would be. "Do you want to make some calls to the lab first?" She was referring to his old colleagues at the university. Maybe they could send one of the younger professors to handle the bagging and freezing. She didn't want her father back in the dam.

Charlie, the chief of police and longtime family friend, broke free from a couple bystanders and joined them. He was a decade younger than her father, and word around town was that he'd planned to retire at the end of the year. She wondered who would fill Charlie's position when he was gone. Mountain Springs was small, so small they had only the chief and four full-time cops. The others were part-time, a total of eight in all.

"What do you make of this, Doc?" Charlie asked.

"It's hard to say." Pop removed his spectacles and wiped his eyes. His hand was shaking. "We'll have to run some tests of course. I'll need to get back into the lab at the university."

"But what's your best guess?" He nodded to the people gathering, gossiping, speculating about what could've caused so many birds to fall from the sky. A commotion at the public dock drew their attention. Hugh was preparing to talk live on camera. He had two people standing next to him waiting to be interviewed, the view of the dead geese floating in the water behind them.

"I can't say for certain what caused this," Pop said. He put his spectacles back on, taking the time to wrap the ends of the curled handles around his ears. He spoke with a little more confidence and stood a little straighter than he had when she'd first seen him up to his knees in the water.

"Do we need to call somebody in health services?" Charlie asked.

"I can't rule out disease, if that's what you're asking," Pop said.

"That's exactly what I'm asking. I don't want to have some kind of mass hysteria on my hands. You tell people a bunch of diseased birds dropped into our little watering hole, and you're going to create panic. Not to mention scaring the tourists away for sure."

"There are other possible causes," Pop said.

"Arkansas." Linnet chimed in. "Hundreds of blackbirds dropped dead after the town's big fireworks display."

"That's true," Pop said.

"Well, hell, that made national news." Charlie ran his hand down his face.

Linnet looked to the sky. Several snow geese flew overhead in perfect V formation, the loud honking interrupting their conversation. When the birds continued to pass them by, she looked at Pop. "They're not stopping," she said to him.

He was also looking up, watching them fly away.

She checked her phone again. "I've got to get back to the house. I've got guests coming this afternoon and two more checking in this evening." She turned toward Pop. "Why don't I walk you back?" She had wanted to take him inside over an hour ago to warm him up and dry him off. She'd never forgive herself if she'd allowed him to get sick because of this.

He nodded without protesting, much to her relief. "I'll make some calls to the university," he said. "They'll want to send someone here right away."

"Make those calls," Charlie said. "And I'll handle this." He motioned to Hugh, who had since trekked around the dam along with several other bystanders. They were heading in their direction.

Linnet took Pop by the elbow with the understanding Charlie didn't want him talking to the press until they had a better idea of what had happened to the birds. She directed Pop toward the path that would lead them through the patch of woods to their yard.

He stopped suddenly.

"We'll need some plastic bags to collect the birds," he said, reminding her again.

"I've got some at the house," she said, noticing how tired he looked. His face was drawn, the skin around his eyes sagging and dark. "Are you sure you're up for this?" she asked.

He waved her off.

They continued toward the path. Her wet feet squished inside her sneakers with each step. Her khakis clung to her calves. Pop's feet were bare.

"Your shoes," she said to him. She'd been so distracted by

the dead birds and the crowd that she'd forgotten all about his socks and loafers. She turned to race back to the dock to retrieve them, nearly bumping into Susan from the market and several of the other onlookers. Before she knew what was happening, the mob had overtaken Charlie, and she and Pop were surrounded.

Dale, a neighbor, fired off the first question. "What happened to the birds?" he asked.

"What should we do?" Susan asked. "Are we in danger?"

They were crowding them. Pop put his arms up to shield his face. Where was Charlie? She couldn't see past the throng of people.

"You're the Bird Man! Tell us what you know!" another man shouted.

"Give him space," Linnet said, not making eye contact with anyone. She knew what people thought of him now, although she suspected most secretly still respected him. But she couldn't deny he wasn't the man he once was. His memory lapses had gotten worse, especially in the last few months. He'd become the very thing the kids in school had teased her and Myna about, the crazy old Bird Man. Kids in their class had been relentless, squawking and flapping their arms, making fun of how he'd dressed up every Halloween as a goose, honking, marching in the town's parade. He'd meant for it to be fun, and when they were little it was, but as they got older, it was embarrassing. Kids were cruel.

She tried to guide Pop through the crowd that was quickly increasing in numbers. Someone reached out and grabbed his bicep.

"Is it the bird flu?"

"Maybe it's the water," Terry said.

"All right." Charlie's voice rose above the crowd. He pushed people aside as he made his way to them. "Everyone calm down," he said, and handed Pop the socks and loafers he'd left on the dock. "The first thing I want to do is make sure nobody touches the birds."

"It *is* a disease!" a woman shrieked.

"No." Charlie shook his head. "I'm not saying that. In fact, I'm sure it's not that at all." He glanced at Pop. Pop's face was pale, waxy.

Charlie continued. "But we need to take precautions just to be safe."

"Is that an official order?" Hugh asked, breaking through the crowd and shoving the microphone toward Charlie.

Charlie faltered for a second, and then he said, "Yes. Picking up the birds without permission is illegal. They are protected. Don't touch them. It's for your own safety as well as theirs."

"But they're already dead," someone said.

The crowd collectively murmured their assent.

"You heard it here first, directly from the chief's mouth. Do not touch the birds." Hugh talked into the camera. "I repeat, do not touch the birds."

Charlie grabbed the microphone before Hugh could continue. "Turn that thing off," he said to the cameraman. Charlie turned to Pop and asked in a low voice, "How soon can you get someone here?"

"A couple of hours, maybe," Pop said.

"What are you whispering about?" Susan asked, tugging the cuff of Pop's cardigan.

Hugh gave the signal to his cameraman to keep rolling.

"There's nothing more to see here," Charlie said, and nodded at Linnet and Pop. "I'll meet you both at the house." He turned toward Susan and the others. "Show's over. I want everyone to go back to your homes or your jobs or wherever else you're supposed to be. Let's go. Move along." He corralled the mob.

There were protests from some of the men and women. Linnet turned toward Pop and took his arm. "Come on." She tried to lead him through the people that were reluctant to go. Hugh and his cameraman had managed to avoid Charlie. Hugh stuck his microphone in front of Pop's face.

"Dr. Henry Jenkins," Hugh said, looking at the camera. "Also known as Mountain Springs's very own Bird Man."

"No more questions," Linnet said, scowling at the camera. She took hold of Pop again and started pulling him away, but he was clumsy and slow. Hugh and his microphone were back in his face.

"I just have one question," Hugh said, turning toward the camera and giving his viewers a sly smile. "You are a bird expert, so tell us, what caused hundreds of snow geese to drop from the sky and turn up dead in the dam?"

"I, I don't know," Pop said.

"Give us your best guess. Is it some kind of bird disease? Should the people of Mountain Springs be worried? What kind of precautions should we be taking?"

"I, I don't know," Pop said again.

"Come on, you must know something," Hugh said. "Should people boil their water?"

"I don't know," he said for a third time. "I don't know anything yet."

"Leave him alone," Linnet said. "He said he doesn't know." A part of her wanted him to explain everything away, to prove to these people he was intelligent, he was an expert in all things birds, his mind wasn't failing him. If only they'd give him a chance. Let him do his job.

"Who's going to get all those dead birds out of the dam?" Hugh asked.

"Yes," Pop said, nodding. "They'll have to get the birds out of the dam."

"So you're saying the water is unsafe?"

"Yes." He shook his head. "No." He looked around, becoming more disoriented by the second.

"What *can* you tell us, Professor?" Hugh asked. "Can you give us anything at all?"

"Claire," Pop said, his face stricken suddenly. "Claire," he called Linnet's mother's name again and raised his arms, knocking Hugh's microphone out of his hand and sending it to the ground with a clunk.

"It's okay, Pop." She stepped in front of the cameraman, blocking his shot, so all Pop could see was her face. "It's Linnet. Remember? I'm right here."

Hugh picked up the microphone.

She held on to Pop's hand and pulled him away. When they were clear of the men, she looked over her shoulder and said to them, "You should be ashamed of yourself."

Linnet and Pop scrubbed their hands in the kitchen sink. Even though they had both worn latex gloves when they'd handled the geese, it was recommended by the National Wildlife Health Center that you wash your hands thoroughly as an added precaution. You didn't live with the Bird Man your entire life and not know these things.

She helped him dry his hands on a tea towel, taking extra care to massage his knuckles where the arthritis had settled. "Why don't you go and sit down?" she said. "I'll bring you the phone."

He shuffled to his favorite chair, the one with the well-worn armrests and faded cushion. It looked like a professor's chair, stately and old. He sat. She knelt in front of him with a clean pair of socks and a pair of old loafers.

"I don't have any answers for them," he said in the soft way he'd always spoken.

"I know you don't, Pop." She looked up at him from her position on the floor, his foot in her hand. His spectacles had slid down his nose despite the handles wrapped around his ears that were meant to keep them in place. "But you will."

"There were so many," he said, his eyes glassy. He was talking about the birds.

"Yes," she said, and squeezed his hand.

"I should make those calls."

"Yes," she said, and wiped her own eyes with the back of her arm.

He hesitated. "It's not the first time a large number of birds in a flock turned up dead. All through history there are reports of this very occurrence. The reasons vary, but it's not as uncommon as people think."

Her shoulders relaxed a little. "Thank you for telling me. It might be something you want to share with Charlie. I have a feeling things are going to get out of hand and fast. More than what we just saw now."

"I'll have to run some tests. Do you think they'll let me back in the lab?" He looked so hopeful.

"I don't see why not," she said but, in truth, she had no idea. They'd all but forced his retirement after he'd failed to show for classes, forgetting the time on numerous occasions, making multiple mistakes in the lab back when they hadn't known he'd suffered from the onset of dementia.

He nodded and reached for the phone.

While he made his calls, she slipped on another pair of latex gloves and picked up the garbage bag with the two dead geese that she'd laid inside the door earlier that morning. They were the freshest pair as far as she was concerned. She began the process of double bagging each one, making sure to slip a note between the carcasses explaining she'd seen them drop, where they'd fallen, time of death.

By the time Pop had hung up the phone, she was emptying the ice trays into a large cooler she'd dragged from the shed.

"We're going to need more ice," she said, dumping the last tray on top of the bagged birds.

"They're sending someone," Pop said. "Professor Coyle." He looked upset. "I've never heard of him."

"Well, it's been some time since you've retired. I'm sure there are lots of new professors at the university that you don't know."

"Yes," he said, his brow furrowed. "How long has it been?"

"Six years," she said.

"It's been that long?" he asked.

"Mmm-hmm." She touched his shoulder. "I'm going to run up to the house and grab more ice. I'll be right back."

"Six years," he said, looking at his hand where the veins bulged underneath wrinkled skin.

Linnet walked through the yard, scanning the grounds. A few dandelions sprouted between the newly green grass. It was nearly impossible to get all of the weeds without using what she thought of as toxic chemicals. Al emerged from the path through the woods. He was wearing the typical plaid flannel shirt, work pants, and boots.

"I'm glad I bumped into you," she said. "I've noticed some dandelions. Is there anything organic we can use to get rid of them?

And I'm going to need you to trim some of the trees. Thin them out so the guests have a better view of the water." Her words tapered off, finally registering the expression on Al's face.

"You were at the dam," she said.

"I've never seen anything like it," he said. "When I stopped to fill up the truck and mower with gas, I heard a few people in town saying something about seeing a bunch of dead birds. I guess I didn't really believe it."

"I know. It's shocking." She looked past him, glimpsing the water through the trees. "Can you do me a favor?" she asked. "Can you run to Jesse's Market and pick up some bags of ice for me?"

"Sure," he said. "What's the ice for?"

"We have to freeze some of the birds so they can run tests and figure out why this happened."

Al looked down at his phone. "You know I took a couple of pictures," he said. "I don't know why I did. I've just never seen anything like it. Is that morbid? It is, isn't it? Maybe I should delete them."

Charlie walked through the yard to where they were standing. His hand rested on his sidearm, worry etched in the lines around his eyes. "What's this about pictures?"

"I took some pictures of the birds," Al said.

"Well, keep them to yourself. That's all we need is for this thing to spread across the Internet." He turned to Linnet. "How's your dad?"

"He's hanging in there. One of the professors from the university is on his way." She pointed toward the house. "I'm going to get more ice. Al?"

"I'm on it," he said, and dashed for his truck. She sprinted toward the house, leaving Charlie alone in the yard looking toward the sky.

CHAPTER FOUR

Jake Mann held his father's old cell phone in his hand. It was black, nondescript, with limited features by today's standards. It looked more like a small walkie-talkie and was one of the first mass-produced cellular phones of the early 1990s.

He turned it over and ran his fingers over the rough scratches all along the back, the result of having skid across the pavement while in his father's possession at the time of the car accident. It was the only distinguishable feature he could find that connected the phone to his dad. Phones back then had lacked the personality of their owners: no fancy cases or personalized screens or myriad of photos.

Jake had found the phone two days ago while sorting through his mother's belongings in the small single-family home where he'd grown up. It had taken him two months before he could set foot back inside her house, before he'd felt ready to confront the memories of his childhood—most of which were happy, one that was not.

He'd been sitting on the floor in the basement, alone, going through the boxes one item at a time, wondering why the heck his mother had kept so many odd things—bent, twisted wreaths,

one for each season, that had hung on the front door at inter-
mittent times throughout his adolescence, glass jars filled with
buttons from shirts long discarded, faded Christmas decorations that she hadn't displayed since he was a toddler. His
mother wasn't a packrat by any standards. The rest of the house,
her cupboards and closets, had been cleaned out. She'd been
preparing for what was coming. Even in the end she'd thought
of him, wanting to make things easier for him by not leaving a
house full of items he'd have to sort, to save him from having to
decide what to keep and what to dispose of after she had gone.

"If you don't want it, sell it," she'd said about the house and
furniture. "Donate my clothes to the women's shelter. You
know the one, *The Second Chance* place."

He'd swallowed hard, holding back tears that had threatened
to spill down his cheeks.

"And my wigs." She'd touched the scarf on her head. "Bring
those to the cancer center. They'll know where they're needed
most."

"Of course," he'd said. "Whatever you want."

When she'd finished going over her last wishes, right down to
the hymns she'd wanted sung at the funeral, he'd walked out of
her bedroom, no longer able to contain the overflowing tears
streaming down his face. He'd made his way to the stairs, passing
old photos from his first day of kindergarten to college gradua-
tion and beyond, all framed and hanging throughout the narrow hallway. Behind the pictures, the wallpaper had yellowed
and peeled, marking in another way the passage of time.

But his mother had never gotten around to sorting through
the boxes in the basement. She'd done a lot in those last few
months, probably too much, but this was where her efforts had
ended. So here he was, kneeling on the cement floor among
the Easter decorations, the plastic eggs she'd placed quarters

in until he'd turned nine years old, the shiny green grass that had lined his baskets and would be found on the kitchen table and floor long after the holiday had ended. It was amidst these happy memories that he'd found the bag containing his father's personal effects.

He sank until his bottom rested on the cold dusty floor, the clear plastic bag in his lap. He didn't open it right away, but he could see there wasn't much inside—a brown leather wallet, a black cell phone, a gold ring, a silver watch. Why would his father's things be there in the basement in a box of Easter decorations? The only sense he could make of it was that his mother had packed them with the decorations without realizing it. She'd been in a state of shock that spring, gripped by terrible grief. They'd stopped celebrating Easter after that. Jake had been nine years old, old enough not to believe in the Easter Bunny anyway.

When he felt ready, or at least as ready as he'd ever be, he opened the bag. He took the wallet out first, the leather smooth with wear. There was sixty bucks inside, an expired credit card, a gas card, and a picture of Jake as a toddler sitting in his mother's lap on their front stoop. He didn't remember the picture being taken, but there was no mistaking by the laughing smiles on their faces that they'd been happy.

He put everything back in the wallet, including the money and the photo, and set it aside. Next he grabbed the cell phone, noticing the scrapes on the back. The battery was dead. He knew it would be, but still he tried to turn it on anyway, wondering how he would feel if he were able to hear his father's prerecorded voice after all this time. Would it hurt too much? Did cell phones even have voice-mail back then? He was sure he could find out. He did a lot of research as a journalist. It wouldn't be hard to dig around, search for an old charger, plug it in and listen.

He set the phone down, feeling an old ache mixed with excitement at the possibility of reconnecting with his old man in some small way.

He pulled the last two items out of the bag. The wristwatch, the kind with the metal band that pinched your skin and pulled your arm hair out whenever you took it on or off, and the championship football ring his father had worn on his pinky finger. The knuckle on his ring finger had been freakishly large after having broken it on numerous occasions playing the sport.

Jake rubbed his own misshapen knuckles, similarly injured from having played the game his dad had loved. Jake had suffered hit after hard hit, absorbing the blows to his kidneys and ribs, the aches and pains in his hips and knees, the strain of his shoulder, the broken bones in his hand, leaving everything he'd had on the field, pushing to break his father's records, wanting him to be proud, only to fall short in the end.

Now, Jake slipped the championship ring onto his pinky finger, wanting to feel close to him again the way he had on the football field when he was in high school, closer in a way than he had in a longtime.

Forty-eight hours later, Jake was at his desk in the small cubicle he occupied in the newspaper's office, the old Nokia cell phone in front of him. He'd searched online for some time, finally locating a charger that was compatible. He'd had to pay for the entire vintage box set—another phone, a new battery, and what he really needed, a charger—spending a couple hundred bucks. But he didn't care about the money. You couldn't hang a price on matters of the heart.

The old Nokia had taken the new battery and several minutes to charge until the screen flickered once, twice, and then lit up. Jake wiped his clammy hands on his pants before picking it up. The features were limited, nothing in voice-mail, and after pushing a few buttons and playing around with it, the only thing he could find was a single phone number he didn't recognize. The screen flickered again, and he jotted the number down quickly before he lost it. The phone was obviously damaged. He continued playing with it while he had the chance, searching for the answers to the questions the boy inside of him wanted to ask, the *how* and *why* types of questions that, when dealing with a tragic accident, there were no real answers to.

The phone died two minutes later. He pressed buttons and then he shook it because that was what you did when your phone wasn't working. But no amount of pressing and shaking and charging would resuscitate it.

To say he was disappointed wouldn't even come close to describing the heaviness weighing inside his chest. He stared at the number he'd written down, wondering why his father wouldn't have had their old house number as the ICE contact. Why weren't there any other numbers listed? It was strange.

Because Jake was who he was, he knew he couldn't let it go. Besides, he'd come this far, so why the hell not? He picked up his phone and dialed the number only to learn it was no longer in service. He wasn't deterred. A good journalist was only as good as his sources. He pulled his chair closer to the desk and typed an e-mail. *Who did this phone number belong to in 1994?* He typed the ten-digit number and hit Send.

"Knock, knock," Dennis said, and poked his head inside Jake's cubicle. "I've got a bunch of dead birds in a town near the Poconos. It could make national news. It's yours if you want it."

Jake spun around in his chair to face him. Dennis had one of those long faces that were all sharp points and edges. He had a hard look about him, but he was all soft and squishy on the inside.

He'd attended Jake's mom's funeral, and you would've thought it was Dennis's mother they were burying by the amount of tears and compassion he'd showed for Jake. Jake was touched. Dennis was a good guy. And Jake had had months to prepare himself for the loss, whereas most of the people at the service—a few family members and friends—had not.

"This has you written all over it," Dennis said.

"What kind of birds? How many?"

Dennis stepped into the tiny office, big enough for a desk and chair and not much else. "Snow geese. A hundred, maybe more." He checked the sheet of paper in his hand. "In some-place called Mountain Springs."

"Let me see that," Jake said, and Dennis handed him the sheet of paper. It couldn't be the same Mountain Springs. "I'll be damned," he muttered.

Jake's e-mail pinged. He turned back around to check it. Kim was fast, he'd give her that. She worked for an insurance company in the IT department. She was the best damn hacker Jake had ever met.

"Is that an old Nokia?" Dennis asked, and picked up the black cell phone from Jake's desk. "Man, I haven't seen one of these in years. It's like a dinosaur compared to phones nowadays."

Jake mumbled something. He wasn't sure what because he wasn't paying attention to Dennis. The sight of Kim's e-mail address in his in-box had spiked his pulse. He didn't know if it was because he was anxious about what she'd found or the simple fact that she'd responded. Most of their interactions were through e-mails, carefully protected against spyware. But just last month he'd taken her to lunch as a way of thanking her for helping him with some information on another story he'd been working on. He had to admit the times when he'd been in her presence there was something about her voice that had made his heart race, something about the curve of her lips, the sway of her hips that had the potential to knock him sideways and leave him breathless.

"What's the story on it?" Dennis asked about the phone, turning it over, running his fingers over the scratches like Jake had done.

"It's nothing," he said absently, and opened Kim's e-mail. It read *Northampton County area code.*

He knew that much. *Whose number?* He typed and hit Send.

I'm working on it.

Call my cell as soon as you find out.

He took the old cell phone from Dennis's hand and shoved it in his computer bag. Maybe the universe was trying to tell him something. Maybe he'd get some answers after all. Maybe he wasn't completely mad and wasting his time. Maybe.

He packed up his laptop and grabbed his jacket.

"Where are you going?" Dennis asked.

"Mountain Springs," he said.

CHAPTER FIVE

Myna was standing on the pier wrapped in a cardigan. She held the collar of her sweater tight against the breeze coming off the water. She'd been standing there for the last thirty minutes waiting, watching the brown pelicans dive-bomb for small fish. When she'd first moved to Florida, she'd been fascinated by the prehistoric-looking birds, feeling as though she'd stepped onto the set of *Jurassic Park*. She'd taken pictures and videos of them on the bay or flying past the balcony of the condo, captivated by their oversize bills, the large folds of their wings. She took some photos now. Pop was delighted to have them, and it gave her something to do, a welcome distraction.

She'd rushed home after her last class had ended, showering quickly only to have to sit and wait, and then later, she'd paced the length of the living room before making her way to the dock. Ben had never walked out on her before. Sure, they'd fought in the past, but not like this. Their fights were more of the typical nothing kinds of things couples fought about after having lived together for a period of time—who forgot to put the cap back on the toothpaste, who left the milk out, where was the remote control for the TV?

But they'd never fought about their relationship or the future of it.

After a few minutes more, and half a dozen photos, Ben's boat finally came into view, making its way back from the open sea. The closer he got, the more shallow her breathing became. She pulled the sweater tightly once again, holding it closed at her neck. Ben was sure to have noticed her, but he hadn't acknowledged her presence. Instead, he concentrated on steering the vessel into the slip, giving the last bit of instructions to the family who'd chartered his boat for the afternoon. His first mate and friend, Pete, jumped onto the pier to tie the forty-foot fishing boat down for the night.

"Hey, Myna," Pete said, and waved. He helped the family's two boys onto the dock and then offered his hand to their mother. The father spent an extra few minutes with Ben.

"Good trip?" Myna asked the family as they passed by.

"Fabulous," the woman said. "But I'm so glad I took something for motion sickness. All that rocking." She motioned to her husband, who looked a little green. He'd finished talking with Ben and had joined his family on the pier.

Ben and Pete busied themselves preparing for the next charter in the morning. They exchanged a few words, some of which Myna overheard.

"I'll finish tying her down," Pete said about the boat. "Go on and talk to her. She's here, isn't she?"

Ben put his hand on Pete's shoulder, a way of saying thank you. Then Ben made his way over to her. He lifted his baseball cap and wiped his brow.

She didn't know what to say. Maybe he didn't either. She extended her hand, a peace offering. He took it. Slowly, they walked the next couple blocks toward home in silence. Some of the desperation she'd felt earlier, the unease, faded away. This had to be a sign he'd forgiven her, saw things her way.

They stepped through the door, and she wrapped her arms around his waist. He smelled like the ocean breeze mixed with the faint scent of fish and sweat, but not a bad scent by any means.

He pressed his cheek to hers and whispered in her ear, "I guess this means you've changed your mind."

She stepped back, her hands lingering on his hips. "I thought you changed *your* mind."

The tension between them returned, bubbling and hot. She stared at him.

He took her wrists and removed her hands from his hips. "I'm taking a shower." He turned to go.

"Wait." She was really starting to hate the way he kept walking away from her. She followed him into the bedroom. He'd already turned on the TV. He couldn't be in a room without the darn television turned on. It was funny how something that had never agitated her before could suddenly make her want to explode.

He strode to the master bath. "I'm going to shower and clear my head. It was a long day." He disappeared behind the door.

She dropped onto the bed and crossed her arms. The shower turned on. What was wrong with her? Any other woman would be thrilled if the man she loved had proposed. And in some ways she was happy.

But in a bigger way, she wasn't.

"Tell us again," a seven-year-old Myna had said, poking Pop in his side. He'd been sitting on the bench next to her. Linnet had been sitting on the other side of him. They were waiting for the arrival of the first snow geese on the dam. It was late winter and the air was cold. Myna and Linnet were wrapped in their winter coats and scarves. Myna breathed into her hands to keep her fingers from going numb.

"If you insist," Pop said, his red cheeks rising up and meeting his eyes when he smiled.

"I do insist," Myna said, and Linnet leaned forward, nodding in agreement.

"It was a warm spring day," he said.

"And you were sitting in the canoe with Mommy," Linnet said.

He held up his pointer finger. "But she wasn't your mommy, yet. First, she had to agree to be my wife."

"What about the birds?" Myna asked.

"Right. The birds." He continued. "Most of the flock had thinned by then. But there must've been fifty snow geese left on the water. They were all around us. It was very romantic."

"Because the birds were in pairs," Myna said.

"Because snow geese mate for life," Linnet said.

"That's right," he said, the smile never leaving his face. "Your mother was wearing a yellow sundress. She had a sweater draped over her shoulders. She was always cold, even under a hot sun. She was so very young and so very pretty."

"And you were scared," Linnet said.

"Because you were old," Myna said.

He pretended to be offended. "I wasn't that old." He looked down for a moment. "I was twelve years older than her. And yes, I was scared. What if she said no?" He put his hand over his heart in an overly dramatic way, and the girls giggled. "I reached into my jacket pocket for the small box, the one with the diamond ring inside. But it wasn't there."

"And you panicked," Linnet said.

"I did. I thought I might've lost it and stood up too fast, forgetting I was sitting in a canoe. The boat rocked left and right and left again."

"Mommy held on to the sides, and you fell out," Myna said.

"I lost my balance and fell right into the water. But thank goodness the water was shallow and only came up to my waist. You can imagine how embarrassed I was."

"And Mommy laughed," Linnet said.

"She did. She said I was the funniest, most handsome man she'd ever met."

"And that's when you remembered the box was in your pants pocket," Myna said.

"Right. I had moved it thinking it would be safer in my pants pocket, and because I was so nervous, I'd forgotten. So there I was standing in the water, soaked through to the skin, and I thought it was now or never. I took the ring out right there and then, and I said, 'Claire Reynolds, would you do me the honor of marrying me?'"

"And she said yes!" Myna squealed.

"And jumped into the water and into your arms," Linnet said.

He laughed. "Who's telling this story anyway?"

"We all are," Myna said. "It's a fun story to tell."

He put his arms around both girls' shoulders and pulled them close.

"And you lived happily ever after," Linnet said.

"Happily ever after," Myna echoed, believing in the fairy tale.

"Look," he said, and pointed to the sky at the geese flying overhead. "Here they come. The first flock of the season."

Myna lay on the bed, waiting for Ben to get out of the bathroom, her arms locked firmly across her chest. She was half paying attention to the television, trying to figure out what she could say or do to get him to drop the idea of marriage, when the program switched to a special news report. She recognized the face on the screen. She sat up straight. *Pop?* He was surrounded by a crowd of people. Someone shoved a microphone in his face.

She turned the volume up. Her father said, "I don't know." The reporter, Myna couldn't remember the guy's name. *Oh, what was it?* Hugh something-or-other. He was talking about dead geese and boiling water. Linnet appeared. "Leave him alone," she said. "He said he doesn't know." More words were exchanged, something about removing the birds from the dam. Pop became agitated, calling for their mother, Claire, knocking the microphone out of the reporter's hand just as the segment ended.

What the hell? Myna yanked the cell phone from her pocket. It had to be the reason why Linnet had tried calling earlier. She'd forgotten all about it, so upset with the disagreement between her and Ben. She checked her messages. There was a missed text message from Hank received ten minutes ago. *Did you hear what happened?*

She walked into the kitchen, texting him back. *I caught a little bit on the news. What's going on? Are you guys okay?*

She sat at the kitchen table waiting for Hank's reply, her leg bouncing up and down. Maybe she shouldn't wait for Hank. Maybe she should just call Linnet and find out what the hell was going on. Why was Pop on the news saying their mother's name as though she were still alive? Why had he looked, what was the word—confused? She was about to dial when her phone buzzed.

No, I'm not okay, Hank replied.

Skype me, she typed back.

She pulled the laptop from her bag. Hank had all the technology skills of young kids today. She'd watched him grow up mostly online through instant messages, Instagram, and Skype. It was times like this that she wished she would've gotten home more often than she did so that she could be in the same room with him and see for herself just how much he'd grown. Although she hadn't talked to Linnet much in the last few years, she and Hank had chatted regularly. Whether or not Linnet knew this, Myna couldn't say. Her leg continued to bounce as she waited for her nephew's face to appear on her screen.

"Hey kiddo, what's going on up there?" she asked. He looked so much like Ian, his white-blond hair and splattering of freckles across the bridge of his nose and cheeks. She remembered Linnet's early complaints about how when Hank had been a toddler her guests at the B&B had thought she was his babysitter rather than his mother. Myna caught herself searching her nephew's face. There had to be some resemblance to her sister in there somewhere, some resemblance to Myna. But nothing about him had changed since the last time they'd Skyped.

"There are, like, dead birds everywhere," Hank said. "In the dam. In the yard. Dad and I even saw one on the street on the way to school this morning. But mostly they're in the dam." He was excited and anxious and scared. He was moving around so much it was making her nauseous.

"Slow down," she said. "What birds? The snow geese?" She found she was just as anxious as he was.

"Yeah, like a hundred of them all floating facedown in the dam. Did you know they don't sink when they're dead? They're, like, floating on top of the water. It's really sad."

"It is," she said, trying to keep her face neutral and not show how upset she was to hear this about her father's birds. "How's Pop?" she asked. This had to be killing him.

"He's not good. It's like he doesn't understand what's going on. He gets all confused, and he acts weird. I can tell Mom's really worried about him." Hank wiped his nose with the back of his arm.

"Confused? How do you mean?" But she'd seen it for herself in that one minute he was on the TV.

"It's like he forgets stuff. Or he's forgetting more stuff. Stuff that just happened, or, I don't know. He eats all his meals with us now. I think Mom's afraid he'll burn the guesthouse down if he tries to cook anything on his own."

"Why didn't you say anything to me about this before?"

"What do you mean? The birds just died."

"I mean about Pop."

He shrugged.

She shouldn't be asking him these things. It wasn't Hank's responsibility to report back to her about her own father and his mental state. She had always been careful about not asking Hank a lot of questions, not wanting it to seem as though she were pumping him for information. Besides, Linnet should've been the one to tell her if Pop had gotten worse. Why hadn't she? But she knew why. It was because Linnet still saw her as a child and not a grown, capable woman.

"Aunt Myna," Hank said, and wiped his eyes. "Can you come here?"

Maybe it was hearing about the birds or Pop's condition, or maybe it was seeing her nephew upset. Maybe it was all of those things separately and combined that made her say, "I'll book the next flight out."

After Skyping with Hank and buying an airline ticket, Myna returned to the bedroom. She stood on her tiptoes, reaching for the shoe box on the back shelf of the walk-in closet. The tile was cold and hard beneath her feet. Her fingertips grazed the bottom of the box just enough to push it askew. She stretched another centimeter, touching her pointer finger to the lid, inching it toward her until she was able to pull it down.

The box itself was light, and anyone else might've assumed it was empty. *As light as a feather*, she mused. She removed the lid and took out the one item inside: a snow goose feather. She sat on the floor, spinning the quill slowly, thoughtfully, between her thumb and finger. It was a feather from a wing, mostly white but for the tip where it was stained black.

She couldn't shake the thought of all those dead birds, her poor father. And she couldn't help but think of her mother.

"Myna?" Ben emerged from the shower. He was wearing boxer shorts. The bath towel was hanging around his neck. He motioned to her suitcase on the bed. "Where are you going?" he asked.

"Home," she said, and stood. She left the empty shoe box on the floor in the closet and carried the feather over to the bed. She laid it carefully on top of the sweater she'd packed. She touched the silky barbules.

She turned to the dresser and pulled out a couple pairs of jeans from the bottom drawer.

"Look, if it's the way I did it, I can do it again, better." He tossed the wet towel on the floor. "I can do it in a more romantic way if that's what you want."

She pulled open another drawer, searching for socks. She'd have to bring her old sneakers. It was always so muddy in springtime around the dam. "It's not that," she said. "It's not how you did it."

"Then what is it? Help me out here. I'm trying to understand." He slipped on a pair of gym shorts and a T-shirt. His bangs, damp from the shower, fell into his eyes. The tops of his cheeks were pink, the rest of him was more or less tan—the kind of tan you get when you're out on a boat all day.

"I'm not leaving because of the whole marriage thing." She decided to put the feather inside the sweater as a way to protect it so it wouldn't get smashed. Then she placed the jeans on top. She never was any good at packing, stuffing her suitcases with whatever clothes would fit and then dashing away. She turned to Ben, hands on hips. "My father and sister were interviewed on the news. It has something to do with a bunch of snow geese turning up dead in the dam."

"Your father's birds?"

"Well, technically, they're not his birds, but yes." She touched her forehead. "It's more than just the birds. Hank said something about Pop. It sounds like he's getting worse. And Hank, well, he was just so upset."

Normally, whenever she was distressed, Ben would cross the room and pull her into his arms, comfort her, and do all those things only he could do to put her mind at ease. But he stayed where he was across the room, eying her.

"Do you want me to go with you?" he asked.

"No, it's okay. Maybe it's better if we spend some time apart," she said. If she gave him some space, gave him the opportunity to miss her, maybe he'd realize he'd want her in his life no matter what. "I know you have a bunch of tours scheduled. And I'm on spring break, so I really can't think of any reason why I shouldn't go."

"Or you can't think of any reason why you should stay," he said.

She looked away from him. She'd never seen this side of him before, but then again she'd never hurt him before. She was sorry. So, so sorry. But she didn't think she could give him what he was asking of her.

"I'd better get going if I'm going to make my flight." She zipped up the suitcase. He followed her out of the bedroom. She slung her big purse and computer bag over her shoulder.

She stopped at the door and turned around. "Let's not make any decisions right now."

"I already know what I want," he said. "You're the one who needs to decide what *you* want."

She lingered in the entranceway, looking back at him over her shoulder. He was always so sure of who he was and what he wanted. It was one of the reasons she'd fallen in love with him.

And yet all she could do in that moment was jump on a plane and fly away.

CHAPTER SIX

Linnet was in the kitchen with Cora, her part-time cook, when she heard a car pull into the driveway. "What am I going to tell them?"

"Tell them the truth. You can't control nature," Cora said. She was stout, with thick nimble fingers. A green apron was tied securely around her waist. She'd been working for Linnet the last eight years, taking over the breakfast and lunch menus, preparing hors d'oeuvres for happy hours. Cora had been a godsend, her cooking to die for. Business couldn't have been better.

"The truth it is," Linnet said, and pushed off the counter where she was leaning. Although she didn't know what the truth was at this point, whether the geese perished from a natural phenomenon or something much worse.

She stepped outside.

"Welcome back." She extended her hand to Mr. Rapp. He shook it hard. He was getting up there in age although his grip was strong. She guessed he must be pushing sixty.

"You're just in time for happy hour." Her plan was to get them settled in their room, drinks in their hands, food in their stomachs, before she told them not to go to the dam and see the birds.

Mr. Rapp helped his wife from the car. Linnet noticed Mrs. Rapp held a cane.

She lifted the silver stick to show Linnet. "I turned my ankle," she said. "It's just a sprain, but I'm afraid we won't be doing much hiking this year." She was referring to the Appalachian Trail and the smaller trails that led to the various waterfalls and mountain views.

"I'm sorry to hear that," Linnet said, sorrier than Mrs. Rapp could know. The Rapps had been staying at The Snow Goose for the last four years. Mr. Rapp was fascinated with the geese, while Mrs. Rapp loved the hiking. And now they were both going to be disappointed this trip. And Linnet didn't like her guests to be dissatisfied. "Let's get you settled in your room then."

"How many geese do we have on the dam?" Mr. Rapp asked. "I bought a new camera, and I'm eager to try it out."

Before Linnet could answer, another car pulled into the driveway. They all turned to stare. A man jumped out from the driver's seat. He was young and thin. His nose was narrow and sharp like a beak.

"I'm looking for Dr. Jenkins," he said in a rush. "It's about the dead birds." He wasn't making eye contact with anyone. He was looking over their shoulders into the backyard.

"I'll be with you in a moment," Linnet said, trying to usher the Rapps into the house. She noticed the university's parking permit hanging from the car's rearview mirror. He had to be the young professor Pop was expecting.

"What's this about dead birds?" Mr. Rapp asked.

She let out a slow breath. She didn't want to lose her regulars over this. *Truth.* "There are some dead geese on the dam," she said. "Quite a lot of them, actually. We're not sure yet what happened." She turned toward the young man. "I'm assuming you're from the university?"

"Professor Coyle." He extended his hand, and she took it. He continued pumping her arm up and down excitedly. He was jumpy, wiry, and full of energy. The opposite of what she'd expected. She couldn't say why, but she'd expected a soft-spoken, gentle kind of man. Someone more like her father.

By the time Linnet turned back around to see about getting the Rapps into their room, Mr. Rapp had already crossed the backyard on the way to the path that would lead him through the woods. He didn't wait for his wife, who hobbled along several steps behind.

"Come on," Linnet said to the professor. They both jogged to catch up.

They reached the dam in no time, poor Mrs. Rapp struggling to keep up. Linnet stood shoulder to shoulder with her guests and the professor on the grassy bank overlooking the water. Her sneakers sunk in the wet soft earth. The current had pushed most of the geese against the shoreline, a hundred birds floating facedown. The sight was still shocking and devastating all at once. She looked away, up at the blue sky, the clouds like wisps of white ribbon. There she saw a hawk circling. But where were the geese in their V formations? Why weren't they flying overhead?

The Rapps were silent. Perhaps they couldn't think of what to say. Professor Coyle crouched at the water's edge. "I'm going to need to see Dr. Jenkins," he said. "And then we need to get a couple of these birds on ice so I can transport them back to the lab."

"I've already got two geese in a cooler for you," she said.

The Rapps gave her an accusing look, one that asked why she hadn't contacted them before now about what had happened.

"Excellent. I'll just need a couple more." Professor Coyle stood and pointed to the trees. "Do you hear the robins?" He paused and turned his head as though he were listening hard for something else. "Blackbirds." He closed his eyes. "And maybe a cardinal or two."

Linnet hadn't noticed the sounds of the other birds in the woods. She'd been listening for the geese and nothing else. But now that she paid attention she could hear their songs as well as the faint breeze rustling the leaves.

"My guess is that whatever happened here is contained to the flock."

"How do you know?" Mr. Rapp asked.

"I don't know for sure," Professor Coyle said. "But the other bird species in the area don't seem to be affected, or we'd see them on the ground, too." He motioned to the dam. "And I'm not seeing any fish belly-up, so that's another good sign that it's probably not the water. Now, I'll have to run some tests, of course, to confirm anything."

"Of course," Linnet said. Pop should've been able to make the same observations. He should've told the reporter, the townspeople, what the young professor was telling them now. It could've reestablished their confidence in him. Or rather was it *her* faith in him that needed to be restored?

Professor Coyle picked up a stick and moved closer to the water's edge. His left foot sunk in the mud, but he didn't seem to notice. He used the stick and lifted the head of one of the geese, bending over to take a closer look.

From across the dam someone yelled, "Hello, there!" He was waving his arms in their direction. A bag was slung across his shoulder and chest.

Linnet looked behind her to check if there was anyone else around, but there wasn't. Apparently, he was talking to them.

"How can I get across?" the man yelled.

"Who is that?" Mrs. Rapp asked.

"He's a journalist," Professor Coyle said, and dropped the

stick. He wiped his hands on his pants. "He was in town asking questions about the birds."

"You stopped in town?" Linnet asked, but either Professor Coyle didn't hear her or he didn't want to answer.

"Wait right there," the journalist hollered, holding up his pointer finger.

"We have nothing to say to you," Linnet shouted back. She took Professor Coyle by the arm and helped him up the muddy bank. "I'll take you to see my father," she said to him. "But first, let's get you two settled," she said to the Rapps.

She directed her guests and the professor toward the path through the woods, pausing once to look over her shoulder at the journalist standing on the public dock. The crowd that was there earlier had dispersed, and he was alone. He looked to be from out of town. *Christ*, news traveled fast.

After Linnet had gotten the Rapps checked into their room and drinks in their hands, she helped the professor unload his gear. He came prepared to transport several birds back to the university's lab. The box in Linnet's arms was full of test tubes, plastic bags, and a small carton of latex gloves.

She pushed the front door of the guesthouse open with her foot, balancing the box in her arms. "Pop," she called. "Professor Coyle is here."

Pop stood from his chair when they entered the living room. Professor Coyle shook his hand and pumped his arm, saying over and over again what a pleasure it was to meet him although he wished it was under better circumstances.

"I came as soon as I could," Professor Coyle said. "My students were taking their exams today before spring break, and then I had to run a few errands. I couldn't get here until now."

He continued to explain his late arrival, his voice falling away when they disappeared into the study, where they'd both feel at home surrounded by books and journals and maps.

"I'm going back up to the house," Linnet called. Neither man answered her. It was just as well. She set the box down on the floor and closed the door behind her. She took the stone path to the main house, trying to remember the names of the young newly-weds who were expected to arrive anytime. Maybe she should've phoned all of her guests that morning when she'd first learned about the birds and given the couples the option of canceling their reservations. She walked with purpose, taking long strides, trying to figure out if she'd really messed up or not when a man stepped onto the path in front of her, sending her reeling backward.

"Shoot," she said. "You startled me."

"I didn't mean to. I was looking for a way to get to the dam."

The way he was staring at her made her uncomfortable. He was tall and his shoulders were broad. He blocked her way. "This is private property," she said. "You have to go around the other side for public access."

"I was over there, but it seems most of the dead geese have drifted over here."

She glared at him, taking an immediate dislike to him and his cavalier comment about her father's birds.

"Where are my manners?" he said, and reached into his jacket pocket and pulled out a business card. "I'm Jake Mann, journalist for the Lehigh Valley newspaper." He held out his card, but she refused to take it, realizing he was the journalist who had waved to them from across the way.

"Do you live here?" he asked.

"Yes."

"The B&B, right there?" He motioned to the main house that was at least twenty yards away.

"Yes," she said again. "Now get out of my way." She pushed past him.

He matched her stride. "Do you have a room I could rent?"

"No."

His steps faltered, but he rushed to catch up with her. "Wait."

"We're all booked."

"Will you at least take my card?" he asked. "Maybe something will open up."

"Why would something open up? Or are you planning on scaring people away with some fabricated story about the birds?"

"What? No," he said, and looked insulted that she would think he was the kind of journalist who would do something like that. But she didn't know him.

"Is there a problem?" Al appeared from around the corner of the house. He was holding pruning shears in his hand, finally getting around to shaping the rose bushes on the far side of the wraparound porch. Al was tall and strong, and the sharp shears made him look threatening. She'd never tell Ian or anyone else, but sometimes she'd catch something in Al's eyes when he looked at her, a lustful look that he'd flushed over on more than one occasion. Maybe she was being silly and the looks had been nothing. She hoped so.

"No problem here," she said. "Mr. Mann, was it?"

"Call me Jake," he said.

"Mr. Mann was just leaving," she said, and marched to the side door. She entered the kitchen just in time for Hank to burst into the room. He was a cyclone of energy when he came home from school and baseball practice. He threw his glove onto the table and dumped his backpack onto the chair. Ian was right behind him. They both wore baseball caps and smelled like the field, wet and dirty. Hank went right to the refrigerator in search of food. He was hungry all the time. At his recent physical, the pediatrician had said it was normal for growing boys to eat a lot. But the way he put away food was astounding. And where did it all go? He was thin, all knobs and bones.

Hank pulled out a small covered plate with a note from Cora on top. She'd made him a snack, knowing he'd be starving. It appeared she'd left for the day, and she wouldn't be back until the morning.

"Hello," someone called from the main entrance.

"That must be the new guests," she said to Ian. "A young couple." She left the kitchen to greet them. And oh, were they ever young. A twig of a girl clung to a boy's arm. The boy's cheeks were red. The girl hid behind his shoulder. Linnet had the distinct feeling she'd interrupted something. There was a small suitcase on the floor by their feet and what looked to be a bottle of champagne.

"I'm Mick." The boy touched his sunken chest. "And this is my wife, Emmy." He grinned. Emmy giggled. They looked like a couple of kids pretending to be grown-ups, but Linnet supposed if they were old enough to drink alcohol, then they were old enough to get married.

After all, Linnet had married Ian when she'd been only twenty-two, having met in college, saying I do three months after the ink on their diplomas had dried. They'd met her senior year. She and Myna had drifted so far apart by then; Linnet had been so vulnerable and lonely. She'd found Ian had been just as lonely, an only child and the kind of math genius that hadn't lent itself to having a lot of friends. He'd been prone to spending long hours alone working equations on the chalkboard in an empty classroom, which is where Linnet had stumbled upon him while on an errand for her father. She couldn't remember why she'd entered that particular room. Ian had been facing the chalkboard, his back to her, and he hadn't realized she'd barged in. She'd watched him, his long arm extending across the board, the way he'd cocked his head to the side as though he were deep in thought, the freckles on his earlobes. There had been something familiar about his intensity, a trait she'd found endearing in her own father. She hadn't been able to look away, but when he'd turned around and caught her staring, her heart seemed to have stopped.

For the next several months they'd worked side by side, making plans on how to improve The Snow Goose, crunching numbers, spending every free moment together, falling in love. At the same time, Ian had been pursued by financial investment and consulting firms across the United States, the salaries growing larger and larger the longer he'd held out. But in the end, all he'd really wanted was to teach. It had been Pop who had suggested the teaching position at Mountain Springs High School.

"Welcome to The Snow Goose," Linnet said to the young couple now. "If you want to follow me, I'll show you to your room. Cocktails are being served in the dining hall." They climbed the stairs. "I can give you a list of restaurants in the area and some places to visit while you're here." She hesitated. This was the part where she'd give her spiel about the snow geese.

"Oh, that's okay," Mick said wearing a sheepish grin. "We probably won't get out much. Well, at least not tonight anyway."

Emmy buried her face in his shoulder. "Mick, you're embarrassing me."

Linnet held up her hands. "Say no more." She stopped outside room number two and opened the door. "If you have any questions or you need anything, you can always find me in the kitchen at the back of the house."

There was an awkward silence.

"Enjoy your stay," Linnet said, and darted down the hall, hearing the door close and the click of the lock. At least some of her guests weren't here for the birds.

Ian was hanging up the phone by the time she returned to the kitchen. She hadn't heard it ring. Ian's face was pulled tight. She recognized the look of bad news.

"What is it?" she asked.

"The other couple that was supposed to arrive tonight just canceled."

Her body tensed. She didn't even realize she'd put her back up against the counter, arms folded defensively. There was more he had to tell her, but in typical Ian style he'd parcel out the bad news one snippet at a time so the hits came in succession, small and manageable, rather than one massive blow all at once.

She exhaled. They'd had cancelations before—someone gets ill, babysitting falls through, couples split—life happens.

"They heard about the birds," Ian said. "I think they were scared there might be something infectious around here. I didn't know what to tell them." He shrugged. "So they're not coming. It's not like it's the end of the world."

"Okay." She nodded. He was right. It wasn't the end of the world. Or maybe it was if you believed in the apocalyptic signs found in the Bible about birds falling from the sky, which Linnet did not. She was a scientist's daughter who believed in factual data. It was only a matter of time before Pop or the wiry young professor provided a reasonable explanation for the fallen birds.

Ian stared at her, his soft blue eyes searching hers.

"What else?" She pulled in a deep breath and waited for the final hit.

"You and Pop made the national news."

CHAPTER SEVEN

Jake was sitting at the bar in the Loose Goose. It was an old establishment by the looks of the scars on the wood and the heavy varnish attempting to conceal them, not to mention the hundred-year-old barn beams dissecting the ceiling. There was even an old dartboard hanging on the corner wall with metal darts pinned to its face. Peanut shells covered the floor. The place smelled of yeast and bodies and a hint of disinfectant. It had the feel of being well-loved, a favorite hangout for the locals.

Jake had rented a room above the pub for a measly eighty bucks a night. The room itself looked to be straight out of the seventies: rust-colored carpet, burnt orange bedcover, cracked toilet seat. Even the television was older than Jake. But he didn't care. He wasn't here to sit around and watch TV. He wasn't here to sleep one off, which was what he'd imagined was the purpose of the shabby accommodations upstairs.

He hadn't bothered with the fancier hotel in the center of town, the Mountain Springs Inn. He found if he wanted to get to the bottom of a story, it was best to mingle with the locals and steer clear of tourists. The locals were the ones with inside information, the juicier pieces of the events that made the news interesting. What better place to get the scoop about the dead birds, or about his father's car accident, than the neighborhood bar?

He drank from a frosted mug. His laptop was open in front of him. A stack of brochures boasting about nearby waterfalls, trails, and outdoor parks was piled to his side. But he wasn't interested in the other tourist attractions the Blue Mountains had to offer. He was only concerned with the dam and the snow geese for his article.

And the mountain road.

The dam was a seventy-eight-acre shallow waterway anywhere from four to five feet deep with the maximum depth of eight feet in the center, giving it a spoon-like shape. It was big, but not huge, packed with aquatic weeds, shallow vegetation, and grasses, an optimal food supply for hosting thousands of migrating snow geese. There was a public boat launch next to the gravel parking lot, the same lot he'd pulled into when he'd first arrived in town only to find most of the birds had drifted to the other side. The few locals that had remained lingering near the launch and dock had refused to answer his questions. He'd gotten back into his car, taking a winding road around the waterway only to get kicked off a certain B&B's property. So far his interactions with the people in Mountain Springs were far from welcoming.

He continued reading. Gas motors were prohibited on the dam, and electric motors were to be used with caution due to the shallow, weedy waters. The message was clear—manpowered boats were preferred. Oddly, he'd found only one listing for boat rentals in the area: Leo's, a canoe-and-rowboat rental shop. "Small-town monopoly," he grunted, and continued searching for more information, but all he found was the surface kind of stuff anybody with Internet access could pull up.

He checked his phone for messages from Kim. Nothing. He set it back down on the bar next to the laptop and stared at the article on the screen.

Who was he kidding?

He hadn't come for the birds, not really, although how convenient for them to have dropped from the sky at the exact time he needed to be in Mountain Springs.

He reached in his pocket and pulled out the old Nokia, rubbing his finger along the deep grooves in the back where it had been scratched.

"Your father would've been so proud of you." Jake's mother had come up behind him where he'd been sitting at the dining room table next to several letters and a stack of brochures. She placed her hand on his shoulder. He'd been accepted to all three colleges where he'd applied.

"I didn't expect you home until later," he said. He thought she'd be working until the library closed at 7 P.M. He tried to look casual, putting his arm over the brochure in front of him, covering it from her view.

"What's this?" she'd asked, and had removed it from under his forearm. She was petite and thin. Her hands were no bigger than a child's. She still wore her wedding ring. He couldn't meet her eyes.

"Me and some of the guys were hoping to go away for senior week."

She shook her head. "Find someplace else to go," she said, dropping the Blue Mountain brochure on the table. "You can't go there. I can't . . ." She broke off. "You just can't."

He covered it with his arm again. Why couldn't she understand this wasn't about her? This was about him. The very reason she didn't want him to go was the very reason he *longed* to go. She was scared. He was curious. His father had done a lot of traveling as a salesman, selling roofing and siding for old and new homes alike. He'd rarely been home. He'd been traveling when the car accident occurred in Mountain Springs on some godforsaken road, and Jake just wanted to see the place where he'd lost him.

"Why don't you go to the Jersey shore or Ocean City, Maryland?"

"It's cheaper to go to the mountains," he said, feeling defiant and, at the same time, ashamed. The few memories he had of his father were fading, and he was grasping at anything, terrified he'd wake up one day only to realize he'd forgotten everything about him.

"Please," she said, her voice cracking. "Pick somewhere else to spend the week."

Jake drained his beer and signaled Rodney, the bartender who'd rented him the room, for another draft. He was the only customer at the moment if he didn't count the two old men at the other end of the bar who looked as though they were permanent fixtures in the place.

Rodney refilled the mug, lingering, waiting for Jake to look up from his computer.

"What's that?" Rodney asked. He was short and thick around the middle. His dark eyes were kind. He motioned to Jake's left hand. "Is that a championship ring?"

"This?" Jake lifted his hand. "Yeah. It was my dad's."

Rodney poured himself a beer.

Jake wondered if Rodney should be drinking, but figured the man owned the place and could do whatever he wanted. "My dad wore it on his pinky because his ring finger was banged up from playing. I think he might've had some arthritis because of it." His words came out in a rush. "My father was killed in a car accident near here on the mountain road."

The door to the pub swung open. They both turned to see who had walked in. A guy in work pants and a flannel shirt sauntered over. Jake recognized him as the man who'd been holding the pruning shears earlier at the B&B.

"Al," Rodney said, and poured him a cold one.

"Did you hear about the geese?" Al asked.

"It's a damn shame," Rodney said.

"I took some pictures," Al said, and held up his phone.

Rodney shooed the phone away. Jake had the feeling he was trying to tell Al to be careful about what he said next. Al took a long, hard look at Jake.

Jake turned on his stool and stuck his hand out. "Jake Mann. Journalist from the Lehigh Valley newspaper."

Al shook his hand. "I remember you," he said. "You're the guy Linnet chased out of her yard today."

"Linnet is the woman from the B&B?" Jake asked.

"That's right."

"Then that would be me." He pointed to Al's phone. "Do you mind if I take a look?"

Al stuck his phone in his back pocket and picked up his beer.

"Or not," Jake said, and turned toward the bar and lifted his own mug.

"Just so you're aware, The Snow Goose is private property," Al said, and wiped his mouth with the back of his arm. "I'm the groundskeeper, and unless you're a guest of Linnet's, you've got no business being there or asking her any questions. Am I making myself clear?"

"I'm not looking for any trouble. I'm just here to report the news." *What was this guy's problem anyway?*

"Yeah, well, there's a lot of you reporters poking around," Al said. "There's a whole bunch of you at the Inn. I bet you can't wait to tell everybody the water is contaminated or it's some new bird disease or some other kind of bullshit. You scare people half to death and then move on to some other town, some other story, and scare everybody there, too."

"All right, Al," Rodney said.

Al finished his beer, wiping his mouth on his forearm for a second time. He tossed a couple bills onto the bar and walked toward the door. He stopped and looked over his shoulder. "Well, aren't you coming?" he asked Jake. "All your buddies are lining up at the town hall waiting for the mayor to speak."

"Shit." Jake threw some cash onto the bar. He hadn't heard about the town meeting. He packed up his laptop and picked up his phone. No messages. He raced out the door after Al, who was already halfway down the block.

"Hold up," Jake called, but it was apparent Al wasn't going to wait. Jake slowed his pace and decided he'd have to follow several paces behind.

Al had made it pretty clear. Jake was the outsider here.

Mountain Springs Town Hall looked like any other municipal building in any other town: square-shaped, layered in brick, and lacking any character. The water fountain in the courtyard with the two bronze snow geese was the only identifying feature. Reporters and their cameramen vied for spots near the sculpture preparing to go live with the news. People milled around. Some carried shopping bags. Others were bent over smartphones.

Jake recognized the local news team from the Lehigh Valley. Others were from the station in Lackawanna County. A couple of news vans were from out of state—two from New Jersey and one from New York. But the biggest attention was being paid to a crew from CNN, with people crowding around the reporter, waving into the camera, claiming their five seconds of fame. Jake couldn't help but think this could be trouble for Mountain Springs. Yes, the small town would get national attention, but the kind of attention they'd attract, possibly from environmentalists or end-of-the-world religious fanatics, wouldn't be what they'd want hanging around their watering hole, gawking at their precious birds.

He took the steps two at a time and entered the building, taking in its stale air and polished floors. He found a seat in the back of the room, where everyone was quieting down now that the mayor appeared behind the podium. The chief of police stood next to him, a much taller, older man. The chief's stature alone sent the signal that order would be maintained.

Jake looked around, searching for someone or something. He was half-listening to the mayor's speech. He wasn't sure what he was looking for, a hint or clue of some kind. He spied Al leaning against the far wall. Sitting in a chair across from Al was the woman from the B&B, Linnet. Jake recognized her straight dark hair, the pale skin of her face and neck. He suspected she was a couple of years older than him, but she wasn't a bad-looking woman. No, he'd say she was quite attractive. Although the way she was sitting, erect and stiff, made her look harder than he imagined she was. She looked as if she were preparing for a fight.

Jake jotted down what notes he'd need for his article. Someone from the National Wildlife Health Center was expected tomorrow. Plans were being made about the best method to dispose of the carcasses. Another warning was issued to the townspeople about not touching the birds as a safety precaution.

"We'll let the experts handle this," the mayor said.

"What about the doc?" someone called from the back of the room. More chatter erupted about someone they referred to as the Bird Man. "What does he have to say about all of this?"

"Where is he anyway?" another man asked. "Shouldn't he be here?"

Jake leaned toward the man sitting next to him. It was obvious he wasn't a journalist since he wasn't holding a notepad or a recorder or other electronic device; instead, he worried his hands in his lap.

"Who's the Bird Man?" Jake asked him at the same time Linnet spoke up.

"My father's working with a professor from the university now," Linnet began. The room grew quiet. All eyes were focused on her. "He'll have the answers you're looking for as soon as he can."

Someone behind Jake whispered, "I wouldn't count on it. Not after what I saw of him this morning."

Jake turned around. "What does that mean?"

The man sitting next to Jake shouted, "What about fishing season? We're coming up on opening day. The dam has to be cleaned of those birds by then."

There were more outbursts from the crowd. The mayor was trying to calm everyone down.

Jake looked up in time to catch Linnet slipping out the back door.

CHAPTER EIGHT

Linnet had taken firm control over any and all decisions the sisters made around the time she'd turned ten years old. It had started one day in early fall when the leaves on the trees had begun to change. She and Myna had been playing hopscotch on the sidewalk in front of the elementary school. Linnet had been clearly beating Myna by two squares, but she'd purposely tossed her rock outside the lines to give her sister a chance to catch her.

Myna stuck her tongue out the side of her mouth, concentrating hard on her next toss, when the hollering started. There was yelling, voices coming from the playground behind the building. They stopped the game to listen.

"Come on," Linnet said, and dropped her rock. Their mother was late picking them up again. They both knew it would be awhile before she'd remember she had two daughters who needed a ride home. Every third Wednesday, Linnet and Myna stayed after school to work on an art project, a mosaic that would cover a section of the outside wall on the side of the building. Only the best artists in school were asked to participate. Today had been the sisters' day to take part in the school's beautification project.

They snuck along the side of the building, staying close to the brick wall. Linnet's arm scraped the rough surface, scratching her skin, but she pretended not to notice. They peeked around the corner.

A few of the boys from Linnet's class were standing in a circle. One of them had a ball tucked under his arm. A cloud of dust kicked up around their feet and billowed around their legs. Skyler, a boy she recognized from gym class, picked up a stone and threw it. Another boy that looked much older darted from the group and picked up more stones. Some of the others copied him.

"Look," Myna said, and pointed to the center of the circle. "It's a robin."

The boys started chucking rocks at the small bird, laughing and yelling, "Come on, you stupid bird, fly!"

"Yeah, fly!"

"Why doesn't it fly?" Skyler asked, and threw another stone. The robin fluttered its wings, but it wasn't flying away. More rocks were thrown. More of the boys shouted, "Fly, you stupid bird!"

Linnet had never seen something so horrible, so ugly. She wasn't thinking when she rushed onto the playground, screaming for the boys to stop. Myna was by her side, arms flailing, shouting. The boys stopped to stare. Myna continued shrieking, tears on her cheeks. Blue chalk stained the front of her white T-shirt. Her curls stuck up in all directions.

"Gonna run home and tell your daddy, cry baby?" the older boy said, pointing at Myna and laughing.

Linnet shoved him. The other boys laughed and continued throwing stones at the injured robin.

"Knock it off," she said, pushing the boys, trying to get them to stop. When they wouldn't, she ran into the center of their circle to protect the bird, putting her own body in harm's way.

A stone struck her cheek. More stones were hurled, pelting her arms and legs. Before she realized what was happening, Myna had darted behind her and snatched up the small robin in her hands. The next thing she knew, Myna was running and yelling for her to follow. Linnet took off after her, but not before the last stone struck her in the back of the head. For a moment, everything went black. "Babies!" someone called. When her vision cleared, she ran to the front of the school, where their mother's car sat idling.

"What do you have there?" their mother asked. She was wearing her bathrobe.

"It's a robin, and it's injured," Myna said, holding the bird up for her to see.

"Well, what are you waiting for then? Get in."

"The bird, too?" Myna asked.

"Yes, the bird, too."

Linnet picked up their backpacks and blue chalk. Myna held the robin in her lap in the backseat.

"You're bleeding," Myna said, and pointed to Linnet's face.

Linnet touched her cheek. Her fingers came away bloody. She caught her mother looking at her in the rearview mirror. Their eyes met. Linnet turned away, toward the bird perched between her sister's legs, and gently stroked the feathers on its back.

When the car stopped in the driveway, both sisters scooted out. "We need to find a shoe box," Myna said. "And fill it with grass."

Their mother got out of the car and came to stand beside them. She not only was in her ratty old bathrobe but she was also wearing her worn, fuzzy slippers. She lifted Linnet's chin with her finger and inspected the cut on her cheek. Her breath smelled stale.

"Come inside and let me clean that up for you," she said.

Linnet and Myna exchanged a look before following her into

the house. Myna carried the bird to their bedroom in search of a shoe box, while Linnet followed their mother into the bathroom. She hoisted herself onto the counter at the sink. Her mother wiped the blood and dirt away with a soft wet towel. Then she dabbed at the cut on Linnet's cheek with Bactine.

"Do you want to tell me what happened?" she asked.

Linnet shook her head. She didn't want to talk about the mean boys and ruin the moment of having her mother near and doing the kinds of things she used to do when Linnet was younger, covering scrapes with Band-Aids, reading her books, holding her close, all the things she'd stopped doing around the same time she began locking herself away, unable to leave her bedroom.

Her mother caught her staring. "What is it?" she asked, and looked over Linnet's shoulder at her reflection in the mirror. She touched her hair, the dark strands limp and oily. Something sad moved across her face. She pulled Linnet into her arms and kissed the top of her head. Then she stepped back and wiped her watery eyes. "You better go find your sister and take that bird to your father." She helped Linnet down from the countertop. She shooed her out the bathroom door.

Linnet stood for a moment in the hall, hearing the click of the lock. She reached for the knob, wanting to tell her mother to please let her back in, to tell her why she'd been so sad these last months and what she could do to make her happy again. But she stopped herself for reasons she couldn't fully explain.

She made her way to the kitchen, where she found Myna sitting at the table with the bird in a shoe box.

"Are you okay?" Myna asked.

She touched her cheek below the cut. "Yes," she said, looking back over her shoulder toward the hall and bathroom. "Let's go find Pop."

Myna picked up the box and followed her outside. They

walked the stone path to his study. A breeze blew. The first autumn leaves fell to the ground.

"Should we tell him that Mom picked us up late again, and she was wearing her bathrobe and slippers?" Myna asked.

"No," she said. "It will only upset him." It felt like something they should keep to themselves, something private and wrong that shouldn't be talked about, not even with Pop.

They burst through the door of the guesthouse. "Pop!" they called.

It would be the first of many secrets the sisters kept.

Linnet returned home from the town hall meeting to find Ian waiting for her on the front porch swing with a bottle of wine. She plopped down next to him and rested her head on his shoulder. The scent of him, the cologne he wore in the daytime, lingered on his skin. The smell was so soothing she wished she could curl up inside it, never leave the safety of his arms.

"Did Hank get his homework done?" she asked. She hadn't seen Hank for more than a couple of minutes. The day had been one thing after another. She'd felt Hank pulling away from her in the last few months. It was a normal part of growing up, but on occasion, if she was lucky enough to get him alone, the little boy she'd remembered would show up, relaying the gossip of the school day, giving her a play-by-play of baseball practice. "Maybe I should go check on him."

"He's fine," Ian said. "A little more tired than usual, but it was a long day."

"All the more reason I should check on him." She went to get up, but Ian pulled her back down.

"Just sit for a minute." He handed her a glass of wine. The swing rocked slow and steady. "What happened at the meeting?"

"There's not much to tell. The Wildlife Health Center was contacted. They're expected to send someone tomorrow. They're going to start the cleanup then." She'd left the meeting relatively unnoticed. There was a moment when someone had mentioned Pop and her heart had leapt into her throat, but she'd responded calmly. The conversation had then been redirected, people shouting over each other. No one was being heard. Reporters were everywhere. She'd recognized the journalist she'd chased off her property earlier in the day. There was something about his face that was strangely familiar, unsettling even, but she was almost certain they'd never met before.

She rested her head against Ian's shoulder again, balancing the glass on her thigh. "How's Pop?"

"He seemed good when I saw him about an hour ago. The younger guy, Professor Coyle, he's still with him."

"Okay," she said. At least Pop wasn't alone. "That's good."

Ian continued. "The Rapps have gone out for the evening," he said. "And I don't think that other couple has left the room."

"I'm not surprised."

They were quiet. The chains on the swing creaked. The crickets chirped. Darkness, thick and black, spread across the sky. The two big maple trees and the cherry blossoms blocked the view of the mountain road.

"This is going to hurt the town, isn't it?" she asked. She didn't buy into the theory that any attention whether, it was good or bad, was a positive thing. All of those news vans parked in front of the town hall and all of those reporters rushing around with their cameramen created chaos, panic. Fear.

"I don't think it's going to be good for business," Ian said, no doubt checking the numbers of the guests that had already canceled for the weekend, the money they'd lost. He was a numbers guy after all. "And it's not just our business that's going to be affected either."

The swing continued to rock.

She thought about the boat rental shop, the stores and restaurants in town that counted on the birds to bring in the tourists. She thought about her own B&B, and what it would mean to her and her family if they were to lose more reservations. But what troubled her most was how the snow geese continued to pass them over throughout the long day. Climate impacted migration patterns, but a dam full of dead geese could have the same effect.

"What if the birds stop coming?" she asked, allowing a much deeper concern to surface.

"Let's not get ahead of ourselves," Ian said. "Let's wait and see what kind of explanation the lab comes up with. Things may turn around once the dam is cleaned up."

He was right, of course. They'd have to wait and see, but waiting wasn't her strength.

Headlights cut across the yard. She lifted her head from his shoulder. A car pulled into their driveway.

"Who the heck is that at this hour?" he asked.

But Linnet knew who it was. She'd felt it all day underneath her skin, deep inside her bones, the essence of the other half of her, the presence that had been silent for far too long. She squeezed his thigh. "It's Myna," she said.

Her sister had come home.

CHAPTER NINE

Myna had been so preoccupied during the flight thinking about Ben, about what he'd asked of her, that she hadn't been prepared for the rush of memories that flooded her when she pulled into the driveway of The Snow Goose. It had been five years since she'd stopped coming home. She was at once struck with a physical ache, a kind of homesickness she hadn't felt since the day she'd left. The feeling was so strong she clutched her chest.

By the time she stepped out of the car, she was hit with another wave of emotion, but this one was much deeper, darker.

She unloaded her luggage from the trunk of the rental, a hideous neon blue compact, and debated whether or not she should use the kitchen entrance on the side of the house or use the front door like a guest. Technically, she was an unexpected visitor in her sister's home, unless of course Hank had warned his mom she was coming.

She decided it was best to use the front door since she wasn't sure what kind of reception she'd receive. She used the walkway toward the porch, rolling the suitcase behind her, struggling with the wheels on the pavers, tripping the motion detectors.

Another large bag containing her laptop was slung across her shoulder, weighing her down on one side.

"You're right. It's her," she heard her brother-in-law say.

The chains on the porch swing creaked. Ian rushed down the steps. "Well, this is a surprise." He took the shoulder bag from her.

"Hank told me what happened, but I gather he didn't tell you I was coming." She looked past Ian, finding Linnet standing on the porch leaning against a post. She couldn't read Linnet's face. There was a time when all the sisters had to do was look at each other and they'd know what the other was thinking, feeling. Tonight, she blamed the shadows, the dark night, for her inability to interpret her sister's mood.

Ian glanced over his shoulder, motioning to Linnet, coaxing her off of the porch. He didn't understand the sisters' relationship. That much was clear. He'd told them once after they had gone through a long silence that had lasted for months that he thought they'd made it more complicated than it had to be. *But there was so much he didn't know*, Myna thought now. The things between sisters they'd never share.

Linnet smoothed her straightened hair. Myna was suddenly conscious of her own unruly curls crowding her face and neck, the flyaway strands breaking free in the damp air.

"Aunt Myna!" Hank called, and burst out the door, running down the steps and into her outstretched arms. She pulled him close. "I missed you guys," she said, and looked up at her sister, who hadn't moved from the porch.

"I thought you were in bed," Linnet said to Hank.

"Come on," Ian said, taking the handle of the suitcase. "Let's all go inside."

They walked up the steps to where Linnet was waiting. She gave Myna a quick hug. Then Linnet picked up a bottle of wine she and Ian must've been sharing before Myna had crashed their party. Hank grabbed Myna's arm and pulled her inside.

She stepped into the familiar foyer that opened into the grand living room and den where the guests were welcome to spend time. The heavy draperies, the woodwork, the leather furniture had a warmth that was inviting, and yet she'd spent very little time here. Her memories were stacked in the kitchen, where she and Linnet had shared meals and played card games, spied on their mother. Other memories were tucked safely inside the bedroom, where she'd slept in the same bed with her sister until she'd moved out after graduating college. Those two rooms had been her home. The rest of the house had belonged to the strangers who had visited.

Myna plopped down in one of the chairs at the big kitchen table. "So tell me about the birds," she said.

Ian and Hank sat across from her. Linnet took a position by the counter.

"There are hundreds of them in the dam, and they're all facedown like they're looking for something, but they're not, you know? They're not looking for anything anymore," Hank said, sinking lower in the chair.

Linnet went to him. She put her arm around him. He pulled away. Myna wondered if there was something else going on with Hank that she didn't know about.

Ian began filling Myna in on the recent events. So far, Linnet had avoided talking to her directly.

"What does Pop have to say about it?" She looked to her sister to answer.

Linnet had moved back against the counter again, putting distance between them. "He doesn't know. They have to collect samples, run tests. But he did say it's not as unusual as people might think. Large flocks of birds have dropped dead from the sky throughout history. The causes vary. Some known. Some unknown."

"Well, Pop would know," Myna said. "He must be really upset. Maybe I should go see him now." She stood up.

"I don't think that's a good idea," Linnet said.

"Why not?"

"He's with a professor from the university. And you know how Pop doesn't like to be disturbed when he's working."

She stared at Linnet, trying to decide whether her sister was right. But of course she was. When was her sister ever wrong about anything? *Once*, she thought. Her sister was so very wrong, once.

"Okay," Myna said, and sat back down. "I guess I can wait until the morning." She turned to Hank, redirecting the conversation to avoid the uneasiness she sensed in the room. "So tell me what you've been up to?" She peppered him with questions about school and baseball. When she mentioned girls, he replied, "Ew, gross." *So he isn't there, yet*, Myna thought with a smile. He was still a boy in many ways despite how much bigger he looked now that she was finally in the same room with him, face-to-face. He was in that awkward stage, his arms and legs lanky, all folded in sharp angles.

When the conversation died down, Ian ushered Hank upstairs, giving the sisters some time alone. Not that either one had asked for it. The kitchen was quiet without the guys. Myna was the youngest, so naturally she expected Linnet to speak first.

"So you're home," Linnet said.

"I'm home," Myna said. "Is that okay?"

"Why wouldn't it be?"

"I don't know. It's just the way you said it, *so you're home*."

"I didn't mean anything by it," Linnet said. She looked tired.

Her eyes were plagued with the dark circles of a stressful day. "You can have the guest room on the right at the end of the hall." Linnet and Ian had taken over the master bedroom, and Hank slept in the room the sisters had shared. The four guest rooms were located on the third floor at the opposite end of the house.

Myna played with her fingernail. Then she smoothed the long wrap skirt that had bunched up in her lap. Her face and arms were tan from the Florida sun except for the oblong discoloration on her left forearm. It was bleached white. Their mother had the same blemish. Myna suspected Linnet used to envy the birthmark, a connection that had once belonged to Myna and their mother alone.

Now, she bet her sister was glad she didn't have a constant reminder branded on her skin.

"That will be great," Myna said about the room.

Neither one spoke after that. The silence between them became unbearable.

"If you don't mind, it's been a long day," Linnet said. "Breakfast is at nine if you want to join us."

"Great. Thanks." She returned to picking her nail.

"Well, good night," Linnet said, pausing outside the kitchen doorway and turning back to stare at her. She was finally giving Myna a look she recognized, the older-sister glare, saying, *There's something you're not telling me.*

Her sister wanted to know the real reason why Myna had come running home.

CHAPTER TEN

Linnet was in the kitchen helping Cora prepare breakfast for the Rapps and the young couple, who had requested a tray be sent to their room. Hank hadn't gotten up yet, and Linnet had no idea if Myna was awake or not. She wanted to knock on her sister's door and ask if she'd be joining them for breakfast, but she didn't want to sound, what? Pushy? Bossy?

Too much like a big sister.

The house smelled of eggs and bacon and Saturday mornings. It was Linnet's favorite day of the week, when she could sit at the kitchen table with her family and they could talk over a leisurely meal without either of her guys having to rush out the door for work and school.

She wiped her hands on a tea towel after buttering a stack of toast. "I'm going to get Pop," she told Cora.

Ian walked into the kitchen, freshly showered and wearing a grin. "I'll go get him for you," he said. Last night she'd been so tired, but she'd been unable to fall asleep. First the birds and then her sister's arrival had both surprised and hurt her, each in a different way, leaving her feeling open and raw. She'd reached for Ian for comfort, wanting his long, lean body to envelop every inch of her, to wrap her in the safety of his love. She'd cried out louder than she'd intended, not wanting to wake up Hank, but she'd been overwhelmed with desire, the physical need to be as close to Ian as she could be. She hadn't been that uninhibited in the bedroom in quite some time. Ian hadn't complained.

She watched out the garden window as he strolled across the backyard. His hands were in his pockets, and she could've sworn he was whistling. She smiled to herself and picked up the plate of toast. She was about to turn around to put it on the table when she noticed he stopped walking suddenly. She paused, wondering what it was that caught his attention, the plate in her hand hanging in midair. He craned his neck toward the path that led through the woods to the dam. His stride lengthened as he made his way over to whatever it was. Her breath stalled and her pulse raced. It was the way he moved, fast and purposeful, that she sensed something was wrong, the way you knew it was bad before you even understood what had happened.

He knelt on one knee, looking at something on the ground. He shook whatever it was as though he were trying to wake it up.

"What is it?" she asked, although he obviously couldn't hear her.

Cora turned from the stove, the spatula in her hand dripping grease onto the floor. "What's wrong?"

Ian looked toward the house. His face was pale where a minute ago it had been flushed with happiness. Now he appeared as though he were going to be sick. He caught sight of Linnet in the garden window.

"What is it?" she shouted, dropping the plate of toast when another thought cut across her mind. *Pop.* She raced through the kitchen and flung herself out the side door, running toward Ian, who had started rushing toward her. He met her halfway in the yard and caught her in his arms.

"Hang on," he said.

"Pop!" She peered over his shoulder, struggling to get around him.

"No," he said, and grabbed her arms. "It's the young professor. What's his name? Professor Coyle."

"It's not Pop?"

Ian shook his head. "It's not Pop."

"I was so scared." She exhaled, her lungs deflating like a leaky balloon. Ian's grip on her biceps loosened now that she had calmed down. She swallowed hard. "Is he okay?" she asked about Professor Coyle, who was clearly not okay.

His body lay motionless on the ground.

Ian shook his head and pulled out his cell phone. "Hello, yes, I need an ambulance," he said, and gave the address for the B&B. He looked in Linnet's eyes as he said to whomever was on the other line, "And I think you better send the police."

Ian waited in the backyard for the ambulance or the police—whomever would arrive first. Linnet headed to the guesthouse as the sun made its way over the mountain. The air smelled damp and earthy, mixed with something rotten. In the not far distance, she heard sirens. She hadn't said anything to Ian outright, but she was worried about how Pop would react to the commotion, the news of Professor Coyle. She and Ian had had numerous conversations and some disagreements in the last few weeks about Pop's increasing forgetfulness.

"It's not something that gets better," Ian had said. "There is no cure. You shouldn't be expected to care for him and make all the decisions where he's concerned. It's your sister's responsibility, too."

"She doesn't know how bad it's gotten. Besides, he lives here with *me*. Us," she quickly corrected herself and then added, "I won't put him in a home."

An exasperated look had crossed Ian's face. The topic of her father and sister had become an instant blemish on their otherwise happy marriage.

She knocked on the door and called, "Pop." *Please, let this be one of your good days*, she thought, before letting herself in with the key she always kept in her front pocket. She nearly tripped over the cooler with the frozen birds inside, bumping her shin in the process. *Ouch.* It blocked the entranceway along with the young professor's boxes and another cooler that must've belonged to him as well. It took her a second to process why his things would still be stacked by the door. It became apparent he hadn't left last night like he'd planned. Otherwise, the samples of water he'd collected and the geese would've been at the university lab. She didn't know why, but she'd assumed whatever had happened to him had taken place this morning, but it appeared that wasn't the case at all. Somewhere in the back of her mind, she recalled seeing his car in the driveway wet with dew when she'd rushed outside thinking it had been Pop on the ground in the yard. At the time, she hadn't processed what it had meant. The professor's car had sat there all night, another sign he'd never left.

"Pop," she called again, a knot forming in her chest. She scooted around the boxes. She found him in his study, his spectacles perched on his nose, an open book in his hands. He was up and dressed, his wavy white hair combed. A good sign.

"What are you reading?" She couldn't blurt out what had happened. She'd have to ease into it so she wouldn't upset him.

"I was reading up on a case in Oregon. They had a similar situation with dead geese on Staats Lake in Keizer."

"That's interesting," she said. Outside the sirens grew louder and louder. She was running out of time. "Did they say what caused them to die?"

"Inconclusive evidence."

"Did you tell Professor Coyle about it?"

"No, no."

He remembered the young professor. Another good sign. "Wasn't he supposed to take the birds to the lab last night?" she asked, pinching the bridge of her nose, hoping for a reasonable answer.

"Yes. He didn't?"

"No, he didn't."

"He must have. He isn't here." He looked around the room.

"No, he's not." She rubbed her brow. The sirens were so loud she couldn't hear herself think. "We need to go up to the house now," she said, having to yell to be heard.

"I was wondering if you would drive me to the university today," he yelled back, and then paused. "Those sirens are awfully close," he shouted. "I hope someone didn't get hurt on the mountain road. You know how dangerous it can be."

"I know. But the accident didn't happen on the mountain road," she hollered back. The sirens stopped. Men's voices were coming from the backyard. "It happened here, Pop," she said in her normal voice. "Right outside."

"Oh." His eyebrows rose.

"Professor Coyle is hurt." She took him by the elbow and guided him out of the study to the living room.

"Is he going to be okay?" he asked.

"I don't know," she said. "I don't think so."

"He forgot the birds." He motioned to the coolers and boxes in the foyer. "And the samples."

"I know."

"We have to get them to the lab."

"We will, I promise, but right now we have to go."

She led him outside. Charlie was talking with Ian. She was glad that it had been Charlie who had arrived first. But of course, he lived only ten minutes down the road. Two of his officers were with him. One of them held a roll of yellow crime scene tape.

She met Charlie's gaze. "I'm going to take Pop up to the main house if that's okay."

He nodded.

She looked at Ian. "Hank?"

"As far as I know, he's still sleeping."

She couldn't see how with all the noise. "Come on, Pop. Let's go check on Hank." She slipped her arm through his as they headed toward the house. She needed to prepare him for one more surprise. "You'll never guess who came to visit," she said.

"Myna's here," Pop said as soon as he stepped into the kitchen. Myna was standing with her back to the garden window, her arm wrapped around Hank's shoulder. They were both in their pajamas.

"Hi, Pop," Myna said, and rushed into his arms.

"What's going on?" Hank asked. "Aunt Myna wouldn't let me go outside with Dad. Is it the birds?"

"No, it's not the birds." Linnet put her hand on his shoulder. "The young professor from the university, the one who came to help with the geese? . . . He had an accident."

"Is he going to be okay?"

Linnet felt both Myna and Pop's eyes on her. She bent down so that she was eye level with Hank. "It's nothing for you to worry about. Accidents happen. And Charlie's going to take care of everything." When she stood, she found Cora in the kitchen doorway, her apron knotted around her thick waist. The Rapps were behind her along with the newlyweds.

"We heard the sirens. What are the police doing here?" Mr. Rapp asked. "We were afraid to go outside."

"It's going to be okay," she said, and opened her arms wide, herding them back into the dining room. "There was an accident. That's all." She motioned to Cora to continue with breakfast. Cora nodded and opened the refrigerator door, pulling out a pitcher of orange juice.

While Linnet focused on her guests, she heard Myna say to Hank, "Come on, let's get dressed. We'll get something to eat when we come back down."

Linnet glanced at her sister; thankful she'd been there for Hank and had not let him outside where the professor's body lay in the yard.

Charlie gathered everyone together in The Snow Goose and directed them to have a seat in the grand living room. Linnet sat on the big leather couch next to Ian. She gripped his hand. Her other hand rested on Hank's leg. Myna sat on the other side of Hank, hugging one of the throw pillows to her chest. Pop sat next to Myna. "Myna's home," he'd said repeatedly for the last hour.

The Rapps were seated in the two armchairs across from them. The newlyweds were wrapped around each other on the love seat. Cora slouched in one of the chairs they'd pulled from the dining room table.

Charlie was about to speak when one of his men called him back outside. "Stay put," he said in a tone Linnet recognized as his cop voice. There had been times when he'd answered a call on police matters in their presence, and his words came out crisper, sharper, more commanding.

They waited in silence for Charlie to come back. Linnet resisted the urge to open the heavy draperies to let the sunlight in. The room was dark, but she didn't want Hank to see where the police had blocked off their yard with yellow crime scene tape. Poor Professor Coyle's body was still out there while Charlie's men processed the scene.

After a few more minutes of uncomfortable quiet, Charlie returned. "We're treating it like a crime scene," he said, "until we can figure out what happened here."

"So it is possible he could've had a heart attack or something?" Ian asked.

"Or it's possible he might've slipped and fallen," Linnet said.

Charlie pinned his gaze on her. "What makes you think that?"

"I don't know." She just said it, trying to come up with something, anything to reason away a deeper fear that had started niggling away at her ever since she'd stepped into her father's study. "The yard is always a little damp and muddy this time of year. And we had a bad thunderstorm the other night."

Charlie nodded. "I'm not ruling anything out at this point."

Hank's stomach rumbled. He'd barely touched his eggs.

"We'll get you something to eat soon," she said, reassuring him this would all be over shortly.

Charlie asked each one of them questions about their activities in the last twenty-four hours. The Rapps confirmed they'd gone out for the evening, supplying the name of the restaurant in town. The newlyweds admitted to never leaving their room. Cora was home with her family all evening.

"Why are you treating us like suspects?" Linnet asked Charlie. "It has to be some kind of accident."

But Charlie ignored her and kept going down the line with his questions, everyone stating they hadn't left their rooms after going to bed. He stopped his interrogation when he came to Pop. He pulled another chair from the dining room table and set it next to him at the end of the couch.

"What about you, Doc?" he asked in a careful voice. "When was the last time you saw Professor Coyle?"

"Well, I don't know," Pop said.

"Think, Pop," Linnet said. Her heart thrummed. "It's important."

"I don't know. I don't remember." He looked at Linnet, asking for her help, but she couldn't give it to him. Not this time.

"Tell him what you *do* remember," she said.

"I don't remember what time it was, but I remember getting ready for bed, brushing my teeth, putting my pajamas on." He kept looking to Linnet, double checking he was giving the correct answer. "Oh, I took my slippers off and put them next to the bed like you're always telling me to do." He looked pleased with himself for remembering the last part.

"Okay, Doc," Charlie said, as patient as ever, but Linnet could see the frustration on the chief's face.

"That's good, Pop. But what time did you last see Professor Coyle? I think that's what Charlie is asking," Linnet said in *her* most patient voice.

"Yes, Professor Coyle. He came from the university about the dead geese."

"That's right, he did," Charlie said. "Do you recall the last time you spoke with him?"

Pop shook his head, puckering his face as though he were trying really hard to remember. "No, I don't," he said, looking disappointed with himself. "I don't remember."

"Why does it matter?" Myna asked, jumping in suddenly. "He said he can't remember right this minute, but he'll remember eventually. Won't you, Pop?"

"I don't know," he said.

Linnet could see the concern on Myna's face. She hadn't a clue about Pop's steady decline, about the things he remembered and the things he didn't. Maybe Ian had been right and Linnet should've warned her, said something about the unraveling of his memory, how it had been rapidly progressing in recent months.

"Okay, Doc," Charlie said. "You can let me know later." He turned his attention to Linnet's guests. She'd become so focused on her own family the last few minutes, she'd almost forgotten they were there.

Charlie slapped the tops of his knees before standing. "How long are you folks in town?" he asked the Rapps and the young couple. "I'm going to need some information from you in case I have any further questions down the road. I'll need to know how to contact you."

They gave Charlie the information he needed. "Well, then," he said. "Stay out of the backyard until my men finish up."

The Rapps stood. Mr. Rapp mentioned going into town and seeing the cherry blossoms since they couldn't enjoy the ones on the B&B's property. The great trees lined the streets of Mountain Springs, sharing their pretty pink flowers for all to see. As much as the town was known for its birds, it was also known for its majestic flowering trees. There were four cherry blossoms on the B&B property, their flowers giving off the mildest of fragrances every spring. Although Linnet hadn't noticed any scent at all, not from the fruitless trees nor from the rose bushes planted on the side of the house. Nothing had smelled right since the aroma of decaying geese had taken hold.

The newlyweds retreated back to their room. *Surprise, surprise.* Charlie followed Linnet and the rest of the family to the kitchen. Myna slipped her arm through Pop's and walked with him. She rested her head on his shoulder. She looked so young to Linnet, so vulnerable.

Linnet handed Charlie a cup of coffee. Ian took Hank upstairs to get ready for his baseball game. She had all but forgotten he had a game that afternoon.

Cora opened the refrigerator and pulled out onions and tomatoes, vinegar and oil. She went to work preparing a light lunch. Myna and Pop sat at the table.

"Is there anybody else who might've been on the property in the last twenty-four hours? Any other guests?" Charlie asked, sipping from the mug.

"No," Linnet said. "This is it." Then she added, "Well, there's Al. He was trimming the rose bushes yesterday afternoon. I did see him at the town hall meeting last night."

"Did he come back here with you?"

"No."

"Okay." Charlie motioned to the backyard. "I don't want this to turn into a damn media circus. My suggestion to all of you is to act as if nothing happened here. Go about your day as usual as best you can. At least until I have some answers." He set his mug in the sink. "Thanks for the coffee. I better get back." He paused. "If you think of anybody else who might've been on the property, you let me know."

He was almost out the door when Linnet stopped him.

"There was a journalist here late yesterday afternoon. He tried to give me his card. He wanted to ask me questions about the geese. I chased him away."

"Do you remember his name?" Charlie asked.

"Jack or John Mann or something. I would recognize him if I saw him again."

"Well, if you can find out his name, that would help."

"Okay," she said. "I know you said you have to treat this like it's a crime scene at this point, but you don't really believe this was something more than an accident, do you? I mean, what happened to Professor Coyle was just an awful, horrible accident, right?"

"I won't know for sure until I get the medical examiner's report," Charlie said. He pulled her aside. Linnet could feel her sister's eyes on them.

"Do me a favor," he said in a low voice so that only she could hear. "Try to get your dad to remember the last time he saw the professor."

No one moved after Charlie left. The idea that Professor Coyle's death was something other than an accident had them shaken. No one was hungry for the onion and tomato salad Cora prepared, all of which was covered with plastic wrap and put in the refrigerator.

"It's time I go to the university," Pop said, breaking the silence. "I have to bring them the samples. It has to be today. It can't wait." He was still sitting at the kitchen table next to Myna.

"It will have to wait a few more hours until I get back from Hank's baseball game, Pop." Linnet knew he was right, they needed to get the birds to the lab, but Charlie had said they should go about their day as planned. And under the circumstances, she strongly believed that Hank needed to be on the field with his teammates, behaving like a kid. And she'd never missed one of his games. She wasn't about to start now.

"I'll take Pop to the lab," Myna said. "I'm assuming I can catch another one of Hank's games while I'm here?"

"That depends. How long are you staying?" Linnet asked, hating the way it sounded as though she wanted her sister gone. It wasn't what she'd meant. Myna could stay forever if she wanted. "You never said," she added.

"A week if that's okay. I'm on spring break."

Linnet shrugged as though she were saying, *sure, whatever.* "Hank's got a couple more games in the next few days, so maybe it's best you take Pop and the geese to the university now." It was important not only to her and Pop to know what had killed the geese, but it was also important to the town. "Just be careful on the mountain road," she added, meeting her sister's gaze.

CHAPTER ELEVEN

Jake opened the hood of the car. White clouds of steam poured from the engine. He waved his hand in front of his face and took a step back. When some of the smoke cleared, he reached for the radiator cap, yanking his hand away instantly, nearly burning his fingers. The last hill up the mountain had been too much for the little four-cylinder engine. The car had one hundred and fifty thousand miles on it and was due for a tune-up. He'd scheduled an appointment at the repair shop for the week after next, but it hadn't been soon enough. He'd put one too many miles on the old girl, driving her all over the Lehigh Valley and beyond, chasing the news.

He leaned against the rear bumper. He'd let his AAA membership lapse, of all the stupid things to do. He didn't have a friend close by that he could call for help. Besides, he could barely get a signal on his cell phone if he did. There was nothing he could do but wait.

He wondered how long it would take for another vehicle to pass by. The road was deserted, isolated. He looked over his shoulder. The mountains loomed large. Maybe he should start walking back toward town. The thought of trekking up the steep incline wasn't the least bit appealing. Besides, maybe the whole thing was fate. He was here for a reason, and if he was going to break down somewhere, it might as well be in the exact spot he was searching for to begin with, the exact location on the stretch of mountain road between two steep hills and one wickedly sharp right turn.

He reached in his back pocket and pulled out the police report he'd requested from the Mountain Springs Police Department.

He climbed onto the trunk, resting his feet on the bumper, and reread the accident report from beginning to end. The sun warmed his back although there was a nip in the air as if winter refused to leave without clinging to one last breath. The trees were thick with leaves, the branches arching over the road in a kind of tunnel, cradling him in the safety of their arms, nestling him inside the vertical, rocky hills. He pulled at his collar, feeling a little claustrophobic, and took a deep breath of fresh air, tasting the scent of the great outdoors.

But what should've been a pleasant view had the opposite effect. This very spot was where his father had crashed his car. The police report confirmed the location. Single vehicle accident. Driver DOA. Based on the skid marks on the pavement, the vehicle was traveling at a high rate of speed when it flipped onto its roof.

Jake looked at the impossible bend in the road. Did his father miss the sharp turn? Where was he going in such a hurry? Why didn't anyone find him before it was too late? He wanted the answers to the questions his mother had refused to discuss, the details that had been too painful for her to talk about.

All that remained of Jake's memories of his father were snapshots. He wasn't sure if they were real memories or ones he'd fabricated in his nine-year-old mind. What he remembered most was his father coming home after his lengthy travels and the entire family celebrating his return. His mother would fix her hair and paint her lips. She'd put on one of her flower-print dresses. "So he sees me at my best," she'd said.

When it had been just the two of them, her wardrobe had consisted of pants and blouses and ankle-long skirts, her hair pulled into a bun, a hint of mascara on her eyelashes. She had been a librarian, and for better or worse, she'd dressed the part.

But it was the last time his father had come home from a business trip, the last time Jake had seen him, that had remained sharpest in his mind.

"He'll be here any minute," his mother said, and untied the apron from around her waist. She'd made pot roast. His father had been gone a long two weeks, and Jake had the nervous, excited feeling in his stomach he'd get whenever he was expected home.

"Go on." She shooed Jake from the kitchen. "Wash up," she said, giddy with anticipation.

The front door swung open. "Hello!" his father called.

His mother rushed to the small foyer and fell into his father's arms. He spun her around as though it had been years since he'd last seen her rather than a few days. He'd brought gifts—flowers and jewelry, candy and toys.

He handed his mother a pink-and-white-striped bag and whispered, "You might want to wait and open this one later." He turned to Jake. "And this is for you." He handed Jake a new Nerf football since Jake had left his old one out in the yard and the neighbor's dog had chewed it to pieces.

They sat around the dining room table. Jake watched his dad cut his meat into small pieces and then stuff each one into his mouth, chewing his food thoroughly without looking up. Every now and again he'd say, "Mmm. Mmm," making a big show out of Jake's mother's cooking. At one point he stabbed a chunk of roast with the knife and held it in the air as though he had some great revelation, but instead of sharing his thoughts, he ate the piece of meat off the tip of the blade and grinned. "Mmm."

Jake's mother beamed.

After dinner he and Jake went outside and played a game of catch with his new ball until the sun went down, and it became too dark to see. And later that night, his father tucked him into bed, kissing his forehead before saying good night. Jake lay awake, thinking he was the luckiest boy alive with the best dad ever. He listened to his mother giggling, the creaking of their bed, his parents playing the tickling game they always played whenever his father was home.

Jake rolled to his side, happy and secure, unaware of what lie ahead.

Jake tucked the police report back inside his pocket. He rubbed the crick in his neck. The bed in the room he'd rented above the bar sucked. It was hard as shit. The fact he'd stayed up late hunched over his laptop typing up his article for the paper hadn't helped. At least he'd made the front page with the headline *Snow Geese Fall From Blue Mountain Skies*. From what he'd gathered at the town hall meeting, the experts were baffled. The hundreds of dead geese remained a mystery.

Other headlines had gone national. CNN ran a special report: *Birds Fall From Sky, The Third Apocalyptic Sign*.

The only good news to come from the tragedy as far as Jake was concerned was Dennis insisting he stay and see the story through. What Dennis didn't know was that Jake had no intention of leaving, not while he had so many unanswered questions about this place, this town.

His phone started ringing. He reached in his front pocket and fished it out. The signal was weak, with only a single bar showing.

"So is it the end of the world or what?" Kim asked.

Jake smiled. "Not from where I'm sitting."

"Good. I wasn't finished with this life yet," she said. "I read your article in the paper this morning."

"And?" He liked that she read his work. "What did you think?" But he hated that he sounded needy, maybe even a little sensitive. It was a part of his personality he wished he could change. If only he could be more confident like his peers. But he didn't have the ego for it. Then again, it was his lack of ego which helped people open up and tell him their stories.

"It's good," she said about his article. "It's interesting, and you can empathize with the town and what happened to those poor snow geese without scaring the bejesus out of people. That's what I like about your style of reporting."

His heart fluttered, and he felt a little weak in his legs. Good thing he was sitting down. "Thanks," was all he could muster. For a moment he heard nothing but static. The connection was poor. It had to be from the fact he was sitting at the bottom of a narrow gap between two enormous hills.

"Listen, about the phone number you wanted me to research," Kim said. "I got tied up at work yesterday. And the usual tinkering around didn't turn up anything, but I'll keep working on it."

"I appreciate it," he said, trying to think of how to keep her on the phone. More static crackled in his ear.

"Where are you? I can hardly hear you," she said.

"I think I'm losing you." He wasn't ready to hang up, but he wasn't about to tell her he was stranded on the mountain road, and it was starting to freak him out a little. His phone crackled some more as the connection faded in and out. He looked at the mountains as if they were trying to tell him something. "Call me as soon as you find out anything."

"I will," she said, and then she was gone.

He stuffed the phone back into his pocket and bowed his head. He should've brought something with him, flowers or one of those crosses you see on the side of the road where someone else's loved one had lost their life. But he was here, wasn't he? It should count for something. Better late than never. *I miss you, Dad. Mom, too.* He didn't know if he believed in Heaven or even Hell for that matter, but wherever his parents were, he liked to think they were together.

He looked up when he heard the sound of another car approaching, a neon-blue rinky-dink thing. He jumped off the trunk and stepped into the road, waving his arms in the air.

CHAPTER TWELVE

Myna stood on the bank of the dam, the sight more horrifying than she'd ever imagined. She brought her hand to the hollow of her throat. "There are so many," she said to Pop about the dead snow geese. It had been one thing to hear it on the news and quite another to see it.

He was kneeling in the mud, filling test tubes with water. He wanted to take extra samples to the lab. After Charlie had completed his investigation, he'd allowed them to take an inventory of Professor Coyle's boxes, the items the young professor had amassed yesterday that had never made it over the mountain to the university. They'd packed her rental car with the coolers containing the iced birds, but they had to collect more water and plant samples.

Pop worked methodically, recording the date, time, and location of the samples. He looked like the father Myna had remembered from childhood, focused and thorough, a man in control of his faculties, unlike the man she'd witnessed earlier when he'd struggled to answer Charlie's questions about events the night before.

So much had happened since she'd been away. She placed her

hand on his back, feeling the soft cotton from the well-worn cardigan. "I'm sorry."

He looked up at her through his spectacles, his eyes gentle and kind. "Yes," he said. "But there's an explanation for it. We just have to figure out what it is." He was talking about the birds, of course. He had no way of knowing she was apologizing for so much more.

"Are we ready to go?" she asked, and helped him stand. She'd called the university earlier to let them know to expect them.

They walked the path through the woods, having to duck under the yellow crime scene tape that was left hanging in the yard. When they reached the driveway and her rental car, she put the new samples in the trunk with the coolers.

Linnet's minivan was gone. They'd left for Hank's baseball game an hour ago. The police had towed the young professor's vehicle away.

Myna got in on the driver's side of the rental car, and then she helped Pop with his seat belt. She took the mountain road slowly. The tiny engine sputtered and groaned up the steep hills and coasted like a sigh of relief on the downward slopes. They were halfway over the mountain coming up on a sharp right turn. As she rounded the corner, a man stepped out in front of her, waving his arms. She slammed her foot on the brake. The car skidded, swerving left and then right, before stopping on the shoulder of the road. Her heart hammered against her rib cage. She was panting, gripping the steering wheel so hard that her fingers ached. It took her a moment to calm down, to focus, before throwing the car in park.

"Are you all right?" she asked Pop.

"Fine," he said, fixing his spectacles that had been knocked askew.

They both turned and peered over their shoulders at the man

who had jumped out in front of them. He was slowly walking toward the car, trying to look into the windows.

"Wait here," she said, unbuckling her seat belt and getting out, not thinking it through, reacting on adrenalin. "Are you crazy?" she shouted at the guy. He looked to be close to her age, maybe a few years younger, and handsome. "I almost hit you!" She was shaking.

"I was just trying to flag you down." He pointed to his car, the one she just now noticed parked on the shoulder of the road with the hood up. "I broke down, and I could use a ride back to town."

She opened her mouth to say no, but nothing came out. He was going to get himself killed if he continued jumping out in front of traffic the way he had.

"Please," he said. "You're the first car I've seen all day."

"What seems to be the problem?"

"The engine overheated," he said.

"All right," she said, and took out her phone. "I can call someone in town to give you a tow." She knew of only one shop in Mountain Springs, Chicky's Auto Repairs. Chicky serviced everyone's car in the area unless you drove over the mountain to one of the dealerships. She held her phone up, trying to get a signal.

"The signal has been sketchy for me, too," he said, and stepped closer to her.

She gave up on the phone. She glanced at Pop in the front passenger seat, wondering what she should do. He rolled down his window. "We have to go," he said, sounding anxious.

"Look," she said to the guy. "We have to get to the university. I'm sure once we get over the mountain I can get a signal, and then I'll call the repair shop for you and let them know about your car."

"You're going to leave me here?"

Well, no, she couldn't do that. Could she? What if the next vehicle that came barreling around the bend hit him?

"I'm Jake, by the way."

"Myna," she said, and shook his hand. "This is my father, Dr. Jenkins."

"Myna," Pop said, growing more impatient.

"Right. Well." She hesitated, remembering the promise she'd made to herself, hearing Ben's accusations about her taking in strays. She looked at the windy stretch of road, the looming mountain. She couldn't leave the guy stranded. Not here. She checked the bars on her phone. Still no signal. "Okay," she said to Jake, reluctantly. "Get in." She slid behind the wheel. Jake climbed into the backseat. "We're taking the snow geese to the lab for tests. You did hear about the dead geese, didn't you?" She couldn't imagine anyone who hadn't heard by now. She pulled back onto the road.

Jake leaned forward. "I did," he said. "What do you specialize in, Doc?"

"Ornithology," she said, answering for him.

"Is that right?" Jake pulled himself up so he could get a better look into the front seat. "What do you think killed the birds?" he asked.

"I don't know," Pop said. He sounded weary. She wondered if he was tired of people asking him the same question over and over again.

"We're hoping to get some answers soon," she said. She met Jake's eyes in the rearview mirror. There was something about him she thought she recognized, but she couldn't say what it was. "Where are you from?" she asked.

"Allentown," he said. "I'm a journalist for the Lehigh Valley newspaper." He passed her his business card.

"Ah," she said, and stuffed it into her back pocket without taking her eyes off the road. "Well, this must be your lucky day."

"Why's that?"

"Do you know how many journalists are trying to get to my father right now? And here you are riding with him *and* the birds."

"I don't know anything yet," Pop said.

"But you will," she said, reassuring him.

Jake sat back in the seat. She kept glancing at him in the mirror. It was his face that seemed familiar, but why? For the first time since she'd picked him up, she felt uneasy.

"I noticed this is a rental," Jake said. "I'm gathering you don't live around here either."

"I'm home visiting," she said, thinking of Ben once again. She hadn't been able to talk with him that morning before he'd taken his clients out to sea. His boat was chartered for the weekend. She had so much she wanted to say, so much she wanted to tell him about the condition she'd found Pop in, the young professor dying, but she still couldn't tell him the one thing he wanted to hear. *It shouldn't be this hard*, she thought. And yet, it was.

"So you grew up in Mountain Springs?" Jake asked.

"Yes."

"I can see why you moved," he muttered.

"What was that?"

"Where do you live now?"

"Florida," she said.

"Aren't you kind of young to live in Florida?"

"Ha ha. You'd be surprised how many young people live there now. And families with kids. It's not all senior citizens, you know."

Pop was quiet, staring out the passenger-side window. She

expected Jake to direct more questions at him about the geese and their trip to the lab, but Jake had fallen silent, too.

They crested the last hill. After driving a few more minutes through town, they reached the university. Myna knew the way to the lab, having visited with Pop enough times when she'd been a kid and later when she'd been a student here. She parked in front of the brick building where two other professors, a handful of students, and several reporters—two with television cameras—were waiting.

"What are they doing here?" she asked, referring to the news media.

Jake pulled himself up and stuck his head between the two front seats. "I'm sure the school called them to draw attention to their program. And you know what they say about publicity. The school probably views this as good publicity."

Pop nodded. "He's right."

One of the professors, the one wearing a white lab coat, opened the passenger side door. She couldn't tell if her father knew him or not. He seemed confused about so many things lately.

She popped the trunk, and she and Jake hopped out of the car. She exchanged handshakes with the university professors and they made a quick round of introductions, but she hadn't been able to catch their names. The reporters surrounded them, firing off questions. They tried their best to ignore them.

"Where's James?" the lab-coated professor asked. "When you called, I assumed he would be coming with you."

"Who's James?" Pop looked to her to explain, as she'd noticed he'd done with Linnet frequently since she'd arrived.

"Professor Coyle," the lab-coated professor added.

Charlie hadn't wanted the news of the professor's death to get out to the media yet. She imagined the professor's family had to be notified first as well. She pointed to the trunk of the car, avoiding the question. "We have the birds in the coolers."

Jake remained quiet as he was being jostled by the other reporters. He didn't seem bothered by it. He went as far as calling one of them by their first name. *They're his peers*, she reminded herself.

The lab-coated professor walked around to the back of the car and lifted one of the boxes from the trunk. The students began taking out the other boxes and the two coolers with the birds. The cameras were turned on, and the reporters were talking, filming the kids carrying some of the evidence inside the building.

"We'll take it from here," the professor said, and put his hand on Pop's shoulder. She understood they were dismissing him. They weren't going to let him inside the lab.

"I have a theory," Pop said, pleading, sounding like a child. "I need to run some tests." He started following the students toward the building and doors.

"Dr. Jenkins, please," the professor said, and grabbed his arm.

"Get your hands off of me." Pop tried pulling his arm away.

"I can't let you in. The university has rules."

"Why aren't you allowed inside, Doctor?" one of the reporters asked, motioning to his cameraman to keep rolling.

"Get off me," Pop said again, flapping his arm, struggling to get free.

They argued. The reporters started pushing and shoving. Myna didn't know what to do. Everything was happening so quickly. Jake stepped in front of the camera, trying to cover the lens with his hand. When that didn't work, he pried the lab-coated professor off Pop. Then he slipped his arm around Pop, shielding him from the throng of reporters and directed him to where she was standing, stunned.

She draped her arm around Pop's other shoulder, embarrassed she'd allowed the situation to get out of control and sure that Linnet would've handled it better.

"I'll take some questions," the lab-coated professor said, straightening his collar, drawing the reporters' attention, commenting about when they could expect the results.

"Why won't they let me in?" Pop asked.

She frowned. "Let's get you home."

Jake helped her put Pop in the car. He acted as though he were a friend. She had to remind herself that she didn't know anything about him. His car broke down. That was all. The uneasy feeling she'd had earlier had disappeared, and then it reversed, turned the corner, and came back again.

The lab-coated professor continued talking with the television reporters live on camera, and then he followed his colleague into the brick building, disappearing inside along with the students and coolers full of frozen geese. The reporters hung around the doors before they turned and caught sight of Myna and Jake still lingering by the car.

Myna immediately jumped in the driver's side and started the engine, knowing she had to get Pop out of there before the press got to him again. She figured Jake could get a ride with one of his colleagues. But instead, Jake dove into the backseat as she started to pull away, the flock of reporters chasing after them.

CHAPTER THIRTEEN

Linnet tried to focus on the baseball game. Twice she'd clapped and hollered encouraging words to the opposing team when they'd been up to bat. Ian had gently lowered her hands and held them in her lap.

"I know it's hard to concentrate," he said. "But Hank keeps looking toward the bleachers. We need to be strong for him, let him know everything is going to be fine." He kept his eyes on the field as he spoke.

He was right. Poor Hank had struck out twice, and then he'd dropped a ball in center field. It wasn't like him. Her son was distracted, too. Maybe it had been a mistake to ask him to play today, but they were here now, and it wasn't like she could march onto the field and drag him home.

"Do you think he had some kind of medical condition we don't know about?" she asked, her mind on Professor Coyle. The professor was so young, but it wasn't unheard of for even young people to drop dead over from a heart attack or some kind of epileptic seizure. She might've been stretching a bit here, but she didn't want to accept the other possibility.

"Maybe, but not likely," Ian said. "Do you think Pop could

have . . . ?" He broke off. "I wish he could remember something. Anything."

Ian almost said what she'd been thinking all along.

And then there was Myna, the complicated look on her face when she'd left to take Pop to the dam for more samples. Her sister had accused her of withholding information about his mental state, and she'd done it without ever having to utter a word.

But Linnet had refused to feel guilty about it. If Myna had wanted to know how he was doing, then she shouldn't have left home in the first place.

She flinched at the sound of the ball striking the bat. She stood with the crowd, watching it fly deep into left field, adding to another home run for the other team. She plopped back down on the bleachers. Ian laced his fingers through hers, squeezing her hand, a reassuring gesture, she knew, that had nothing to do with baseball. His patience had been tested these last few months where Pop was concerned, yet still he was trying hard to help with his care without complaint. But how much more could she ask of him, or of Hank, if Pop were involved somehow in the professor's death?

She knew inside her heart he was still the father she'd always known. The one who'd left his study to cook dinner for her and Myna when he'd learned their mother hadn't been able to leave her room and that they'd been eating stale crackers and bread. Or the time she'd caught him sewing buttons on Myna's princess costume so she'd have something to wear to the school's Halloween party when he should've been at the university teaching a class. He'd taken them hiking where they'd pretended to be explorers, playing the I Spy game. And once when she'd twisted her ankle, he'd carried her the half mile down the mountain to home, where they'd spent the rest of the weekend eating popcorn and watching old movies while she'd kept her leg elevated.

Ian let go of her hand. They both clapped and yelled encouraging words as Hank's team came up to bat. And somewhere in the back of her mind, the child inside of her whispered, *Pop had never failed her before. Not like her mother had.*

"Are we having company?" a sixteen-year-old Linnet asked.

Her mother was standing at the kitchen sink peeling potatoes, which wasn't unusual. Linnet often found her at the sink cutting or chopping fruits and vegetables, preparing breakfasts for the guests her father had insisted would come, but hadn't.

"If you're too afraid to leave the house," Pop had said one night when he'd come home from the university and found his wife locked inside their bedroom for the seventh day in a row, "then we'll bring the people to you." He'd had it in his head that whatever had plagued her mother could be cured if she had someone or something to take care of other than herself. He'd concocted a plan to turn their big, colonial home into a bed-and-breakfast.

Linnet had loved the idea of entertaining guests, sharing the beauty of the dam and snow geese with visitors. Any doubts she'd had about Pop's plan—and the gnawing questions around how in the world her mother, who had become incapable of caring for her own daughters, would take care of houseguests—she'd kept to herself. She'd been too excited about the prospect of parties.

"This will give her a reason to get out of bed," he'd said to Linnet. And once Pop had made up his mind this would cure her mother, construction on The Snow Goose had begun.

Now, while her mother prepared food for the nonexistent guests, she paused, the knife gripped in her hand, and stared out the garden window through the array of potted plants she'd never got around to planting outside. Linnet peeked out the window to glimpse at whatever had captured her mother's attention, but all she could see was their backyard, the same old cherry blossoms and shrubs, the stone trail that led to the guest-house and Pop's study, the winding path through the woods that led to the dam.

But the most remarkable thing about finding her mother at the kitchen sink this morning was that she was showered and dressed. She'd replaced the ratty old nightgown, worn robe, and slippers with a pair of khakis and a button-down shirt.

"Yes, we're getting company today," her mother said. "A salesman."

"Really?" Linnet said. The B&B had been vacant for so long, it was strange to think of someone actually staying in their house. For the first few years, Pop had been right, and her mother had really tried to make a go of it. But as time passed, her enthusiasm had waned, and she'd started distancing herself from the family and the business, giving in more and more to whatever had tor-mented her mind. Eventually, the guests had stopped coming. A room had been rented here and there for an off weekend. Twice a couple of businessmen had stayed when the hotel in town had been booked to capacity during the height of the snow geese migration. The B&B could've been successful if only her mother had put her heart into it, but she had put her heart into so little, it was no wonder it was failing.

Myna walked into the kitchen, nudging Linnet in the arm. "Go on," she said. "Ask her."

Linnet had started driving two months ago, although Myna had acted like she was the one with the driver's permit. "If you ask to take the car out, then we won't be stuck here all day," Myna had said not five minutes ago.

Linnet cleared her throat. "I thought we could take the car out today, and I could practice driving around town." But now that she'd asked her mother, she wondered if she'd made a mistake. The woman couldn't even focus on peeling the potato in front of her. She was staring out the window again.

"What is it, Mom?" Myna asked. She looked over their mother's shoulder. "Oh!" she said. "The snow geese are in the yard."

Linnet peered over their mother's other shoulder, spying a pair of geese, a male and a female. Unlike ducks, the males have the same coloring as females, but she could tell the males apart by their larger size.

"I really do hate them," their mother said.

The sisters exchanged a glance behind her back. Linnet silently begged Myna not to ask why. There were some questions a child shouldn't ask a parent, some answers a child shouldn't know. Once you knew the answer then it was out there, and you could never take it back.

"Why?" Myna asked. "Why do you hate them so much?"

Linnet balled her hands into fists, digging her nails into her palms, trying to hold on to something that was much too slippery. The tighter she squeezed, the more it slid through her fingers. Why couldn't Myna keep her mouth shut? But that was why her father had named her Myna. She behaved like the small talking bird, unable to keep her trap shut since she'd been born; reproducing sounds in her environment by the time she'd slid from the birth canal. Linnet was named after a common linnet in a poem by Yeats, her father's favorite poet.

"I didn't always hate them," she said, giving them a sad smile. "I don't know when it changed. Or even why. I guess there are some things you just can't explain." She looked down at the knife and went back to peeling.

Try explaining it, Linnet wanted to say to her, but the words wouldn't come out.

It seemed the sisters' roles had reversed, and Myna was the one urging Linnet to let it go. She took Linnet's hand, opening her fist, entwining their fingers together. She pulled her toward the side door and out to the yard. They didn't speak as they walked hand in hand. The two geese they'd been watching from the window waddled away as they approached the path through the woods. Squirrels scattered up trees. The wind nipped at their ears.

Myna climbed into the row boat. "Maybe we can take the car tomorrow," she said.

Linnet nodded and untied the rope from the dock's post before joining her in the boat. She rowed to the middle of the dam. The snow geese milled around, ducking their heads underwater and pulling up the plant life from the shallow, murky bottom.

Linnet dangled her legs over the side, her sneakers nearly getting wet. She propped the life jacket behind her head like a pillow and tilted her face toward the late March sun. Myna sprawled out beside her. She was so used to having her sister's body next to her, touching her, overlapping with her own that sometimes she didn't know where her sister's body ended and hers began.

The dam smelled cold, holding on to the last days of winter. Not far from where they were floating a bull frog croaked on a lily pad. Ducks toddled on the dock, keeping their distance from the larger geese.

Linnet closed her eyes, listening to the water lap against the side of the boat. Their mother hated the birds. *Well, what the hell did their mother like anyway?*

"We can't tell Pop," Myna said about their mother's comment. "Or do you think he knows?"

"No," she said. "I don't think he knows." She believed she was protecting him by not telling him all the ways in which her mother suffered. "He doesn't see how miserable she is. He doesn't see she's sick and that she has problems."

"He loves her," Myna said. "And love is blind."

The baseball game ended, Hank's team losing seven to three. He was quiet as they piled into the van, driving past Christmas tree fields, a smattering of houses. Woods flanked the road the closer they got to home. Within a few minutes, Ian pulled the minivan into the driveway. Linnet turned in her seat and put her hand on Hank's knee.

"Tough loss today, but it's not your fault." She used her most reassuring voice. "You had a lot on your mind. In fact, I think your entire team had a lot on their minds. The last few days around here have been hard, and everyone was having trouble focusing. Don't you think?" she asked Ian.

"Agreed," he said, glancing in the rearview mirror at Hank.

"Whatever," Hank said. "Can I go and get something to eat?"

She nodded. He got out of the van and dragged his feet into the house.

"Your sister just pulled in," Ian said, and opened the driver's side door.

They got out of the car and stood in the driveway. She was dismayed to see Pop get out of the rental car. She'd hoped they would have let him into the lab. It had been a lot to ask, she knew. He'd get in the way. He'd retired because they'd forced him to.

A strange guy climbed out of the backseat of Myna's car. It took Linnet a moment before she recognized him as the journalist she'd chased off her property. *What the hell?* She marched toward her sister and was caught off guard by Mr. Rapp wheeling his suitcase down the front porch stairs. She pointed at the newspaper guy and looked at Myna as she walked by. "What is *he* doing here?"

"Who?" Myna asked, but she knew damn well who Linnet was referring to.

"Mr. Rapp," Linnet said. "What's going on?" Ian walked over to stand by her side.

"We're leaving," Mr. Rapp said.

"I don't understand," she said.

"It's too much," Mr. Rapp said. "First the birds and then that poor professor."

"Yes," she said. *It was too much.*

"Have you been to the dam?" he asked. "Have you seen them out there in their hazmat suits, for chrissakes? It's downright creepy. This is not the long weekend we had in mind, I can tell you that."

"No, of course it isn't," she said.

Mrs. Rapp appeared on the porch, fumbling with a bag on her arm and hobbling with the cane in her hand.

"Let me help you," Ian said, and took the bag from Mrs. Rapp, helping her down the stairs. He gave Linnet a look that said, *Let them go.*

"I'll give you a refund, of course," she said to Mr. Rapp.

"I should hope so." He put the suitcases in his trunk.

Ian placed the bag he was carrying in the backseat of their car. "I'm sure there's a reasonable explanation for all of it," he said to the Rapps.

"I'm sure there is," Mrs. Rapp said, trying to apologize for her husband's foul mood. "And we do hope to come back next year. Don't we, Dear?"

"We'll have to see," he grumbled, and helped his wife into the car. "It's just so disappointing," he said to Linnet.

"It is," she agreed, and watched as Mr. Rapp got in on the driver's side and drove away.

"They'll be back," Ian said.

"The geese or the Rapps?" she asked.

"Both," he said, and put his arm around her. Myna and Pop came to stand next to them.

"I'm sorry about your guests," Myna said.

"Why is he here with you?" Linnet asked in a low voice, referring to the newspaper guy. He was lingering in the driveway, staring at his phone.

"His car broke down on the mountain road, and, well, it's a long story."

"With everything going on, do you really think it was smart to pick up a stranger and give him a ride?" She had this way of talking to Myna as though she was her mother rather than her sister, but she couldn't stop herself when her sister behaved like a child. "And a journalist, no less!" The thoughts she'd been trying to circumvent, the ones about Pop being involved somehow in the young professor's death, clawed their way front and center. *What if Pop had said something he shouldn't have to that journalist?*

Myna gazed in the guy's direction. "His name is Jake," she said. "He seems all right to me."

"Oh, well, if he seems all right to you, then he must be." Ian squeezed her shoulder, signaling her to calm down. He was right. This wasn't worth fighting over. She was on edge, and having a journalist around, especially this guy who was familiar in some way, wasn't helping matters.

"I'm going to the dam," Pop said, and started walking toward the yard.

"Maybe we should go take a look while Hank's occupied inside," Ian said. "And see what this hazmat suit business is about."

Linnet nodded. She did want to see what the Wildlife Health Center was doing with the birds. Ian kept his arm around her as they walked. Myna tagged along. Linnet hesitated, then called over her shoulder, "Aren't you coming?" If Jake was going to be on her property, she was going to make damn sure she kept her eye on him.

He jogged to catch up, taking his place next to her sister. "What's up with the crime scene tape?" he asked, pointing to a tree where a piece had been left dangling.

"There was an accident on the property with the professor from the university," Myna said. "I don't think it's public knowledge yet."

Linnet glared at her.

"What kind of accident?" Jake asked.

"If you want to know anything else about it," Linnet snapped, "you'll have to talk to the police."

Jake didn't say anything. He seemed to be deep inside his own thoughts, which bothered Linnet more than if he'd asked a bunch of questions. Weren't journalists supposed to be pushy and irritating? Jake seemed reflective and thoughtful.

The cardinals and robins flitted about the trees, hollering at the intrusion of so many unwanted guests. Three crows chased a hawk in the sky. But what Linnet noticed most once they'd reached the dam was the lack of geese flying overhead, the unnatural way they floated on the water.

"They're not wearing hazmat suits," she said, and shook her head at Mr. Rapp's description. The men from the health center wore waders and used poles with claws to pick up the dead geese, much like the pole Professor Coyle had had in the trunk of his car. Other men walked up and down the muddy embankment collecting the birds on the ground.

Jake used his phone to take pictures. Across the dam in the public parking lot, several TV cameras were documenting the cleanup.

"CNN," Ian said. "I can't believe it."

She snorted. "Maybe this is the last of it. Maybe they'll go away once the geese are taken care of."

"They'll go away when a more shocking story comes along," Jake said.

"So we're supposed to hope for another tragedy?" Linnet asked, thinking of how they already had another one with Professor Coyle, and how things happened in threes.

"Only if you want them out of your town," Jake said, and stepped away to talk with one of the men from the center. Linnet was surprised when the man wearing waders and lifting a dead goose with the clawed pole stopped to answer Jake's questions.

After watching the cleanup at the dam, they returned to the B&B and gathered in the kitchen. Linnet was trying to think of a way she could get Pop alone so she could ask him questions about Professor Coyle. She'd buried the terrible thoughts as best she could throughout the day, but the longer she waited to confront him, the more urgent the situation seemed. And now with Jake hanging around, she felt the need to be extra careful about everything she said and did.

Ian hung up the phone. "Chicky's going to meet us at your car in an hour," he said to Jake. "He'll bring radiator fluid to see if that will get it started. Otherwise, he'll have to tow it to his shop."

"Okay," Jake said.

Myna was sitting at the table with Hank. They were bent over his iPad playing something called *Five Nights at Freddy's*. Every now and again Myna would squeal and laugh and tap the iPad furiously with her finger. Hank laughed along with her. Linnet smiled, but it was quickly replaced with a scowl when she realized Jake was also watching them and grinning.

Linnet wanted to pinch him, tell him her sister was spoken

for. Although she'd only ever met Ben once, she knew instantly that he was different from the other guys Myna had dated. Linnet and Ian had taken Hank to Disney World for a family vacation not two years ago. During their stay, Myna and Ben had driven the hour and a half to spend the day with them, going on the rides, eating fried food and cotton candy, getting their pictures taken with Goofy.

It had been Linnet's idea to have her sister join them, although Myna hadn't made up her mind until the last minute whether or not she would. And then she'd brought Ben with her. Linnet had studied the two together, looking for something in her sister, a signal alerting her that she was unhappy and wished to move home. But there was nothing Linnet could find wrong with her sister's life, nothing bad she could say about Ben. Talking with Ian later that night, she'd admitted she'd never seen her sister happier, the truth of it making her glad, but somehow sad at the same time, realizing that her sister wouldn't be coming home anytime soon.

When their time together had ended, and Myna and Ben had headed to their car for the long drive home, Linnet had been convinced Ben was right for her sister. She wondered if Myna had known. It hadn't been something she'd felt comfortable asking her then and still wasn't now.

She glared at Jake, who was still grinning at the sight of her sister and son playing games. "She has a boyfriend," she said to him about Myna in a low voice that only he could hear. "And she's very serious about him." She didn't know if this was true, but it seemed logical. She'd been living with Ben for a few years now.

Jake turned his handsome face toward her. "I'm not surprised," he said, and ran his hand through his hair.

And that's when she noticed the ring.

CHAPTER FOURTEEN

Myna was in the guest room unpacking her suitcase. It was the first chance she'd had to settle in since she'd arrived. She'd hung up with Ben not two minutes before. He'd called her cell phone after watching the six o'clock news and learning the young professor had been found dead on their property. She'd nearly cried out in relief at the sound of his voice. She hadn't realized how much she'd been missing him, how crazy this short time in Mountain Springs had been so far. He'd called because he'd been concerned. He'd wanted to make sure she was all right even though she'd hurt him—although he hadn't admitted that last part. She'd heard it in his tone, the careful way he'd talked as though he were choosing his words deliberately.

"If you need me to come there, I will. I'll cancel my trips," he'd said.

"You don't need to do that," she'd said, but a part of her wished he'd hop on a plane and come anyway. "I need to be with my family, but there's no need for you to miss work because of it."

"Your family," he'd said. "I guess that's part of the problem, isn't it? I'm not a part of your family."

"That's not what I meant," she'd said. Or was it? "It's complicated." She had no other way to describe the situation she'd found herself in with her sister and father.

And also with him.

Their call had ended soon after when the static in their connection had interfered to the point where she could no longer hear. The mountains made it impossible to connect to the outside world for more than a few minutes at a time. She couldn't count how many times Hank's face had frozen on her screen during a lost Skype connection.

She searched for her pajamas—cotton pants and button-down top—thinking she might as well go to bed. She emptied her pockets, finding Jake's business card and setting it on the dresser. The room was warm and cozy, decorated in soft yellows and greens. A wicker chair sat in the corner. The four-poster bed was covered in a hand-stitched quilt one of the women in town had sold to her sister at a craft fair. Linnet had purchased quilts for all four beds, giving the guest rooms a down-home country kind of feel.

It was all very nice, so why did Myna feel as though she were suffocating? She opened one of the windows. A spring breeze blew into the room, knocking the feather she'd packed off the top of the opened suitcase. The gentle breeze lifted it and carried it across the bed before it drifted to the hardwood floor. She picked it up, admiring its beauty, its ability to fly.

There was a rap on the door. "Hey," Linnet said. "Are you up?"

"Yeah." She quickly tucked the feather underneath the sweater. "You can come in."

She kept her back to the suitcase, hiding the feather from her sister and feeling as if she were a little kid caught doing something wrong.

"How's Hank?" she asked. It was a lot for him to take in, first the birds and then the professor.

Linnet stood in the doorway. Her arms were folded. "I just came from saying good night to him. We had a long talk. He'll be okay."

"You're doing a great job with him," Myna said. "He's such a good kid."

"Thanks." She moved to the dresser and picked up Jake's business card. "Interesting guy," she said about Jake. "Good-looking." She looked at Myna as though she were accusing her of something.

"I guess," Myna said. "I haven't really noticed."

"Sure you haven't," Linnet said. She kept the card in her hand, and Myna wondered if her sister was going to tear it up. What was she accusing her of anyway?

She continued. "I have to admit I was a little freaked out about him hanging around us, you know?"

Myna didn't say anything. Her sister had an agenda, and until she knew what it was, it was best to say as little as possible.

"Well, I'm sure it was just a coincidence," Linnet said. "I suppose there are a lot of guys who wear football rings on their pinky fingers."

"What are you talking about?"

"You didn't see the ring?"

"No." Her throat was scratchy, and she suddenly couldn't swallow.

"I'm sure it was nothing," Linnet said. "Like I said, it's probably just a coincidence."

They stared at each other, an old wound beating as though it had been given new life, its thrumming stretching between them.

Myna was the first to speak. "Why didn't you tell me things with Pop have gotten worse?"

Linnet touched her forehead as though she had to think about it. Finally, she said, "I didn't know how to tell you." She looked at the floor. "Besides, what could you have done about it anyway?"

"We could've talked about it. Maybe there was something I could've done to help you. Maybe there's something I can do now that I know."

"Right." She snorted. "What can you do all the way from Florida?"

Myna hated that her sister had a valid point. She was too far away to be of any real help in his care, but she could be supportive, talk things through so her sister wouldn't feel as though she carried the burden alone. "I had a right to know." She wanted to sound firm, but her voice wavered, making her words sound small, weak.

"Maybe if you came around more often, you would've known what was going on."

"That's not fair, and you know it."

"Myna, Myna, Myna. When are you going to learn? Nothing in life is ever fair."

There was so much anger in her sister's words.

Linnet dropped Jake's business card on the dresser. She pulled out her phone, punched in a number, and then pressed the phone to her ear. "Hi, Charlie," she said, keeping her eyes locked on Myna's while she talked. "Remember I told you about a journalist I saw on my property. Right. Well, I have his name, Jake Mann. He's staying at the LG," she informed him, using the local's name for the popular pub. She paused, listening to whatever Charlie was saying on the other end. "Maybe the Inn was booked, but that's where he told Ian he was staying." She was quiet for a moment, and then she said, "Okay, I will. Thanks." She hung up. "Charlie has a few questions for your journalist friend."

"Come on, Linny. You don't really think Jake has anything to do with the professor, do you?"

"Probably not. But he was here that day, and Charlie wanted a list of everyone who was on the property. And he *was* on the property. Trespassing, I might add."

Myna stopped short of rolling her eyes.

"Do me a favor." She tapped the card with her finger. "Don't seek him out. There's something about him I don't trust."

"Because he works for the paper?" She didn't wait for a response. "He seems okay to me. He helped me with Pop this afternoon, and he didn't have to."

"What do you mean? What happened with Pop?"

"The TV crews were outside the lab filming. Pop was confused. I was caught off guard, and I didn't know what to do. Jake helped me get Pop away from them."

"So this is the long story you mentioned earlier about why you brought him back with you? I don't even understand why you picked him up in the first place."

"I couldn't just leave him stranded," she said in a quiet voice.

"Yes, you could have."

But that was where her sister was wrong. She *couldn't*. It was the one big difference between them. All she could think about was what had happened the last time she hadn't helped someone when she should have. They both should have.

"I can't trust you to do anything right, can I?" Linnet asked.

Myna didn't know how to respond. She didn't want to fight. *You can trust me*, she wanted to say, but all she did was shrug.

Linnet shook her head and turned away. "That's what I thought," she said, and disappeared down the hallway.

Myna shut the door, putting her back against it, searching for the lock.

She picked up Jake's business card and turned it over in her hand.

CHAPTER FIFTEEN

Jake found himself once again sitting at the pub with his laptop powered on in front of him. Rodney set another frosty mug of whatever was on tap onto the bar.

"Thanks," Jake said, and took a long swallow of ice cold beer. He was working on his article for the morning paper. He could've easily made the front page for a second day in a row if he'd pressed the sisters about the young professor's accident on their property. He'd seen the six o'clock news. Although he hadn't known it at the time, he'd had an insider's view of the events when the one sister had given him a ride.

Still, it had been a bit of good luck. He couldn't have planned it any better if he'd tried. And yet, he hadn't pushed either sister for information. He'd been touched by the elderly doc, sensing his mind had weakened in his old age, and he'd felt dismayed when they'd refused to let the man into the university's lab.

But the bottom line was that Jake's heart wasn't into the story he was expected to report. His thoughts were elsewhere.

Watching Myna and the young boy, Hank, hovering over the iPad, laughing at some game, had reminded him of the times he'd spent with his own mother, the times they'd played board games on snowy afternoons, how she'd taught him to play poker when he'd been thirteen years old. Sometimes her death seemed to come out of nowhere, hitting him harder than he'd expected.

She'd suffered for three long years. The last four weeks had been unbearable, the pain she'd endured unimaginable. He'd sat by her bedside for days, slipping away to write when he could, returning the second she'd cry out. He'd wished for it to end, for his mother to be at peace. When the day had come and she'd been able to let go, it had been a blessing, and in ways, a relief.

He picked up the mug and took another long swallow. Then he reached for the old Nokia, turning it around in his hand. Someone pulled out the stool next to him and sat down. Out of the corner of his eye, he recognized the blue uniform. He shoved the Nokia in his pocket.

"What can I get you, Chief?" Rodney asked.

"Just a club soda," the chief said. Rodney nodded and stepped away to the other tap at the far end of the bar.

The chief turned in his seat, angling his broad shoulders in Jake's direction. "Jake Mann?" he asked.

"Yes," Jake said, wondering what in the world the chief wanted with him.

"I'd like to ask you a few questions about your whereabouts during the last twenty-four hours." There were lines around the chief's eyes. Deep crevices framed his mouth. He was getting up there in years, but he still looked fit. Intimidating. Maybe the chief saw a little bit of fear in Jake because he added, "It's just standard procedure, son."

"Okay," Jake said. He'd talked to a lot of cops in his line of work, but he'd always been the one asking the questions, not the other way around.

"Were you anywhere near The Snow Goose? You know the one—big white colonial with black shutters, and all those cherry blossoms in the yard? It's about a stone's throw away from the dam where the birds turned up." The chief stopped short of saying where the birds turned up *dead*.

"Yeah, I was there today. One of the sisters, Myna, gave me a lift. My car broke down on the mountain road."

"Was that the first time you've been there?"

Jake shook his head. "No, I met the older sister the day before when I got into town. I went straight to the dam. I'm a journalist."

"I know," the chief said.

"Okay, well, most of the birds had drifted away from the public lot, so I got in my car and headed for the other side. I met the older sister, Linnet, in the backyard of The Snow Goose. I tried to ask her some questions, but she refused to talk with me. I tried to give her my card, but she wouldn't take it and chased me away."

"Did that bother you that she chased you away?"

"I didn't take it personally, if that's what you mean. I just assumed she was upset about the birds and what it meant for her business, which is why I wanted to talk with her in the first place and get a local's point of view for my article."

"Did you stick around after that?" the chief asked.

"No," Jake said. "She asked me to leave, so I left."

"And what time was that?"

Jake scratched his chin. "I can't say for sure, but sometime before I went to the town hall meeting."

"And people saw you at the town hall meeting? They can place you there?" the chief asked.

Jake realized that the chief was asking him questions because it had something to do with the young professor. "Yeah, I think so. I sat next to a guy who smelled a little fishy, like he'd been to the dam and hadn't showered for some time. I didn't catch his name. And I saw Linnet and her groundskeeper guy." He tried to remember the guy's name. He snapped his fingers. "Al. I saw him trimming the rose bushes at the B&B earlier that day. He saw me here before the meeting."

"Okay," the chief said. "What did you do after the meeting?"

"I was on deadline, so I came back here to write my article."

"Just like you are now?" the chief asked, and motioned toward Jake's laptop.

"Well, no. I was tired, so I went straight to my room to work." He pointed toward the ceiling where the shabby room he'd rented was located.

"Did anyone visit you in your room? Or did you go anywhere else that night? See anyone else?"

"No, I was alone in my room all night. I didn't leave. I didn't have any visitors."

The chief kept his eyes on Jake's face as he talked. Jake suspected the chief was watching him closely to see if he was lying. "This is about what happened to the young professor," he said, and a million questions leapt to mind. "Am I a suspect or something?"

"I just need to talk to everyone who was on the property that day," the chief said.

"It wasn't an accident, was it?" He knew the chief wouldn't be wasting his time questioning him if the professor had died from an illness or natural causes. "What can you tell me on the record?" he asked. "I'd like to get a statement from you."

The chief frowned, hesitated, and then he said, "I have no comment until I get the medical examiner's report." He pointed to the laptop again. "Go on and type it in, *No comment.*"

"Sure," Jake said, but he made no attempt to touch the keyboard.

The chief turned toward the bar and sipped from the club

soda Rodney had set down in front of him. "There's something else," he said. "Off the record."

"Okay," Jake said.

"My secretary told me you were in to see her first thing this morning."

"Yes, I was."

"She copied a police report for you."

"Yes." He was beginning to realize just how small this town was, where even a request for a copy of an old auto accident report didn't go unnoticed.

"I think I know why," the chief said.

"I don't understand."

"You're his son, aren't you?"

"You knew my dad?"

"I didn't know him, but I remember him." The chief paused. "We get called to a lot of accidents on the mountain road. Some can be pretty bad."

Jake nodded.

He continued. "But there have been only two fatalities over the last twenty-five years that I've been chief. One was a young girl barely sixteen years old. She was going too fast and missed the turn, sailed right over the guardrail and down the mountain. The rail was twisted where she hit it, but it didn't stop her car from flipping over and over." He motioned with his arm, imitating the projectile of the vehicle. Then he ran his hand down his face. "It about killed me telling her parents what had happened to their little girl. You see, in a small town like Mountain Springs, everyone knows everyone. It was one of the saddest days of my career."

"And my dad?" he asked. "He was the second fatality."

"The other saddest day," the chief said, and picked up his club soda, turning it around in his hand.

"But it had to be different with my dad because he was from out of town."

"Different, yes, but it's not something you ever forget."

"Tell me what happened," Jake said.

"Are you sure?"

"Yes."

"We got a call early that morning. An elderly couple, the Olinskys, were on their way to a doctor's appointment over the mountain for Mr. Olinsky. He was noticing some blood in his urine. They own the hardware store in town. Olinsky Hardware. It's about three blocks down Main Street, not far from the Inn." His voice trailed off. "Never mind. It's not important. Anyway, I got the call there was a vehicle overturned on the mountain road."

Jake steadied himself on the stool, his jaw stiff from holding it rigid as though he were expecting a blow.

"The Olinskys had called it in. They'd found your dad's vehicle on its roof and your dad, well, you know. He was going too fast," the chief said. "We could tell from the skid marks."

Jake nodded.

"But I don't think it was just his speed that caused him to lose control of the car and roll it over. This isn't in the report, because it's all conjecture on my part, you see. It's not the hard facts. Do you understand?"

"Okay," Jake said. "Go on."

"There were a couple of feathers caught in the grille of your dad's car." He rubbed his brow. "There wasn't a dent or any blood on the bumper as far as I could tell, so the feathers might've gotten stuck before the accident. It's not uncommon to find feathers on the cars around here as I'm sure you can imagine. But on the side of the road not far from your dad's car, we found a dead goose."

"You're saying that you think he hit a bird?" Jake asked, unable to keep his voice from shaking.

"Well, I think he might've swerved to miss it, but hit it anyway."

"And that's what caused the accident? He was killed because he didn't want to hit a bird?"

"It's just my opinion. He was driving pretty fast to begin with. And the snow geese are pretty large birds."

They sat in silence. Perhaps he was giving Jake time to process what he believed had caused the accident. When Jake didn't say anything, the chief finished his club soda and then put the empty glass on the bar. He got up from the stool and turned to walk away, pausing to add before he left, "The dead bird's mate," he said, "stayed on the side of the road the entire time we were there. It never left until someone bagged the carcass."

"Why did you tell me this?" Jake asked.

"You're not the only one who lost someone they loved that night. If you ask me, that bird was mourning."

Was that supposed to make Jake feel better? That the bird's mate had died when Jake himself had lost his father? When Jake's mother had lost a husband that she'd loved so much she'd never gotten over it? And all because of some stupid bird in the road?

"Don't leave town," the chief said before he turned to leave. "I may have more questions for you."

Jake stayed at the bar, drinking one beer after another and pounding out the article he had to turn in before midnight. He focused on Professor Coyle's sudden death, an obituary of sorts, because he hadn't much else to go on—single, survived by his parents, master's degree in ornithology, where he spent time in Asia working on his thesis on the spoon-billed sandpiper.

The guy didn't have to go all the way to Asia, Jake thought. *He could've studied the sandpiper right here in the Poconos along the Delaware River.* Jake didn't include this bit of information in his article obviously. He was well aware he wasn't doing his job to the best of his ability. He hadn't asked the questions he should've asked about the police investigation into the young professor's death. Hell, he'd had the chief sitting right next to him. But he'd been distracted, and he struck each key harder than necessary when he got to the part about the National Wildlife Health Center cleaning up the dead snow geese from the dam. He struggled with infusing the empathy he'd felt for the birds in his initial report. But then he thought of the lone goose standing on the side of the road next to its dead mate, and something inside him cracked.

His cell phone buzzed. It was a text from Kim. She was close to getting him a name for the number in his father's old cell phone. *Hang tight,* she'd written. He set his phone down and reached into his pocket for the Nokia, rubbing the deep scratches on the back with his finger over and over again. Something the chief had said turned around in Jake's mind, the idea that in small towns *everyone knows everyone.*

So who did Jake's father know in Mountain Springs?

CHAPTER SIXTEEN

Linnet slipped under the covers and into Ian's arms. His body was warm and inviting.

"He'll be okay," Ian said about Hank. "The dam will be cleaned up by tomorrow, and Charlie will sort out the mess with Professor Coyle. Things will get back to normal. And that goes for Pop, too," he added.

She agreed about Hank. He was a sensitive boy, but he was also resilient like his father. It was one of the things she loved most about Ian, his ability to see past difficult situations and keep them both moving forward. She wasn't so sure about Pop. She had other worries where he was concerned, troubled by the things he remembered, and those he didn't.

"I called Charlie," she said. "I told him Jake was on the property the same day as the professor." She felt the need to defend her actions. Myna had looked at her as though she were crazy for thinking Jake had anything to do with the professor's death. Maybe her sister was right, but maybe she was wrong. Maybe Linnet was grasping at anything and everything that would take the attention away from Pop, who couldn't remember the details of what had happened that night. "Charlie asked for a list of everybody who was here that day. I thought he should know."

"You did the right thing," Ian said, and then added, "Jake seems like an all right guy to me though."

"Yeah," she said. "So everybody keeps telling me." The last part she whispered to herself. There was something about him, something that had tightened her chest and put her on guard. Plus, he was a journalist, and she didn't want anyone from the news media stalking her family.

"I'm beat," Ian said. "Try and get some rest." He stretched his long arms and legs, untangling his limbs from hers.

She rolled to her side, rethinking her conversation with Myna, hating the way she'd sounded defensive, stern. If only she could find a way to talk with her sister, a way to return to the easy rhythm of their youth, when everything wasn't strained and difficult.

She flipped onto her back and stared at the ceiling. Ian snored lightly. She wasn't going to get much sleep. It was going to be a long night.

She turned her head toward the window. The light of the moon sliced through the branches of the trees, making oblong-shaped shadows on the ceiling and walls. Linnet had moved into the master bedroom the day she'd married Ian. Until then, the sisters had shared the room that Hank now occupied. When Myna had graduated from the university, she'd taken the first job offered to her in New Jersey. She'd been determined to live anywhere but Mountain Springs. Linnet had been running the B&B successfully for a year by then, and she and Ian had been making plans for their future. Linnet had no intention of going anywhere. Her life had always been in Mountain Springs, at the B&B with the dam and the snow geese. Her sister had felt differently.

But since Linnet had been determined to stay, she'd had to erase all the sad memories and create new ones, happier ones, with Ian. She'd eradicated any trace of her mother from the room, changing the color of the walls, the area rug, the curtains and furniture. When she'd finished, it had looked nothing like the room it had been—so much so that it had brought Myna to tears.

"But there's nothing left of Mom in here," she'd said.

"That was the point," Linnet had said.

"But it doesn't even smell like her." Myna had wiped her eyes, her long dark eyelashes wet and clumped together.

"No, it doesn't," Linnet had said, wanting to comfort her sister, but instead she'd crossed her arms. She hadn't told her sister that she'd kept the doily that had been on the dresser, the one where their mother had kept her hairbrush and perfume. The lace had held on to their mother's scent, or at least the way she had smelled in the few happy months before everything had changed.

It had been during one of these happier months, November, nearly eight months after her mother had confessed her hatred for the birds, when the students of Mountain Springs High had been let out early from school for holiday break. The autumn air had been crisp. The pewter sky had smelled like rain. Linnet had rounded the corner of the mountain road, and The Snow Goose came into view. *Home.* She breathed a sigh of relief and pulled into the driveway. Myna was already bending down to pick up her backpack from between her legs.

"We've got company again," Linnet said, and nodded in the direction of the car parked in the guest parking space.

"That's the third time he's been here this month," Myna said.

They exchanged a look before getting out of the car and heading to the side door. Linnet dumped her backpack onto the kitchen table. It was heavy, stuffed full with library books to occupy her over the next few days. Myna dropped her backpack onto the floor.

There was a pot of beef stew simmering on the stove, the smell rich and warm. Linnet and Myna eyed the pot suspiciously. Linnet pulled the refrigerator door open, surprised to find a cheese platter that had been picked over. She handed it to Myna.

They helped themselves to the leftover cheese wedges and apple slices, eating in silence, exchanging looks back and forth, listening for sounds of the others.

Myna dipped an apple slice in caramel and stuffed the whole thing into her mouth. Linnet helped herself to another cheddar cube. She didn't have to ask Myna what was up with the soup and platters. It was for the man who had been coming to the B&B the last couple of months. They'd seen him with their mother on the sofa in the grand living room and on the front porch swing, and once up close when they'd bumped into him in the hallway where the family's bedrooms were located and where guests weren't allowed. He'd held up his hands. "I guess I got lost." Linnet had pointed him in the direction of the dining hall.

Today, there was enough food and wine in the house to feed a dozen people. Linnet hoped that meant more guests were coming. The Snow Goose wasn't exactly thriving. You could say that business had been dead if you didn't count that man constantly showing up.

"Do you hear that?" Myna asked.

Linnet shook her head.

"That," Myna said.

It sounded like giggling.

"That's Mom," Myna said.

"It can't be," Linnet said. She couldn't remember the last time she'd heard her mother laugh.

They got up from the table and followed the sound, stopping outside their parents' bedroom door. Myna's eyes grew wide. She opened her mouth to say something, but the only sound that came out was a strangled squeak. Linnet had an overwhelming sense that there was something wrong here. She grabbed her sister's hand and pulled her back down the hall. She didn't stop until they were standing in the kitchen once again.

Myna rubbed the birthmark on her arm, unaware she was doing it. Linnet could swear her sister could connect with their mother telepathically through the damn thing. Maybe that was the reason why Linnet didn't have to ask her if she'd felt it, the injustice of what was happening right now, this very instant, inside their house.

"Come with me," Linnet said, taking her sister's hand again, but this time leading her outside into the cool air, through the yard and woods to the dam. The trees were nearly bare. Most of the leaves had fallen to the ground, the bright yellows and oranges turning varying shades of brown.

She led her down the pier where the rowboat was docked. Linnet untied the rope from the post and climbed in with her sister. She picked up the oars.

Myna stared at the gray sky. "Pop's car wasn't in the driveway," she said.

"I noticed," Linnet said.

Myna slipped her arm through Linnet's. "Look." She pointed at the V formation of geese overhead migrating south for the winter. Neither one spoke until the honking had faded and the birds flew farther and farther away. When the dam was quiet again, Myna said, "Now we know what has been making Mom happy."

"Yes," Linnet said, and closed her eyes, pinching back tears. "Now we know."

Linnet carried a plate of cookies to the guesthouse for Pop. She'd seen his light on in his study when she'd gotten out of bed, unable to sleep. If she ever hoped to get answers from him about what he might know about what had happened to Professor Coyle, the opportunity was now. The fewer people around, the easier time he had of focusing, remembering.

The stone path was cold beneath her feet. She rushed inside the guesthouse to escape the chilly night air. When she opened the door to his study, she expected to find him pouring over books and journals or perhaps peering into the lens of a microscope. She found neither. He was slumped back in the old leather chair behind the desk, fast asleep. His lips made a motorboat sound each time he exhaled. There was a time when he'd be so focused on his research he'd remain awake for hours, sometimes days, never even stopping to eat. She hadn't known then exactly what he'd worked so hard on. Outside of teaching, much of his job had been a mystery, one more thing he'd kept to himself. Sometimes she wondered if a child ever understood the inner lives of their parents. She thought of Hank, of all the things he didn't know about her, and she supposed not.

"Pop," she said, and put the plate of cookies on the desk in front of him. She gently nudged his arm. "Pop."

He opened his eyes, blinking several times.

"I brought you a snack."

He came around, appearing to remember where he was and why. "I must've fallen asleep." He looked at the plate, the papers underneath. "I've barely begun." He motioned to the table on the other side of the room, where more papers were strewn on top of charts containing information about snow geese migration patterns. She picked up what appeared to be some kind of weather map. More maps covered the wall, including a detailed one of Canada and the Northern Alaskan tundra. Pins marked the final stops where the flocks had nested.

In the corner, Gerty peered at them through glass eyes. She was one of the first snow geese her father had tagged for research. He'd followed her for more than seventeen years until the day she'd died, staying behind on the dam one winter while the rest of the flock had moved on. He'd found her not far from the bench where he'd often sit with binoculars, watching them forage the fields, ripping the bulrush from the shallow water. He believed she'd died of old age, although some snow geese were recorded to live twenty-five years or more, the oldest snow goose on record being twenty-seven.

Linnet remembered finding Pop at the dam with tears in his eyes, holding Gerty gently in his arms. He hadn't wanted to let her go, so he'd made the decision to have her stuffed and kept in his study. On occasion, Linnet had caught him talking to the old bird, stroking the silky feathers on her back.

He tapped the mouse, and his computer screen lit up. Weather charts appeared. One in particular showed the radar tracking another storm. It looked to be a few days away but was clearly heading in their direction.

She covered his hand before he could touch the keyboard. If she allowed him to go back to his research, she'd lose him to it. "I need to talk to you about Professor Coyle," she said.

"Young guy, isn't he? He must be around your age," he said.

"I'm thirty-seven, Pop. Almost a decade older."

He searched her face as if he couldn't quite believe so much time had passed. "I'll always see you as my little girl. You and your sister."

She leaned on the desk, bending close to him, smelling the soap on his skin, the scent reminding her of when she was a child curling into his arms. "What happened to the professor?"

"You're different from your sister. You're stronger. You have a level head on your shoulders," he said. "Your sister, well, she's impulsive. She doesn't always think things through. I worry about her."

This was all great, but he wasn't answering her question. "Please, Pop. Tell me what you remember about last night. Tell me so I can help you. When was the last time you saw him?"

"Did I show you the new pictures she sent me of the *Pelecanus occidentalis*?" He searched his desk for the iPad Ian had given him for his birthday two years ago. "It's fascinating watching them plunge-dive for small fish."

"Myna's here, at the main house, do you remember?" she asked. "She came home to visit."

"Yes," he said. She detected a slight irritation in his tone.

"What about Professor Coyle?" She had to get him back on track, in-line with what she'd been asking. "I want to know everything you remember about him."

"Is this another one of your tests?"

"No," she said. When she'd noticed he'd been forgetting more and more of life's daily activities in the last year—like brushing his teeth or changing his clothes—she'd gone online and printed out tests and made flashcards, trying to self-diagnose how far things had progressed. Eventually, she'd taken him to a doctor, under duress, who in the end hadn't been able to tell her anything she hadn't already known. He'd suffered from vascular dementia after a series of minor strokes that had originally gone unde-tected, reducing the blood flow to the brain, the result of which forced him into retirement. "It's not a test. But it is important," she said.

"He was supposed to take the birds to the lab," he said. "And that's the last thing I remember, so stop asking me about it."

"Are you sure there's nothing else you remember about him, about what happened?"

"Yes, I'm sure," he snapped.

"Okay, Pop." If she continued to press him, she'd only keep agitating him, and then she was certain not to get anything more out of him. She believed he didn't know much more than he was saying, or if he did, he wasn't capable of remembering what it was. "Have a cookie."

He picked one up and took a bite. She got up to leave.

"I'll get the plate tomorrow." She paused in the doorway. "Don't stay up too late, okay?"

He waved her off.

She hesitated, watching him, the cookie shaking in his arthritic hand as he brought it to his lips. There was nothing she could think to do. She was powerless over time pecking away at his mind. The feeling of helplessness was so strong; it took everything she had not to fall to the floor at his feet. What kind of daughter was she if she couldn't help her own father?

CHAPTER SEVENTEEN

"I think your honeymooners have come up for air," Myna said to Linnet, and helped herself to a fresh cup of coffee. She'd gotten up early after a cold, restless night, missing the warmth of Ben by her side. She'd slipped on a pair of jeans and a peasant blouse, something that looked as though it came straight out of the seventies. She'd debated whether or not to throw on the only sweater she'd brought, having forgotten how much cooler spring was in the mountains, but in the end had decided against it.

"I almost forgot they were here," Linnet said, and leaned her back against the countertop. She raised a mug to her lips.

"They were wandering around the halls," Myna said. She was aware of treading lightly, testing the waters between them after their exchange the night before. The tension was there, rough but not rocky, nearly gone but not forgotten.

Linnet put her cup in the sink. "I don't have anything prepared. I gave Cora the day off with everything that has been going on around here. And with the Rapps leaving." She opened the refrigerator door. "I'm going to have to whip up some scrambled eggs or something." She pulled out the egg carton. "Maybe some bacon. Are you hungry?" she asked.

Ian and Hank strolled into the room. Hank reached for a bowl and a box of cereal. Linnet handed him the milk and pulled open the silverware drawer for a spoon.

Ian touched Linnet's arm as he moved around her to get to the coffeemaker. He sat at the table with the paper and his cup. The news of Professor Coyle had been plastered on the front page. He scanned the article. "Did you see this?" he asked, before flipping to the sports section.

"Yes," Linnet said.

Myna had read Jake's article on her laptop before she'd gotten out of bed and before the Internet connection had crapped out on her. He'd mentioned The Snow Goose briefly, focusing more on Professor Coyle, the man, his life before it had tragically ended on the B&B's property. Somehow Jake's words made what happened to the professor all the more real.

Linnet turned toward the counter and cracked an egg into a bowl, cursing the pieces of shell she'd dropped into the yolk.

Myna knew her sister was good at hiding her feelings, stowing her emotions away so that her face was unreadable. She'd always been the stronger of the two, but there were times when even she had shown signs of breaking. And Myna was beginning to see the splintering behind her sister's expressionless mask.

She took the eggshell from Linnet's hand. "Why don't I run into town and pick up some bagels and croissants from the bakery? I'm sure they're just looking for something to fill their stomachs."

"You're probably right." Linnet abandoned the bowl with the egg. Hank slurped milk from his spoon. Voices came from the living room area. "I better get Pop," she said absently, and gazed at Ian and the paper once again.

"I'll get Pop for you," Myna said.

"No," Linnet shot back. "I'll get him."

Hank looked up from his cereal bowl.

"Fine," Myna said, putting her hands up in a surrendering gesture and stepping toward the door. "I'll be back with bagels."

Myna hadn't been to town since she'd arrived in Mountain Springs. She didn't count her first night here when it had been late and the streets were bare, the stores dark, the streetlamps her only guide. But now in the morning light, Mountain Springs was exactly as she'd remembered it. The cherry blossoms were in bloom, the branches full of lush pink flowers. The pretty trees lined both sides of the street. A dusting of petals covered the walkways; more were piled high in the gutters, where they had been swept aside by passing cars.

But where were the people walking their dogs? Where were the couples strolling arm in arm? Where were the tourists taking pictures of the blossoms and larger-than-life mountains? The scene was usually quaint with quiet activity.

Something was off.

She reached the center of town, where the news vans were lined up in front of the mayor's office. The sidewalks were littered with pamphlets and napkins and discarded wrappers leftover from the various food trucks that had served the reporters' makeshift arena. Myna could only imagine what the Mountain Springs Inn looked like, a bunch of men and women wearing badges, vying for the latest gossip, pestering the tourists and locals for information.

She drove another two blocks on her way to the bakery. She stopped at one of three traffic lights. A group of people had gathered at the corner. A woman ran up to her window. She was pale and thin. Her nails were painted black. She knocked on the glass.

Myna rolled the window down.

"Prepare yourself," the woman said, and shoved a pamphlet into Myna's hand. "The end of the world is near."

The pamphlet was covered in quotes from the Book of Revelation, an image of the Pale Rider plastered on the front. "Give me a break," Myna said, and tossed it aside. The light turned green, and she proceeded through the intersection, the woman and her cohorts spouting off about the signs, about the birds falling from the sky. She spotted Jake walking down the sidewalk. Several doomsayers surrounded him, waving their propaganda in his face. She should drive by and pretend she hadn't noticed him, but she was more than curious about the ring Linnet had mentioned, the one that had her sister more upset than she'd tried to let on.

Myna pulled over and rolled the window down for a second time, not succumbing to second thoughts, not thinking it through. "Do you need a ride?" she asked. In the back of her mind she heard her sister's voice asking her what she thought she was doing. Sometimes Myna wasn't always aware of why she did certain things. Sometimes she did them out of spite, behaving like the child Linnet had made her out to be. But this was more than rebelling against her sister. This was personal.

Jake looked up from one of the flyers that had no doubt been shoved into his hand by the throng of protestors or whatever they called themselves. He jumped into the car.

"Thanks for saving me," he said, and picked up the pamphlet she'd thrown on the seat.

She pulled from the curb, eager to get away before the crowd surrounded her vehicle. "Where are you headed?" she asked.

"I was on my way to pick up my car from Chicky's," he said, and held up the flyer. "What do you make of this?"

"On or off the record?" she asked, and then added, "I suppose it doesn't matter which it is. I think it's a load of crap. In a couple of days we'll know what happened to the birds, and it won't have anything to do with the end of the world."

"Can I quote you on that?" he asked.

"Sure," she said, and smiled. She didn't care if he did use it in one of his articles. Hell, she was the daughter of the Bird Man, so she should know.

"For the record, I think it's a load of crap, too," he said. "And you can quote *me* on that." He stuck the flyer into the backpack he was carrying. "Still, it makes for a good story."

"Did you see all those news vans hanging around town hall?" she asked. "You'd think they'd be hanging around the dam."

"Oh, I think they're scared to be near the water in case it's contaminated. Some of them are worried it's the bird flu or some other disease."

"If it is then it only affected some of the snow geese out of the tens of thousands that pass through. Not to mention all of the other species of birds alive and kicking around the dam."

"You make a good point," he said. "I'd love to interview your dad. Did he ever tell you his theory?"

"No," she said.

"Do you think you could set up an interview with him for me?" he asked.

"Oh, I don't know," she said, and made two more turns through town. In another two minutes they'd arrive at Chicky's. She hadn't been able to take her eyes off the road to search his hands.

"What if you were there when I talked with him?" Jake asked.

"I don't know."

"How about you set up the interview for me, and I'll let you see the article before I turn it in to my editor? That way if you don't like something I write, you can take it out. You'd have control."

She didn't see any harm in it, especially if she was there with Pop during the interview, and then later if she could edit the piece as she pleased. Jake had treated him with nothing but respect and care the last time they'd been together. And what if the interview could portray Pop as the scholarly scientist he once was? She knew Linnet would never go for it, not with an investigation pending surrounding Professor Coyle, and Pop's memory lapse.

"I'll think about it," she said, and pulled into Chicky's Auto Shop.

Jake checked his phone, and that's when she saw the gold ring on his finger. He reached for the door handle.

She wasn't thinking when she suddenly grabbed his forearm. "Your ring," she said.

He stared at her hand where it pinched his skin.

She released him, embarrassed by her outburst. "It's interesting, that's all," she said.

"It was my dad's," he said.

The blood rushed to her ears. She wasn't able to speak.

After a short pause, he got out of the car. "Let me know what you decide about the interview." He slung his backpack over his shoulder. "Thanks for the lift." He walked into the repair shop, where Chicky was waiting.

She put the car in drive and pulled out of the lot. Her heart beat loudly. She couldn't stop her body from shaking.

CHAPTER EIGHTEEN

Linnet was about to walk down to the guesthouse to bring Pop up for breakfast when Charlie knocked at the side door. He stood on the stoop dressed in blues, his chief's hat in his hands. Her father and Charlie had played chess every Sunday morning for as long as Linnet could remember. Charlie had often worn jeans, a gray sweatshirt, and an old fishing hat, but never his police uniform.

"Charlie," Linnet said, hesitating for a split second, and then stepping aside to let him in. Ian lowered the paper.

"Pop is in his study. I was just about to go and get him."

"Hang on a second," Charlie said. His eyes looked tired. "I want to talk to you first." He glanced at Hank sitting at the table in front of an empty bowl of cereal. "Is there someplace we can talk privately?"

Ian sprung from his chair. "We'll leave you two alone." He motioned to Hank. "Let's head over to the batting cages for a while."

Hank shot up from his seat. "I'll go get my bat," he said, and rushed out of the room.

Thank you, she mouthed to Ian.

He crossed the kitchen and kissed her cheek. "Fill me in later, okay? I'll take Hank out the front," he said, and disappeared to follow their son.

Once they were alone, she motioned for Charlie to sit. She could hear the murmurs of her guests in the next room. They'd migrated to the dining room looking for their promised complimentary meal that came with the weekend package they'd purchased.

"Would you like a cup of coffee?" she asked Charlie, putting off dealing with the newlyweds for the moment. "I'm afraid I don't have anything else to offer you. Myna went to pick up some pastries. She should be back shortly."

"Coffee is good," Charlie said.

She poured him a cup and set it on the table.

"Excuse me," a male voice said from behind her. She turned to find her young guests standing in the doorway of the kitchen. *What was his name?* She searched her memory. "Yes, Mick, good morning." His new wife poked her head out from behind him. "Hello, Emmy," she said.

"We were wondering what time breakfast would be served," Mick said, and touched his stomach. "We skipped dinner, and we're a bit hungry." Emmy hit his arm, smiling behind his back.

"I imagine you are," Linnet said. "Breakfast is going to be a little late this morning." Out of the corner of her eye she caught Charlie shifting his body in the seat in an impatient way. "On second thought," she said to Mick and Emmy, "there's a really good diner in town. Breakfast is on me." She put the coffeepot down and grabbed her purse from the countertop. She pulled a couple of twenty-dollar bills from her wallet and handed them to Mick.

"Are you sure?" Mick asked, taking the money from her hand.

"Of course," she said. "All you have to do is take a left onto the mountain road and follow it straight to town. If you go right you'll end up going over the mountain, and you don't want to do that." *Never mind why*, she thought. "Keep going straight through town. At the second stoplight make another left. Murphy's Diner is on the corner. I apologize for any inconvenience," she added. "It's, uh, not a typical weekend around here. I'm sure you can understand."

Once the newlyweds were gone, she topped off Charlie's coffee. She'd never had to chase her guests away before, but she didn't feel as though she had any other choice.

"Why don't you sit down with me," Charlie said.

There was something in Charlie's voice that made her sit on command, the coffeepot still in her hand.

"I got the medical examiner's report this morning on Professor Coyle. He died of blunt force trauma to the face and head."

She kept still, but she thought she might've gasped. It wasn't some heart condition or other medical condition that had caused his death. "Could he have tripped and fallen?" It was possible. The ground was uneven along the path and at the edge of the yard where the grass met the woods. Tree roots and rocks jutted from the ground. If a person wasn't watching where they were walking, they could trip, turn an ankle, become the victim of an unfortunate accident. She'd warned her guests over the years to watch their step not only on the B&B's property but also around the dam. There was the bird dirt to consider, too. Snow geese eliminated an amazing six to fifteen droppings an hour, and when it was fresh, it was slippery underfoot. Linnet had posted *Watch Your Step* signs at the path and next to the pier. The town had posted their own signs at the public parking lot and boat launch.

Charlie continued. "We believe someone or something struck his face, the force of which sent him falling backwards and subsequently causing a blow to his head."

"I don't understand." Her mouth was dry, arid.

"The trauma to his face and head caused bleeding into his brain. If he had been taken to the hospital right away, who knows, maybe he would've survived. But somehow I don't think so."

She was listening, but at the same time she wanted to cover her ears. Why was the truth so hard to hear and a lie so easy to believe? She suddenly needed a drink to wash away the sand that seemed to coat her tongue. The faucet was only a few feet away, but she didn't move. She stayed seated, composed. "Why are you telling me this?" she asked, putting the coffeepot down. She hadn't realized she'd been holding it the entire time.

"I think your dad may know what happened to Professor Coyle. He might've been the last person to be with him."

"You can't be serious," she said. "Come on, Charlie. Pop may forget what he had for dinner or where he put his slippers, but he's not violent or even hostile. He'd never hurt anybody." *Water.* She needed a glass of water.

"I've known your dad a longtime," he said. "And I agree with you, but the fact remains he was the last one with the professor. Maybe someone else was with him that night. We just don't know unless your dad tells us. I need to talk with him again. It's the only way I can help him."

"You can't force him to remember. That's not how it works." She wouldn't look at him.

"We've got the entire nation watching what we're doing right now," Charlie said. "And once the word gets out this is a homicide investigation people are going to start asking questions."

"Homicide." She couldn't wrap her mind around the word.

"I need for him to try to remember something, anything that will help clear this up. It's important," he said, and touched her forearm. His hand was warm. "I promise to go easy on him."

She pushed back from the table, pulling her arm away, and

went to the sink, filling a glass with water. She gulped it down. When she finished drinking, she set the empty glass on the counter and turned around, meeting his gaze. Concern hung on his face, worry filled his eyes.

"Okay," she said, understanding she didn't really have a choice. "I'll go and get him."

Linnet stood in the doorway of the dining room. Pop had his back to her, so she wasn't sure whether or not he knew she was standing there, listening. Charlie sat opposite him, and every now and again he'd look up from the chess game to glance at her. Thirty minutes in, and he hadn't asked Pop one single question about Professor Coyle. She'd warned him if her father was having a bad day, he wouldn't be much help. If he was having a good day there was a chance he'd remember something about that night, something other than the professor failing to take the geese to the university lab. *Please, Pop, be having a good day,* she thought. *Tell us it was somebody else's fault.* Behind her, the side door slammed.

"Linnet," Myna called. "Where are you?"

Reluctantly, Linnet turned and made her way to the kitchen.

Myna was pulling a box of pastries from a shopping bag along with several bagels and cream cheese. "Sorry I'm late," she said.

"Uh-huh," Linnet said, distracted. She was straining to hear what Charlie was saying in the dining room.

"Did you know there's a group of people passing out flyers about the apocalypse?"

"Why am I not surprised?"

"I bumped into Jake in town."

It wasn't until she mentioned Jake that Linnet noticed how pale her sister's face was.

"I saw the ring," she said. "I asked him about it. He said it was his dad's."

Linnet felt as though the ground shifted below her feet. She steadied herself against the countertop. "So what?" she asked.

"I think it's more than a coincidence."

"What does any of this have to do with us?"

"It has everything to do with us," Myna said, her voice pitching high. "What if he had a son? What if Jake is his son?"

Linnet spread her hands flat on the counter. "So what if he is? Who cares? It means nothing to us. Why are you so hell-bent on stirring things up now? We have enough going on around here." She talked through clenched teeth and pointed to the dining room. "Charlie is in there giving our father the third degree, and you're concerned about some guy who may or may not be who you think he is." She knew which buttons to push with her little sister, and she couldn't stop herself now that she'd started. She hated herself before the words even left her mouth. "Do you think he's good-looking? Is that what this is about? Is he the next guy on your list of men? What about Ben? Or is that why you came running home, because you broke up with him?"

"What? No." Myna took a step back. She looked at the floor, shaking her head, cowering away from her.

Myna had never been one to defend herself, and for once Linnet wished her sister would fight back, show some backbone. Myna's answer to everything was to run away, and Linnet was tired of shouldering all of the weight of this family on her own.

After a long stretch of silence, Myna asked, "What do you mean Charlie is giving Pop the third degree?"

Linnet rubbed her brow. "Professor Coyle's death was ruled a homicide. And Charlie thinks Pop knows something about it."

A ruckus came from the dining room. Linnet raced past her

sister and found both Pop and Charlie on the floor picking up chess pieces.

"What happened?" she asked. Myna rushed in behind her.

"Nothing," Charlie said. "Your dad just bumped the board with his arm."

"It was an accident," Pop said, and looked up at both Linnet and her sister from where he knelt on the floor.

Myna moved past Linnet, bumping into her arm as she did. She slipped her hand underneath Pop's elbow. "Let me help you up."

Linnet stared at Charlie. She knew it was more than Pop simply bumping the chessboard with his arm. When he was frightened or agitated, he acted out. It had been occurring more and more lately. Recently, he'd knocked the microphone out of the news reporter's hand when he'd kept after him, pressuring him with questions.

She also knew Charlie was aware of the new development in Pop's recent behavior.

"Accidents happen," she said.

Linnet and Ian were sitting on the bench by the dam. The moon was high in the sky. A thousand stars sparkled, winking at them from above. The water rippled in the cool breeze. The fallen geese were gone. Only the faintest scent of death lingered, staining the otherwise fresh air.

She told Ian about Charlie's visit. It was the first opportunity she'd had in the long day to talk with him alone. The newlyweds had packed and gone.

Ian had remained quiet while she talked, nodding occasionally, rubbing the back of her neck in a soothing way.

"For what it's worth," Ian said when she'd finished, "I don't think Pop would hurt anybody." He stopped, and she knew what he was thinking without him saying it. *No, Pop wouldn't hurt anyone—not intentionally anyway.*

She rested her head against his shoulder and looked out across the water. The waves lapped against the shore. The air buzzed with silence.

In the quiet, her thoughts wandered to her exchange with Myna earlier that morning. Her sister hadn't mentioned Jake or the ring again, and Linnet hoped she'd heard the last of it.

"Ready to call it a night?" Ian asked after some time had passed. "I've got an early day tomorrow."

They walked hand in hand on the path through the woods and entered the yard. They passed the guesthouse. The small light was on in the back room where Pop slept. She turned to Ian. "I'm just going to check on him," she said.

"Don't be too long," he said, and squeezed her hand before letting her go.

She slipped through the front door, tripping over one of Professor Coyle's boxes that had been left in the foyer. She flicked on the light, staring at the two boxes containing empty test tubes, clean slides, latex gloves. Pop and Myna had taken the samples out and left the rest of the supplies here. She supposed she should call the university and have someone pick them up.

Then she had a thought. What if Charlie's men had missed something? What if she could find something to indicate someone else had been with the young professor that night?

"Pop," she called quietly. She didn't want to startle him or wake him if he were asleep. When he didn't answer, she bent over the boxes and looked through them. Nothing looked out of place or suspicious. The light in the foyer spilled into the living room. She poked around, looking for signs someone other than Pop had been here. She spied the empty plate of cookies from the night before but saw nothing to suggest that he'd had company. The only evidence Professor Coyle had been here at all were the boxes from the university.

She picked her way through the living room and poked her head inside the bedroom. Pop was sitting up with his eyes closed, his spectacles crooked on his nose. Carefully, she removed them from his face and laid them on the nightstand in the exact spot where he'd put them every night so he'd know where to find them in the morning. She gently lifted the journal out from under his arm, the page opened to a picture of a snow goose.

Oh, Pop, I miss them, too. She set the journal on the nightstand next to his spectacles. She turned out the light, closing the door softly behind her, wondering how this gentle man who had loved his birds could have possibly done what Charlie suspected.

A seventeen-year-old Linnet opened the ledger on top of the bed where she'd been lying down. She propped herself on her elbows and poured over the B&B's books her mother was supposed to have been keeping. Myna was lying next to her in the reverse position, her feet next to Linnet's head. She was studying for an algebra test, or trying to anyway. She kept whining about how it was stupid to study math when you either knew how to solve the equation or you didn't. The winter wind blew, rattling the shutters. There were six inches of snow on the ground.

"There's no bullshitting with numbers," Myna said. "There's only one right answer, and that's why I hate it. I like options." She kicked her legs, knocking her feet into Linnet's face.

"Watch it," Linnet said, and pushed her sister's feet away. She didn't like what she was seeing. Her mother had written down names and phone numbers, but very little else about the guests and how they'd paid for their rooms. They'd had so few visitors, it was easy to track the money coming in and out, and still her mother failed at keeping basic records.

Myna sighed and slammed her math book shut. She flipped onto her back. "I hate homework," she said, and stared at the ceiling.

"Look at this." Linnet sat up and put the book in her lap. Myna pulled herself upright and looked at the page where Linnet was pointing to a list of names, sliding her finger to indicate where the money should've been recorded under the credit column. Myna's long curls draped over Linnet's arm, mixing in with Linnet's straight hair, the dark brown matching perfectly together. "There are more here and here." She turned the page. "And here. But there's no documentation of whether or not any money was exchanged. And did you notice there's no mention of that man who's been coming for the last ten months?" Neither sister knew the man's name, only his face, but it was clear he wasn't in the books. It was as though he hadn't existed, and Linnet imagined that was the point. But he did exist.

He did.

"Where did you find this?" Myna asked.

"I found it in the kitchen drawer." It wasn't like she went searching for it. Well, not really. She had a project for a business course she'd added as an elective at the start of the second semester of her senior year in high school. She had to come up with a plan for how she would successfully own and operate a small business. The assignment had excited her. She'd jotted down her ideas on how to improve The Snow Goose, on how to enhance the guests' experiences so they'd keep coming back year after year. She'd envisioned showing her mother the proposal once she'd put it all together, sitting down with her and her sister to discuss her plans. She hadn't shared any of this with her sister yet. She'd wanted to surprise them both.

"Besides," she said to Myna. "If Mom didn't want anyone to see how the business was doing, she would've hid the record book somewhere where no one could find it."

"I guess so," Myna said, glancing at the entries. "It doesn't look good though, does it?"

"No, it doesn't." She agreed.

It came as no surprise their mother wasn't good at running a business or handling money. Linnet couldn't think of one thing their mother was good at lately. But she had been a good mother once, and she made their father happy—or at least she used to.

Linnet tossed the book aside. Her assignment was going to be harder than she thought, but she'd make it work somehow, someway.

They lay quietly for some time listening to the clacking of the electric heat, the wind, and the geese honking outside their window. They were smack in the middle of winter, and the dam was filled with hundreds of the snow geese, their familiar sounds making for a good night's sleep.

There was a moment when everything fell silent, and Linnet heard their mother talking.

"Who's Mom talking to?" she asked.

Myna turned to her side. "Maybe Pop's home."

Linnet stood and looked out the window to the guesthouse. "The light is still on in the study." She crossed the room and opened their bedroom door.

Myna pulled herself up. "Where are you going?"

Linnet crept down the hall.

Her sister followed. "What are you doing?"

"Shh," she said.

Their mother's voice was low and muffled.

"She's on the phone," Linnet said, and snuck farther down the hall toward the steps and kitchen.

Myna trailed her, tugging on the back of Linnet's sweatshirt. "Who could she be talking to this late at night?" she whispered.

"Exactly," Linnet whispered back, and tiptoed to where the cordless phone sat in its cradle on the kitchen countertop. She reached for it.

"You can't be serious," Myna said. "She'll hear you pick up."

"I don't care." Linnet suspected who her mother might be talking to. She eased the phone out of the stand and heard the click as she picked up. A man's deep voice purred in her ear.

The sisters put their heads together, cradling the phone between them, and listened.

"You're serious," their mother said.

"Of course I'm serious," he said. "Run away with me."

"But—" their mother said.

"There are no buts. It's either yes or no. Either we do this or we continue to torture ourselves until the next time we can be together."

"You make it sound so simple."

"It is simple. I love you. You love me. It's not hard."

Linnet and Myna exchanged a nervous glance.

He continued. "What do you say?"

"And we're just going to leave everything behind?"

"Yes," he said. "Everything and everyone." He paused. "Can you do that?"

Linnet pulled the phone away from Myna. Whatever her mother said next, Linnet didn't want Myna to hear. She wanted to protect her younger sister from the hurt her mother was constantly inflicting upon them.

"What are you doing?" Myna hissed, and grabbed for the phone.

Linnet clutched it firmly.

"And you think leaving will help? It will make me better?" their mother asked. *Was she crying?* She sounded as though she were crying, but were they tears of joy or sorrow?

"Just give me a chance, and I promise I'll make you happy."

There was some hesitation on their mother's part. Myna reached for the phone again, and Linnet pulled away from her.

"Okay," their mother said, as though she was trying to convince him, or maybe she was trying to convince herself.

"You'll do it? You'll leave with me?"

"Yes," she whispered.

Linnet lowered the phone from her ear, catching him say he'd need time to tie up some loose ends. She set the phone back in the stand.

Myna stomped her foot. "Well?" she asked. "What did she say?" Her chest rose up and down. "Is she leaving us?" She stomped her foot again. "Is she? Is she running away with him?"

Linnet couldn't answer right away. She didn't want to tell her sister the awful truth, but she couldn't lie to her either. "We might have some time before she goes."

"So she's leaving?" Myna asked.

Linnet watched Myna's face contort in pain and confusion, and then she saw in her sister's eyes a flicker of hope.

"Maybe she'll change her mind," Myna said.

"Maybe," Linnet said, but she didn't believe it.

"Why is she doing this?" Myna asked. "Is she that unhappy here? With us? With Pop?"

"I don't know," she said, and pulled her sister to her. "I really don't know." She held her close, but the strength in Linnet's arms couldn't reach the weakness in her knees, and they sank to the floor, clinging to each other.

CHAPTER NINETEEN

Myna had sent a text to Ben asking him to Skype with her at 10 P.M. She sat on the bed with her laptop opened in front of her, not even realizing she'd been holding her breath, fearing he'd stand her up. But then there he was, his face filling the box on her screen. She exhaled a steady sigh of relief.

"Hey you," he said. There was a lag time and his movements were slow and jerky, but he was there, smiling, filling her heart with an ache so strong she nearly put her hand through the screen, wanting to reach in and pull him to her.

"Hey." It was all she said in return, wishing she could tell him how much she missed him, loved him, but she couldn't. She hadn't changed her position on marriage, and yet she wasn't willing to give him up over their opposing views on the subject.

"How are you holding up?" he asked. "According to the news, it's the end of the world in your neck of the woods."

"So they say." She laughed uneasily. "Things are a little crazy here, but I'm certain there's a rational explanation for all of it."

"You never told me what your dad says about all of this. What does he think happened?"

"I think he has a theory," she said. She didn't mention the homicide investigation surrounding Professor Coyle's death. The idea that Pop had anything to do with it seemed outrageous, ridiculously so. Besides, it hadn't made the national news. Maybe it would all be straightened out by the time the story broke. Instead, she said what she could about her father. "He's having a hard time remembering."

"I'm sorry. That must be hard." His face was tanned, darker than the last time she'd seen him only a few short days ago.

"I miss you," she said.

He nodded and looked away from the screen, unwilling to meet her eyes even through the computer. He was hurting. She watched his Adam's apple rise and fall as he swallowed. *I take it back,* she wanted to say. *I'll marry you if that's what you want. Whatever you want is fine with me.* But she couldn't. Her throat started to close just thinking the words. She felt as trapped as a bird in a cage. *I can't do this. I can't give you what you want. I wish I could.*

Instead, she found herself asking about his chartered trips, the fish they'd caught, and his schedule for the week. He'd added a few more charters now that she wouldn't be around. Originally, he'd taken a couple of days off to be with her during her spring break.

He was breaking up. She knew from Skyping with Hank they'd only have a few more minutes before the mountains intruded, inserting their bulk where it wasn't welcome, and ended their time together.

"How are things with your sister?" he asked, knowing her relationship with Linnet was complicated. The one time he'd asked her why, what had happened between them, she'd said it had been many little things, unwilling to share the one big ugly truth.

"It's as difficult as ever. There's just no talking to her some-times," she said to him now, thinking about Linnet's refusal to discuss Jake and the possibility the ring was much more than a mere coincidence. And yet she'd had glimpses of how things used to be between them, flashes of the sisterhood she longed to reclaim. But the wall between them seemed as high as the tall-est trees. If only she could change the past, the moment that severed them in two. But she couldn't say all of this to Ben. She'd promised Linnet she'd never talk about it with anyone, ever. And no matter what transpired between them, she'd never break their pact.

"Keep in touch," he said through the flickering, and then his face was nothing more than a frozen image on her screen.

"You can count on it," she whispered.

Myna put her laptop aside and got up to wash her face and brush her teeth in the bathroom down the hall, the same bath-room shared by the guests in the rooms next to hers. But there weren't any guests since the young couple had checked out ear-lier that day.

She looked out the open window, the chilly night air send-ing goose bumps up and down her arms. She saw movement, a shadow of a person in the yard. She slipped behind the curtain and peeked out. Whoever it was moved near the storage shed not far from the guesthouse.

Myna reached for her robe to cover the pajama top and bot-toms she wore when she traveled. When she was home with Ben, she'd grown accustomed to sleeping naked. She grabbed her cell phone and stuffed it in her pocket. She felt safer having it with her, although it wouldn't be much help if she couldn't get a signal.

She made her way to the kitchen. The house was quiet and dark. Everyone had gone to bed. She had a fleeting thought about the young professor and an unknown person lurking in the yard. *Oh please, Pop, don't let it be you.* She'd heard about family members wandering away with their memories, found in places they shouldn't be, lost and confused.

Maybe she should wake Linnet and Ian, flood the property with spotlights, and catch whoever it was. It was exactly what she should do, but she didn't. If it was Pop shuffling around out there, she'd help him back to bed and never speak of it. She didn't want to upset her sister or put her under any more stress if it wasn't absolutely necessary. She didn't want to give the police another reason to suspect Pop had anything to do with the professor's death.

She slipped out the side door and made her way under the cherry blossom tree in the backyard. A guy was pulling a ladder from the shed.

"What do you think you're doing?" she asked, figuring it had to be Al. Ian had told her about the groundskeeper Linnet had hired a few years back, the same guy Ian had laughed about when he'd said he'd suspected Al had a crush on his wife.

Al jumped and clutched his chest. "Linnet, is that you?" he asked. "Jesus Christ, you scared me."

"It's Myna. Her sister."

"Oh, right. Linnet said you two looked alike." He pulled off one of the heavy gloves he was wearing and stuck his hand out for her to shake. "I'm Al."

She pulled her robe tight, clutching the collar by her neck. He was handsome in a rugged outdoorsmanlike way.

"The groundskeeper," he added, and put his work glove back on.

"What are you doing here this late at night?"

He continued pulling and tugging at the ladder. "Linnet mentioned something about having some of the trees trimmed."

"You can't possibly be thinking about trimming trees in the dark."

"No," he said. "But I noticed a beehive in one of the maples along the path here at the edge of the yard. It's best to knock it down at night when the bees aren't as active." He picked up the ladder and maneuvered around her. She smelled a strong odor of alcohol.

"Are you sure you should be doing that now?"

He ignored her and carried the ladder across the yard to the maple tree with the hive. He set it against the trunk and stumbled.

"Have you been drinking?" she asked.

"I had a few," he said, and looked around.

"I don't think you should be climbing a ladder in your condition."

"I'm fine." He shook the ladder to make sure it was secure. He looked up at the tree and then once over his shoulder.

"Do you want me to hold that for you?"

"No," he said. "I'm good."

She took a step back.

"You should go back inside now," he said. "I'm not sure how many bees are going to fly out of this thing, and I don't imagine they're going to be happy."

He didn't have to ask her twice.

Myna finished getting ready for bed in the hall bathroom and returned to her room. She put her toothbrush and toothpaste back inside the Dopp kit, wondering if she should close her window in case angry bees were searching for someone to blame for the destruction of their home. She wasn't allergic, so she decided she'd take her chances. She pushed the curtains aside and peered out at the backyard. The mountain air was as cool and soothing as she'd remembered it to be. When she was young, she and Linnet had peeked out every window in the house at one time or another. They'd often played imaginary games in their mother's B&B, Myna being the guest making unrealistic demands while Linnet tried to accommodate every unreasonable request. When Linnet had had enough, she'd tell Myna where to go, and the two would fall to the floor in a fit of giggles.

Myna searched for Al down by the path, trying to see in the dark under a moonlit sky. The shadows from the branches made it darn near impossible. But she could see the ladder propped against the shed. She took it as a sign he hadn't fallen and had finished the job. She hoped that he hadn't decided to drive in his condition and that he'd walked home. And now that she thought about it, he must've done just that since she'd never heard a car pull in or out of the driveway.

She crawled into bed, but she wasn't tired. Reaching for her laptop, she powered it on. She checked her e-mail, answered a couple questions from students about an upcoming assignment, responded a resounding no to a faculty member's bridal shower invitation—someone on the staff she barely knew and who'd probably invited her out of courtesy. Clearing out her in-box distracted her for a few minutes.

She didn't want to think about Jake and the ring. She wanted to do what Linnet had asked and forget about it. But it was no use, not if she planned on getting any sleep. She couldn't push the thoughts away. The guilt she carried would never go away no matter how hard she'd tried or how fast she'd run. It had followed her everywhere—to every city, every job, every relationship, every bed in which she'd slept. She couldn't outrun what was inside her. It was there, always, waiting for her to give it shape and form.

She stared at the computer screen. The Internet connection wavered.

Do you think he's good-looking? Linnet had asked. *Is he the next guy on your list of men? Is that why you came running home, because you broke up with Ben?*

Now, hours later and too late to react to her sister's accusations, she found herself angry. The way Linnet had read her as though she'd slipped inside her mind, glided along the cracks inside her heart, the way she'd fully understood her as only a sister could, was simultaneously brilliant and infuriating.

What if there were a way, Linny, to make up for what we'd done?

She typed Jake's name into the search engine, but hesitated before hitting enter.

It was a risk, and she had no way of knowing how she'd feel once she learned the truth, no way of knowing what the outcome would be, but she had to take some responsibility for her actions even if Linnet never would.

Her finger hovered over the key, thinking she wouldn't push it after all, but then she did, and waited for the search engine to do its thing, for the page to load.

Maybe for once her anger was right on time.

CHAPTER TWENTY

Linnet rested her forehead against the cabinet. "I understand," she said. "Thank you for calling." She hung up the phone and set it on the countertop.

"Who was that, Mom?" Hank asked. He'd finished eating the eggs and buttered toast she'd made him for breakfast. Pop sat next to him crunching a piece of crispy bacon.

She was about to say it was no one important, but she'd hated how her mother had kept the B&B's business private. Hank had grown up sharing his home with strangers, and she was aware of the sacrifices he'd had to make to accommodate their family business. No sleepovers or friends when the B&B had paying guests, no hanging out in the living room to watch television when visitors were reading, relaxing, using the space. He had done this without complaint most of the time. The PlayStation in his bedroom had helped, but she understood it hadn't been ideal.

"It was another cancelation," she said to him. It was the second cancelation she'd taken this morning. One more and The Snow Goose would be empty next weekend, too.

"Oh." He picked up his plate and set it in the sink. "That's bad."

"It's not good, but things will turn around. I bet in another week or two the world will forget all about our little town. The snow geese will be back on the dam, and they'll bring the tourists here like they've always done."

She looked to Pop for confirmation, but he didn't say a word. Some mornings he was so quiet she would almost forget he was there. Almost.

Ian walked into the kitchen dressed for work and carrying his briefcase. "We have to go, kiddo." He looked at Linnet. "Everything okay?"

"Mom had another cancelation," Hank said as he slipped on his backpack.

She handed Hank his lunch. "It's going to be okay." She hadn't told him the worst of it. Losing guests didn't compare to the kind of trouble his grandfather was involved in. "Try and have a good day," she said to him.

"Take your own advice," Ian said, and winked at her, waving to Pop as he and Hank headed out the door.

"Would you like more bacon?" she asked him once Ian and Hank had gone.

He shook his head, taking a bite of toast. "You should listen to your husband," he said. "Your mother had guests cancel. She had empty beds, but she managed to keep it going. So can you."

She ran her hands over the top of her head, smoothing her straight hair back. Oh, the things her father hadn't known about her mother, the things he'd refused to acknowledge if he had. "You're right, Pop," she said. "Mom kept it going, all right."

He took his time chewing. His white hair was messy, and the spectacles slid down his nose no matter how many times he'd had them adjusted. *I'm worried about you*, she longed to say, but what good would it do? Would he understand?

Myna walked into the kitchen. "Good morning, Pop," she said, and kissed him on top of the head. He smiled, his cheeks meeting his eyes. She was wearing jeans with holes up and down her thighs. An oversize sweatshirt hung off her shoulder. Her hair was pulled into a sloppy ponytail, making her look pretty and much younger than her years.

For a second, Linnet envied her sister, her laid-back clothes and easygoing demeanor, the smile she'd brought to their father's face. When was the last time he'd smiled at Linnet that way? It had been as recent as last week when she'd slipped on fresh bird dirt and landed on her butt. He'd chuckled and said, "Watch that."

She scolded herself for being jealous. Petty. She was dressed in her typical khakis and oxford, her hair as sleek as a goose's feather.

Myna sat at the table with a fresh cup of coffee.

"You look like you had a rough night," Linnet said after noticing the dark circles underneath her sister's eyes. She wondered why she'd just pointed this out when a moment ago she'd believed her to look young and pretty. Was she incapable of being kind to the one person she wanted nothing more than to be close to again?

"I didn't get much sleep," Myna said, turning her head, her eyes cast down. She touched the sleeve of her sweatshirt where, underneath the cotton, the birthmark stained her forearm.

Movement outside the garden window drew Linnet's attention. It was Al. He walked across the yard to where a ladder leaned against the shed. He was early. She suspected he wanted to get a jumpstart on trimming those trees today. He turned around and stared at something in the distance. He had a strange look on his face, one she'd never seen before. She leaned over the sink, peering outside. Her father and sister talked quietly behind her. *What is it, Al? What do you see?*

It was Charlie. He held a folded sheet of paper in his left hand. His right hand rested on his belt near his sidearm. Al hadn't moved. He just stood there with that odd expression on his face. Charlie was a big guy with broad shoulders, making Al look smaller than he was.

They exchanged a few words. A rabbit darted from the edge of the yard into the woods. Al motioned to the ladder. Charlie shook his head. A blue jay flew in front of the window and landed in a nearby tree. The sun was up, promising a beautiful spring day. Both men turned toward the house. They were headed in her direction. Linnet's pulse quickened.

"Myna," she said. "Take Pop out for a drive."

"Now?" Myna asked.

"Right now." Linnet walked over to Pop and slipped her arm under his elbow. "Come on," she said, helping him up.

Myna got up. She must've recognized the seriousness of Linnet's tone, the urgency of her request without having to ask for an explanation. Some things between them hadn't changed after all. At least they still shared this.

"You two can take a nice long drive and catch up while I do some chores around here," Linnet said. She directed Pop toward the main hall. "Take him out the front," she said to Myna.

"I'm assuming you're going to tell me later what's going on?" Myna asked in a hushed voice, taking their father's upper arm and guiding him through the hall to the living room and foyer.

"Yes, later," she said. "Go. Go." She hurried them along.

"You two are ushering me around like I'm an invalid," Pop said. "I'll go for a drive, but let me get my notes first." He turned around.

There was a knock at the side door.

"I'll get your notes," Linnet said. "Where are they?"

"On the table," he said.

She rushed back into the kitchen, recognized the silhouette of the man's tall stature and broad shoulders through the curtains. He knocked harder this time. She snatched the notebook off the table and ran to the foyer. She pushed the notebook into Myna's hands, and then she hurried back down the hall. Behind her she heard the front door open and close.

She paused outside the kitchen entrance and ran her hands down the front of her khakis. Then she crossed the room and pulled the door open. "Charlie," she said. Al stood behind him.

"May we come in?" Charlie asked. He'd never asked before, always assumed he'd be welcomed. But not today. No, today was different.

She moved out of the way, and both men stepped inside.

Charlie held up the paper in his hand.

"What is it?" she asked.

"It's a search warrant," he said.

CHAPTER TWENTY-ONE

Myna backed out of the driveway slowly, not wanting to draw attention to the fact she was kidnapping her father and high-tailing it out of there. The pavement was smooth underneath the tires, quiet. She eased onto the mountain road. She passed three police cruisers, but not one of them had given her a second glance, so accustomed to rental vehicles and tourists traveling in and around town. She noticed them, though, the entire Mountain Springs Police Department heading in the direction of the B&B.

She checked the rearview mirror, looking for Charlie, for flashing lights. There was no one behind her. She pressed down on the gas pedal.

"So where do you want to go?" she asked Pop.

He looked over his shoulder. "I think Charlie wanted to talk to me."

"Do you want to talk to him? Do you want me to turn around?" She looked at him out of the corner of her eye, worried he might've remembered something about the night of the young professor's death, and at the same time hopeful that whatever it was would clear him of suspicion.

"He thinks I know something about what happened to Professor Coyle," he said. "But I don't. I don't think I do."

"It's okay," she said, and patted his leg. "Would you like to get some coffee? We could go to Murphy's if you want."

They drove the few miles to town in silence. The streets had the same deserted look as the other day when she'd stopped at the bakery. The tires swept the fallen petals from the cherry blossoms, collecting them in pretty pink piles in the gutter. She pulled to the side of the road and parked at a meter, dropping two hours' worth of quarters into the slot. There was activity farther down the block as the news media converged on town hall.

"Let's get something sweet," she said, and slipped her arm through his. "How about a slice of pie?"

The front door of the diner opened, and people starting pouring out, some young and some old, a little dirty and weathered. They picked up signs from the ground and gathered around a tall woman with streaks of gray in her long black hair. Myna recognized the group as the same picketers from the other day.

"We'll form a line of two people, side by side. When we reach the end of the block"—the tall woman with the graying black hair pointed toward town hall—"we'll split apart—you'll go one way, and your partner will go the other. We'll form a circle and surround them. And, gang, make sure you hold up those signs for the cameras."

The group began to form a line. One of the younger men wearing heavy black eyeliner handed a pamphlet to Pop as he passed by.

"What's this?"

"It's the end of the world," the young man said. "And it's going down right now, right here."

Pop gave him a funny look. "Rubbish," he said, and handed the pamphlet back.

Myna gently steered him through the door and away from the crowd.

"You'll be sorry!" the man shouted.

"Rubbish," her father said again.

They stepped inside. A hush fell over the place. Customers turned to peer at them. The waitstaff paused, putting off orders, holding off refilling coffee cups.

The hostess asked if they'd like to sit at the counter, but before Myna could answer, she leaned in close as though they were confidantes and said, "You know, people around here are saying the birds had something to do with what happened to that professor."

"That's absurd!" her father hollered, startling them both.

He flipped his notebook open, continuing in the same loud voice. "The birds had nothing to do with that man's death." He snapped the pages, turning each one as though he were a lawyer, the birds his clients, and their entire defense written in between the white lines. "This isn't some Hitchcock movie," he bellowed.

"Pop." Myna reached for the notebook. He pulled away and hugged it to his chest. "Please," she said more gently. He acquiesced, allowing her to take it from his hands. "Could we have a booth in the back?" she asked the hostess.

The hostess appeared dumbstruck, her mouth open slightly.

"Could you show us to a booth?" Myna asked again.

"Oh, right," she said, coming around. "This way."

People continued staring until Myna and Pop were seated. Once the hostess walked away, Myna put the notebook on the table between them.

"What's in this, Pop?" she asked, fearing it was nothing more than the ramblings of a once brilliant mind, afraid it held the evidence the police were searching for about the young professor's murder.

"My theory on the geese."

"May I see it?"

They were interrupted by a waitress. "What can I get for you?"

"Two cups of coffee," Myna said. "And a very large slice of lemon meringue pie."

After the waitress walked away, Myna tapped the cover of the notebook. "What's your theory?" she asked, thinking about how he'd mentioned it to her and Jake the other day. Last night when she'd searched for information about Jake on the Internet, she'd found his mother's obituary. And then she'd found his father's. It hadn't been easy seeing his face, learning his name for the first time after all these years. She hadn't been able to sleep after that, confirming Jake was his son. How could she tell Linnet? Would she even listen? It was no longer about the two of them, their family alone. No, it was so much bigger than they'd ever imagined, this thing they'd set in motion.

Pop talked about a thunderstorm the night the birds fell from the sky. He explained how climate had been a big factor in other occurrences similar to the one Mountain Springs had experienced, and thunder in particular. He believed the turbulence in the storm had disoriented the geese, and the rain had chilled them, soaking their feathers so they hadn't been able to maintain flight.

"They'd fall pretty quickly," her father said. "Of course, all of this is just theory. I won't know for sure unless I can get into the lab and run some tests. I have no idea why they won't let me in." He seemed genuinely perplexed.

She covered her father's hand with her own. "I don't know why either," she said, but of course she knew why. And yet here he was, alert, aware of his surroundings. It was hard to reconcile this man, the one she remembered from her childhood, with the one who became addled and confused, childlike, or the one who had lashed out just moments ago when they'd walked into the place.

"I have an idea, Pop," she said, believing she may have found a way to help him and the town out of this bird mess. "If you're up for it." She pulled Jake's business card from her pocket. "How would you feel about talking to that journalist we picked up the other day on the mountain road? Do you remember him?" she asked, already punching Jake's number on her cell phone.

Myna remained silent while the waitress refilled their coffee cups and took Jake's order. He was having two fried eggs over easy, bacon, and hash browns. There was something boyish and sweet about him. Linnet's accusation that Myna had been attracted to him had been all wrong. It wasn't a physical thing, although Jake was handsome. It was more like a kinship.

"I see you've been doing some shopping while you're in town," she said. He was wearing one of the T-shirts sold in the corner shop that said *I'd rather be birding*.

"I was hoping to win over the doc here," he said with a smile, and directed his next statement to Pop. "I'd like to record you if I may. That way I can go over everything again later and make sure I didn't miss anything."

Pop nodded, and she made it clear to Jake she'd shut him down if he asked any questions that didn't pertain to the snow geese.

"Understood," Jake said, and set a small recorder on top of the notebook.

"He might need his notes," she said.

"I don't need them. I know what I'm talking about," Pop said. She played with the spoon in her coffee cup.

"Dr. Jenkins," Jake said, and began to ask him a series of questions regarding his expertise, his years as a professor at the university. And then, without prompting, Pop launched into a discussion about the history of the town and birds.

"The dam was created decades ago when a farmer flooded a cow pasture," he said. "Several creeks serve as tributaries." He went on to talk about the birds, how the dam had become a popular resting spot for the migrating snow geese due to the shallow water and abundant vegetation, how he and his wife, Claire, were the first to invite guests to witness the magic of the sights and sounds of the flock.

Myna perked up at the mention of her mother's name and then slowly tuned out when her father returned to talking about the town's history. They'd seldom discussed her mother— neither her, her father, nor Linnet. At times, Myna had found she'd wanted to talk about her, about why she hadn't been able to leave the house sometimes for weeks on end, about how she'd slipped month after month into a state of nothingness only to be revived for a short period of time before relapsing, falling even farther into the darkness that inevitably claimed her. But she also understood some families didn't talk about certain things, and her family was no different, the reasons as varying as the families themselves.

Besides, there were certain memories she'd prefer to forget. Like the time she'd heard Pop talking to her mother behind the bedroom door, the anger in his voice when he'd said, "You need to pull yourself together, Claire. You can't keep locking yourself up in this room."

She'd mumbled something inaudible.

"If you can't do it for yourself, if you can't do it for me, then I beg you to please, please do it for the kids." It had been one of the few times he'd raised his voice, and the sound rumbled deep within Myna's bones. She'd pressed her back against the wall when the door had flung open and he'd marched down the hall, fists pumping at his sides, unaware his youngest daughter had been listening.

Eventually, Jake asked Pop about his theory. Here she paid attention, making sure he spoke clearly, coherently, proving his mental sharpness was intact.

The two talked for some time. Jake was respectful and seemed genuinely interested in what Pop had to say. She was beginning to like Jake all the more, but it didn't quell her worries. How would she ever explain it to her sister? She didn't know if she could. She wasn't sure she understood it herself. But maybe, just maybe, it would end up being a good thing. Maybe it would erase some of the negative publicity surrounding the birds, The Snow Goose, reestablish their father's reputation as an expert. Maybe it would help Jake in some small way.

"I think that's all the questions I have," Jake said. "I really appreciate your taking the time to talk with me."

The waitress stopped at their table, holding a pot of coffee. "Would you like more coffee?" she asked Jake, smiling more brightly than needed.

"Dr. Jenkins?" Jake asked, and pointed to his cup.

Her father waved the waitress away. "If you'll excuse me," he said, and stood, using the table to pull himself up. "I need to use the restroom."

"The bathroom is that way," Myna said, reminding him in case he'd forgotten.

"Don't get old," he said to Jake, and headed to the men's room.

Once they were alone she said, "Promise me whatever you put in your article about him will be positive. He may get confused sometimes, but he knows what he's talking about when it comes to the birds."

"I promise," Jake said.

"I still want to see it before you send it to your editor or whoever you turn it in to before it's printed."

"Sure." He nodded. "I said I would send it to you, and I will. I'll send you a copy tonight. I have a deadline at midnight."

She gave him her e-mail address, and as she did she realized she'd just come up with an alibi, if she ever needed one, as to why she'd searched his name on her laptop. She could tell anyone who might ask that he'd requested an interview with her father, and she'd wanted to check him out, make sure he was legit. Linnet would never believe it, but she'd go along with it. What other choice did her sister have?

"What are the doc's troubles anyway?" Jake asked.

"Like he said, don't get old. People have a way of treating you differently when you do."

CHAPTER TWENTY-TWO

"Is this really necessary?" Linnet asked Charlie after taking the search warrant from his hand.

"I'm afraid so." He looked just as upset about it as she was. "Where's your dad?" he asked.

"He went for a drive with my sister. I have no idea when they'll be back."

He nodded as though he wasn't sure, but he said, "It's probably for the best."

Al remained quiet, fidgeting with his work gloves. Outside, car doors slammed.

"That's my men," Charlie said. "I've got six of them to help so we can be in and out of here as quickly as possible."

"Six," she said more to herself than to him. Practically the entire Mountain Springs Police Department was in her driveway. "I don't suppose I have a say in any of this."

He shook his head.

"That's what I thought." She took a deep breath. "You might as well do what you came here to do." Her chest tightened at the thought of the men going through her house, her family's personal belongings. Her mind raced. Was there anything she should hide? She wasn't guilty of anything, and yet she was.

But that was a longtime ago. A longtime ago.

She tried very hard to keep the expression on her face neutral and not show any emotion at all. She wasn't sure she was succeeding.

She glanced at Al. His face had drained of color. She went to him, touched his arm. He was warm underneath his flannel shirt. Perspiration dotted his hairline. He scrunched and twisted the gloves in his hands. He worried about her probably more than he should.

"Maybe you should come back tomorrow," she said to him. "The trees can wait."

"I'd prefer it if you did," Charlie said to him. "My men will be working outside as well as in. I don't want you disturbing the grounds. In fact, it's best you take the day off."

"Are you sure?" Al asked Linnet.

She squeezed his arm. "It's okay," she said. "We have nothing to hide." She made a point to glare at Charlie as she spoke.

"If you need me," Al said to her. "You'll call." He looked torn between staying and running out of there.

"I'll call if I need you." She reassured him.

Both she and Charlie watched him leave.

"What about Cora?" Charlie asked. "You might want to tell her not to bother coming in."

"I'm not expecting her. In fact, you reminded me I need to call her. There's a good chance I won't need her this weekend either. I've had more cancelations."

Charlie nodded. He hesitated. "I'm going to start in the guesthouse."

"Fine," she said.

"I am sorry about this, Linnet."

"Are you?"

"Do you want the truth?"

"Yes, I do."

"I debated whether or not I should hand this whole thing over to the state police. My men . . ." he paused. "We don't handle these kinds of investigations often around here, and you know that. It's a good thing. Oh, hell." He took a deep breath. "I was worried I couldn't be impartial. But if your dad is involved in some way . . ."

"He's not."

He held up his hand to stave off her protest. "If he *is* involved, I want him to be handled by a friend who is, shall we say, mindful of his difficulties."

"You mean his dementia," she said. "You can say it, Charlie. It's not a dirty word."

He remained quiet for so long, she wondered what he was thinking or if he'd forgotten about his promise to search her property quickly.

"Okay then," he said. "It's best you wait here."

"I have no intention of going anywhere."

The second Charlie was out the door, Linnet took off for the guest room that Myna was staying in. *Mistake number one, Charlie. Never give a person the opportunity to tamper with evidence.* She slipped inside and closed the door behind her, locking it so she'd have an extra minute if, *when*, Charlie's men came knocking. There was nothing she could do to help Pop now, not with Charlie going through her father's things. But maybe she could figure out what Myna had been up to last night. She knew her sister was hiding something. It had been all over Myna's face, sure as shit, when she'd mentioned she hadn't gotten much sleep. And then the way she'd put her hand over the birthmark on her forearm, another signal something was amiss.

Maybe Linnet could protect them both if she found out what her sister had been doing before anyone else did. It was an awful thing, not trusting her sister in the way she had when they were young. *It's for your own good*, she thought now. *And mine, too.*

She sat down on the unmade bed and fired up Myna's laptop. She checked the history. It had been wiped clean. Of course it would be. Myna was a tech genius. She'd know exactly how to cover her cyber tracks. That was good, especially if Charlie's men decided to poke around in her sister's business. She put the laptop aside and peeked into Myna's suitcase.

The first sweater she pulled from the top of the messy pile smelled like her sister. She brought the fabric to her nose. Memories of her childhood flitted across her mind—Myna curled against Linnet's back while they were sleeping; Myna's hair draped over Linnet's arm, heads together, scheming; Myna's hip pressed against Linnet's when they'd been drifting in the rowboat on the dam, daydreaming. They'd talked about how they'd live together forever in the B&B with their husbands, their kids growing up as though they were siblings rather than cousins. They'd promised each other deep into the night, when their darkest secrets had been shared, that nothing would ever separate them. No one could keep them apart.

But, oh, how they had been so naive, so terribly wrong.

She clutched the sweater to her chest, feeling the kind of ache in her heart one felt after suffering a painful loss. Sometimes she felt the absence of her sister as sharply as if there had been a death.

It wasn't until some time had passed that she was able to place the sweater back into the suitcase. As she did, a feather drifted to the floor by her feet.

"Linnet," Charlie called from somewhere downstairs.

Linnet hurried from her sister's room, making sure to leave everything as she'd found it—except the feather, which she took with her. "Coming!" she called, finding Charlie in the dining room in front of the chess set. "What is it?" she asked. "What's wrong?"

He was holding a clear plastic bag in his hand, the contents a pair of Pop's loafers.

"What are you doing with Pop's shoes?" she asked.

Charlie looked at the bag as though he'd forgotten he'd been carrying it. "Right," he said. "I gather your dad's wearing his other loafers, the brown ones he always wears."

"Yes," she said with certainty. His slippers were placed on the left side of the bed, his brown loafers at the foot near the dresser where he'd find his socks.

"Will you step outside with me for a minute? I want to show you something."

She followed him to the backyard, but first she stuck the feather inside one of the kitchen drawers. Three of Charlie's men were standing on the side of the guesthouse. One of the officers was spraying the vinyl siding. Another officer held a UV light.

"What are they doing?" she asked, but she knew exactly what they were doing. She had watched enough television crime shows to know they were looking for blood.

Charlie ignored her question. "Do you recognize this?" he pointed to a pole on the ground where the brush from the woods had bled into the yard. It had a claw-like hook at the end of it. A numbered identification marker was placed next to it.

"Yes," she said. "It looks like one of the poles they were using to pick up the dead geese."

Charlie looked it over, his brow furrowing. "I thought the same thing," he said.

"What does the pole have to do with anything?" she asked.

"We're trying to figure that out," Charlie said.

"Did it belong to Professor Coyle?" Her breathing became shallow, and she started to feel warm. She'd seen a pole just like this one in the trunk of the professor's car.

"I can't say."

She nodded, or thought she'd nodded. The officers moved around her, but she was no longer processing the scene. There was a certain dreamlike quality to her vision, her thoughts. Everything was blurry, fuzzy around the edges. A dull throb started in the back of her head. "Do we need to get a lawyer?" she asked.

Charlie's expression changed. "I think maybe it's time you did."

CHAPTER TWENTY-THREE

Jake walked out of the diner after interviewing Dr. Jenkins. He'd insisted on paying the bill. Myna had reluctantly agreed.

He'd walked the few blocks to Murphy's after getting her call. He'd needed to gather his thoughts before talking with the doc. Now, he started down the sidewalk back in the direction of the LG and his car. The picketers were coming his way, returning from their earlier march around town hall still holding up their signs, chanting a warning about the impending apocalypse. A woman handed him a pamphlet as she passed by, the same propaganda she'd given him before.

"Got it," he said, and considered interviewing a few of the doomsayers from the group. He dismissed the idea almost immediately, although he stopped to take a few pictures. *A picture's worth a thousand words*, someone once said. And didn't someone else say, *there are two sides to every story?* Who was Jake to argue? He imagined one of his photos in black and white on the front page, while underneath the provocative image, his article of a more scientific nature on Dr. Jenkins's theory, disproving the end of the world was upon us. The newspaper's readers could decide which side of the story they wanted to believe.

The air was cool under the cherry blossoms despite the bright sun. His shoulder bag containing his laptop, notes, and wallet swung at his hip with each step. The bag's strap crossed his chest and pinched his neck. He turned the corner and was surprised to find Myna leaning against her car looking at her phone not two blocks from where he'd left her.

"Is everything okay?" he asked.

"Pop wanted to get his glasses adjusted." She motioned to the eye care center behind him. "I came outside to see if I could get a signal, but no such luck." She tucked the phone into the back pocket of her jeans.

An awkward silence followed.

"Look," she said, finally. "I want to make sure we're clear about my pop. He's having one of his good days. Sometimes when he's having a bad day he seems, oh, I don't know, confused. He's suffering from . . ." She stopped. "This is harder to talk about than I thought."

"Take your time." He liked that she was opening up to him, showing a vulnerable side people so often tried to hide. It was also obvious she was having second thoughts about giving him access to her father.

"I want you to write about the man he was before he started having trouble remembering things. The man he was today." A strand of hair blew across her face, and she pushed it away.

"Of course," he said, thinking how pretty she looked under the blossoming trees. He sensed she needed something else from him, something other than an article showing her father in a positive light. "May I ask you a question?"

She nodded in an unsure way.

He continued. "Why give me the exclusive interview with him? Why not some other journalist from the bigger papers or the reporters from the national news? I'm small potatoes compared to them." His phone went off. "Excuse me." He reached into his jacket pocket and checked the screen. Dennis. He'd been avoiding his texts and phone calls the last few hours. Jake had suspected Dennis wanted him back in the Lehigh Valley to cover other local news, although Jake hadn't heard of anything big going down. The dead geese had been removed from the dam. The word around town was that the national news teams would be packing it in and moving on. It made sense for Jake to return. He had his exclusive with the doc. All he had to do was type it up, and he could do that anywhere.

But Jake wasn't ready to go back to his lonely condominium. His work in Mountain Springs wasn't over. He hadn't learned much about his father's accident outside of what the police chief had told him. And he was still waiting for Kim's call. He had a hunch his father's old Nokia was his biggest lead finding out whatever it was about his father's death that had nagged him all these years. He wasn't going anywhere, he decided, and shoved the phone back in his jacket pocket, unanswered.

"My editor," he said. "I'll get back to him later."

The doc stepped out of the eye care center.

"Remember," she said to Jake, and turned to get in the car. "I want to see what you write before you send anything to that editor of yours."

"You got it," he said, and smiled. She smiled back, but she never did answer his question: *Why him?* But what did it matter? He'd already decided he'd keep his promise to her.

Jake pulled into the parking lot of the Mountain Springs Police Department. The lot was empty of cruisers, which seemed a little strange. The building itself was square and made of brick. He pushed the glass door open and stepped inside. The same secretary he'd spoken to the other day when he'd requested a copy of the police report sat behind a large desk. She looked up from the magazine in front of her. Other than the secretary, the place looked deserted.

"I was wondering if you could help me again," Jake said. "I'm looking for the coroner's office."

"The county coroner? Well, you'd have to go to Easton for that. His office isn't far from the courthouse. Do you know where that is?"

"What about your local coroner?"

"Did someone die? Do you need me to call the chief?"

"No, nothing like that." He was reluctant to give her any more information. He suspected she might be the town's busybody.

"Then you'll want to talk with Chicky."

"The auto repair guy?"

"Yeah, that's him," she said. "Do you know the address?"

"I know it. Thanks for the help." *Jesus*, he thought as he walked out. He'd heard about small towns, how the local grocery store clerk could also be the coroner, elected by the citizens to keep local matters insulated and keep outsiders out. It seemed Chicky, the auto repair guy, was one of these: the guy who pronounced people dead, no medical training required.

Jake hopped in his car and drove the few miles to the auto repair shop. Chicky was wiping his dirty hands on a towel when Jake pulled up and got out of the car.

"More engine trouble?" Chicky asked.

"No, but thanks again for taking care of that radiator leak for me," he said. Chicky was around Jake's age, but Chicky was shorter, stockier. "I was hoping you could help me out with a more personal matter."

Chicky stared at Jake a moment as though he were sizing him up. Music played from somewhere in the back of the garage.

"All right," he finally said and put the greasy towel down on the car he'd been working on, the one with the hood up. "Come on back to the office."

Jake followed him through the garage, where two other cars were waiting to be worked on. Black grime covered the floor. The music got louder as they approached what Chicky had referred to as his office: a small room separated by a glass partition and an entranceway without a door. A girly calendar hung on the wall. The metal desk was surprisingly clean and tidy; a computer sat on top of it next to a cordless phone.

Chicky reached up to turn off an old transistor radio that sat atop the filing cabinet. "My dad's," he said. "It was my grandfather's originally." He shrugged. "I know what you're thinking. There's a lot of great technology out there to play music, but the shop doesn't feel like the shop without the tinny sound of this old radio playing."

"I get it," Jake said. So Chicky had a sentimental side.

"Now, what can I do for you?" Chicky asked.

"I was hoping you had a copy of an old coroner's report, although I think you were probably too young to be the coroner in this case."

"It must have been my dad then. He passed a couple of years ago."

"I'm sorry," Jake said. "So did mine. Except it was long ago, and it's his death records I'm looking for."

"Oh, geez, okay," Chicky said. "When was it?" he asked and turned to the filing cabinet, putting his back to Jake.

"April 1994."

Chicky pulled open a drawer and searched through a folder. "Here it is," he said after looking it over. He handed Jake a single sheet of paper, pointing to a box at the bottom. "You might want to check with the county coroner. Says here the body was transported to them. They might have done an autopsy or toxicology report if they suspected alcohol was involved or anything. If you look here where my dad filled in his statement, he didn't record the time or cause of death. That tells me there was an investigation. The county coroner or medical examiner handles all the cases where an investigation is required."

The report looked as if it had been typed on an old typewriter. Motor vehicle accident was clearly stated at the top, but the cause of death had been left blank like Chicky had said. The county coroner's report would, of course, give Jake the details he was seeking. He wasn't sure what he'd expected from Chicky's dad. Maybe he just wanted to talk with someone who had been there, who had towed his father's car and pronounced his father dead.

"Thanks for everything," Jake said. They shook hands.

Jake climbed back into his car, an old familiar resentment clawing its way up his spine. Chicky had more time with his father, more years to build memories. Jake had found himself envious of a stupid transistor radio. He'd felt like this before, on and off through the years, with his football buddies and later with his college friends. He'd watch them with their fathers after games, the high-fives, the hugs when they were kids, the handshakes when they were young men. He'd watched with longing, an ache so deep he'd thought if anyone had been paying attention they'd have seen right through his rib cage to the hole in his heart.

But he'd had his mother. She'd gone to every game, every big event in Jake's life. He couldn't tell her how he'd felt at the time, happy she'd been there for him, but sad his father hadn't been. He'd never break her heart and let her think she hadn't been enough. He remembered hinting at missing his father only once, when he'd found her cleaning out her bedroom closet five years after his father had passed.

"What are you doing?" he'd asked, guzzling a large glass of

water. Several suit jackets with matching pants had been lying on top of his mother's bed. It had been late August. The days had been long and hot. He'd had to walk the few blocks from the practice field to home carrying his football gear. The coach had worked them extra hard during summer camp, getting them ready for the season. His legs had been tired, rubbery. His shoulders had been sore.

"I'm cleaning out the closet," she'd said, and followed his gaze to the pile of suits. "I thought I'd donate them. They're a bit outdated I suppose, but someone might get some use out of them."

"Why can't I have them?" He'd wanted nothing more than to pull on one of his father's jackets. He'd wanted to remember.

"You're right," his mother had said, and picked up the jackets still on hangers and hung them back up. "I'll just save these then."

He'd upset her. "No, it's okay. You're right. They're old-looking anyway."

She'd kept her back to him, but he saw her bring the sleeve of a jacket to her nose. "I was lucky, you know." She hadn't waited for him to reply before she'd continued. "Your father was a good man. If you remember anything about him, I hope you remember that."

Jake hadn't moved. He'd been used to these sermons by now, about what a wonderful husband his father had been, how his leaving hadn't been his choice. Although Jake had wanted to believe his father had been some great man, his adolescent mind had been starting to suspect that his mother had built him up, created a romanticized version to ease her grief.

She finished hanging up the last of the suits and closed the closet door. He probably wouldn't have been able to fit in them anyway.

CHAPTER TWENTY-FOUR

Charlie and his men had come and gone before Ian and Hank or Myna and Pop had returned home. Now, Linnet was sitting next to Ian on the bleachers at the baseball field, pushing through the day as though nothing were out of the ordinary for Hank's sake. His game was about to start. The teams had just finished warming up. Hank took his position in center field. Dark clouds huddled overhead, and the air was damp. She wondered how many innings they'd get in before the game was rained out, postponed for another day. Every spring they'd had to rearrange their lives around an ever-changing baseball schedule due to inclement weather. And every spring it was getting harder and harder for her to attend his games and keep her guests at the B&B satisfied. Looking back, she'd give her right arm to return to the luxury of such concerns.

She and Ian whispered back and forth. They sat at the very top of the stand in the far corner, away from the other parents. They needed to talk without anyone overhearing their conversation.

"Charlie took his shoes," she said, feeling as though she were reliving a nightmare, telling Ian about a bad dream. "They found prints in the yard. I told them my footprints, yours, Hanks, all of our prints could be found all over the property. It didn't change their minds, and they took his shoes anyway." She showed him the list of lawyer's names she'd collected.

She continued. "I don't know much about any of them," she said. "I stayed away from anyone local, and I searched outside the county." She didn't have to explain the reasons why she didn't want anyone from Mountain Springs representing Pop. No one local would be equipped to handle a case of this magnitude.

"I just can't believe he had anything to do with it," Ian said. "It doesn't fit with the man I know." He paused, and leaned a little closer, so close she could smell the soap on his freckled skin. "What do we know about this Professor Coyle, anyway? What if this guy was involved in something that had nothing to do with the birds or Pop? What if it was just bad luck that it happened on our property?"

"What are you talking about?"

"Awhile back I overheard something in the teacher's lounge, something about him having an affair with one of the teachers."

"Really? A teacher in your school? Who?"

"Do you remember Donna Cowell?"

"Terry's wife?" He'd been in the crowd at the dam the day the dead birds had been found.

"Yeah. Apparently, she met the professor while taking a continuing education course at the university." He wiped his hands on his jeans.

"Why didn't you say something to me before?"

"I shouldn't have said anything now. It was just a rumor." He wasn't one to gossip, and she imagined he didn't want to start now. He fidgeted, clearly uncomfortable for having said anything at all. It wasn't as if Professor Coyle could defend himself against such an accusation.

"There they are," Ian said, spotting Pop and Myna at the far end of the bleachers. He raised his arm to signal them. "Just forget I said anything."

But how could she forget? It opened up the possibility of someone else being involved with the professor and his murder.

"Why the gloomy faces?" Pop asked as he approached, taking his place next to Linnet. She knew immediately that he was having one of his good days. His face was alert, and there was an acute awareness in his eyes, the one that would disappear behind a hazy film on what she thought of as his bad days.

"Not gloomy," she said. The first batter was up. "So what did you two do all afternoon?"

"We stopped for coffee and then drove around town." Myna sat on the bleacher in front of them, turning around to talk. "Pop got his glasses adjusted."

He touched the frames and pushed them up his nose. "I had a nice long conversation with that journalist friend of your sister's. I hope it puts an end to those picketers and their crazy talk."

Linnet leaned in closer. Maybe she hadn't heard him correctly. "What friend was this?" she asked, and felt the cords in her neck strain. Ian put his hand on her thigh and squeezed, his way of saying Stay calm.

"Jake something-or-other," Pop said, and looked to Myna.

Crack! The boy at bat hit a fastball into center field.

"Mann," Myna said, barely above a whisper.

Hank captured the ball in his mitt on the first bounce. The runner rounded first, sliding into second before the ball ever left Hank's hand. Safe.

Linnet tried hard to remain in her seat and pay attention to the game, and to ignore her sister's blatant refusal to do the one thing she'd asked of her: to stay away from Jake.

Oh, forget it. She was too damn angry. "Myna," she said. "Do you mind if I talk to you a minute? Alone." She stood and walked down the side of the bleachers, pausing to look over her shoulder to make sure her sister was following. Behind her she heard Pop say, "Where are they going?"

She marched to the parking lot and stopped next to her car. Myna slowly walked over to her, dragging her feet like a guilty child about to get reprimanded.

"What in the hell were you thinking?" she asked.

"I know you didn't want Pop talking to him," Myna said.

"You're right. I didn't." She couldn't believe her sister could be so stupid. "With everything going on, the last thing Pop should be doing is talking to anyone from the press. And least of all *Jake Mann.*"

"But you should've seen Pop. He was amazing." Myna's head was lowered, but she looked up into Linnet's face as she spoke. "And Jake. He's that man's son. And I wanted to do something nice."

Linnet craned her neck, coming in close to Myna's face. "And how do you know for sure he's his son? Let me guess. You looked him up on the Internet." *And erased your history afterward*, she almost added, but she didn't want Myna to know just how far she'd gone to spy on her. "And then you took it upon yourself to do something *nice* for him. At Pop's expense. Really, Myna? You'd put a total stranger before your own father?"

"No, it's not like that. Jake is going to write about Pop's theory about what happened to the birds, and that's all. Pop was . . . he was good today. It gave him some dignity back."

Linnet covered her forehead where the pressure was building. Why couldn't her sister behave rationally? Why couldn't she think ahead and understand her actions had consequences? If her sister had learned anything from their past experience, it should've been this. "And you believe this guy's going to write up something that makes Pop look good? Is that what you were going for?"

"Yes," Myna said. "He promised me he would."

"He promised you, huh?" Linnet looked to the sky. The clouds were heavier, darker. The crowd on the bleachers clapped at some play Linnet had missed. "And you believed him because, after all, his father was such a trustworthy and honest man."

"That's not fair." The space between Myna's eyebrows creased. "Do you want to know the reason why I did it?" Her jaw set. She spoke through gritted teeth. "Because I think about it every day. Every damn day. And I thought maybe, just maybe, if I did something *nice*, I could get through a few hours without hating myself."

Linnet grabbed Myna's arm. "What I know is that you're messing around in something you shouldn't be. You have no idea what you've done." She was every bit aware of how much she sounded like a mother scolding a child, and she hated herself for it, but Myna was leaving her no choice. "Do you know what Charlie did today? Do you?"

Myna shook her head ever so slightly.

"He searched our property! Our house! He took Pop's shoes!" She hollered. "Do you know what this means? Do you? It means Pop's a suspect." She lowered her voice, scratchy now from the yelling. "He needs a lawyer."

"Pop didn't do anything wrong." The angry knot between her eyebrows relaxed. "And it's crazy to think he did."

"Yes, it is crazy. Crazy for our crazy father," she said before she could stop herself. She didn't mean it.

The umpire yelled, "You're out. That's three." There was more clapping. The teams were changing positions, which meant Hank was coming up to bat.

"I don't understand you," Linnet said. "I thought I did. Or, I used to."

They both fell quiet, listening to the sounds of the game, chatter coming from the bleachers. A light drizzle fell from the sky.

Myna fiddled with the sleeve on her forearm. "They weren't onions," she said.

"What?"

"Mom. She wasn't cutting onions. She never cut onions. She didn't like the way they smelled or how they left an aftertaste in her mouth."

"What are you talking about?"

"That day we were playing our spy game under the kitchen table and she chased us outside. You said she was cutting up onions. But she wasn't, Linny. She wasn't cutting up onions. She was crying."

Thunder rolled, giving way to the black, angry clouds. Parents stood, calling the boys off the field.

Linnet didn't want to discuss their mother unless they were on the same side, but it was apparent they were not. She longed to get back to the place when they once were. She wanted her sister tucked securely by her side, knowing she'd have her back no matter what. She wondered if Myna ever felt the same way. Or was the bond between them so far stretched that one more disagreement, another tug and pull, and whatever was left between them would break in two?

"Will you answer something for me?" she asked, a bitter taste burning the back of her throat. "Why was there a feather in your suitcase?"

CHAPTER TWENTY-FIVE

Myna lay in bed staring at the ceiling, the birds outside the window signaling the arrival of dawn. One robin in particular sang something that sounded strangely like *cheer up, cheerily, cheer up*, which she knew in bird speak meant either he was defending his territory or trying to attract a mate. Only the robin knew for sure. But the bird's chatter wasn't nearly loud enough to dull the buzzing in her ears. There should've been a chorus of honks, high-pitched quacks from goslings, the clap of wings.

It was the absence of the noisy snow geese that perched heavy on her chest, making home feel not quite like home. She'd looked forward to seeing the geese almost as much as she'd looked forward to seeing her family. But the most surprising ache pressing in on her this morning was the longing to return to Florida. How she missed the sights and smells and sensations—the blue of the ocean, the scent of hot sand, the warmth of Ben by her side. They'd chatted briefly on the phone last night, the connection cutting in and out. She'd felt the tension run the length of the miles between them. She'd told him about the journalist who had interviewed Pop. Instincts had told her to leave Jake's name out of the conversation to avoid any uncomfortable questions she couldn't answer. She'd started to tell him about Professor Coyle and the ongoing police investigation, but their time had been running out. "Please don't give up on us," she'd said. The line had gone dead before she'd heard his reply.

A sliver of sunlight snaked through the closed curtains, cutting across the floor where her suitcase had been tossed the night before. The feather she'd saved all these years, the one she'd taken with her from state to state, city to city, was nowhere to be found. She couldn't believe Linnet had gone through her things. The excuse she gave, her concern about what Charlie might have found during his search of the house, was lame. Maddening. It wasn't that she'd violated her privacy. No, it was proof her sister didn't trust her.

Yet, Myna was feeling smug. Jake had e-mailed a copy of his article late last night. It had read beautifully, portraying her father as smart as the town had always known him to be.

She tossed the covers aside. It was clear she wasn't going to get anymore sleep, so she padded down the hall and stairs in her pajamas. She'd barely had the opportunity to spend any time on the water since she'd arrived. Now that the fallen geese had been removed from the dam, she didn't see any reason why she couldn't take the rowboat out and watch the sunrise. She poked her head into the kitchen to find it empty. The house had a hazy feel of sleep, the yawn of morning in its walls and fixtures.

She slipped out the side door. The grass was covered in dew and stuck to her feet. She held the pants of her pajamas up so the bottoms didn't get wet. She picked her way across the lawn and jogged down the path through the woods, watching where she stepped. The usual fresh geese droppings were nowhere to be found, although she spied hard clumps from geese of weeks past.

She reached the end of the path, the dam opening wide in

front of her. The leaves rustled in the trees. The water rippled in the cool breeze, but there was something wrong. She took a tentative step closer. Floating on top of the water were hundreds of fish, belly-up. She recognized the olive green pattern and sharp underbite of chain pickerel, the plumpness of largemouth bass, the ever-so-cuteness of sunfish. She covered her mouth and nose, her hands in prayer. She thought of the picketers outside Murphy's Diner, their claims the end of the world was near, ticking off the signs of the Bible's version of the apocalypse. *What's next*, one of the women had said. *Dead fish.*

There had to be an explanation, a reason grounded in science, just like there was a rational explanation for the fallen birds. *But oh, how awful.*

A grunting sound came from somewhere off to her side. She took a step closer. "Who's there?" she asked, continuing to move toward the noise. Two rowboats were tied to the dock. This second boat had replaced the canoe not long after her mother had died. "Too many memories," Linnet had said when she'd traded it in.

Myna took three more tentative steps. Pop was lying on his back halfway in the water, the other half on the muddy bank. She made the tiniest whimper before yelling, "Pop!" and rushing over to him. The mud squished between her toes. She slipped and nearly landed on top of him.

"Are you hurt?" she asked.

"I'm okay," he said.

"Let me help you up." She grabbed his arm, trying to get her footing, reaching around his waist, sliding in the slick earth. Her left hip hit the squishy ground with a thud, splattering mud up her back and arms.

Once she was able to get him out of the water, he rolled to all fours, crawling to the grass before being able to stand.

She did the same.

They made it to the bench and sat. His pants were soaked from the thighs down. Mud caked his shoes and her feet. His spectacles were crooked. He righted them.

They stared at the water, at the fish drifting in the current, piling up along the shoreline. The sun made its way over the mountain, shining brightly for what should've been a gray day.

"I didn't know how to help her," he said, and looked at Myna, a deep sorrow reflecting in his eyes.

She recognized the pain, the same sorrow she'd often felt whenever she, too, thought about her mother. "I know, Pop. None of us did," she said, and her heart cracked anew, for him, for her mother, for herself. "I know," she said again, and reached for his hand.

They sat on the bench for some time, holding hands. Neither one talked. The day would be full of reporters and picketers, Charlie and the Mountain Springs Police. They took solace in the silence before the chaos enveloped them.

"I thought I'd find you here," Linnet said. She was dressed in her typical khakis and oxford, her hair sleek and straight. She walked toward them, glancing in the direction of the dam and stopped. Something like a gasp escaped from her lips. "No," she said. "Not the fish, too." She gripped the day's newspaper in her hand and marched to the dock, staying clear of the mud, and stepped onto the wooden planks. She surveyed the scene. When she turned around, she looked as though she might throw up at her feet.

"Sit with us," Pop called.

Linnet did as he asked and took her place on the other side of him. For a moment it felt like old times, when Myna had been young, she and her sister flanking their father, their hips pressed against his, waiting patiently for one of his stories.

"I think one of two things happened," he said about the fish. "They could've died from what they call a winterkill, or what happened to them is indirectly related to the geese. Either way, I believe it has something to do with the oxygen levels in the water."

"What's a winterkill?" Myna asked.

"When you have a cold winter like the one we had, and there's not enough non-frozen water for the fish, it becomes not only a water-loss problem, but an oxygen problem."

"Have you tested the water?" Linnet asked.

"My lab might be small, but I can still perform some basic tests."

He was about to continue when a commotion on the other side of the dam drew their attention.

"Here we go again," Linnet said. Several vehicles had pulled into the public parking lot. One of the vehicles was a big old Lincoln Continental. "That's the mayor," she added.

Myna sat up straight to get a better look. Two pickup trucks parked behind the mayor. A couple of fishermen stepped out. Of course, the fishermen had been up before the sun and had seen the dead fish by the time Myna and her father had gotten to the dam. Fishing season wouldn't officially start until the weekend, but the locals often dropped a line for a quick catch for dinner. Illegal, yes, but it was a part of life in Mountain Springs that no one minded. Leo was the next one to pull into the lot, driving a truck with several of his rental canoes strapped to the roof.

The men gathered on the public dock, pointing at the dam and talking. At one point, Leo raised his hand in their direction. Myna waved back.

"Put your hand down," Linnet said to her. "You're still in your pajamas, for goodness sake. And why are you both covered in mud?"

"We slipped on the bank when we were looking at the fish," she said, leaving out the part about finding Pop on his back, up to his thighs in the water. She'd been embarrassed for him; how humiliated he must've felt needing her help to stand. He'd always been such a proud man.

"What were you telling us about winterkill?" Linnet asked him. They were doing their best to ignore the growing crowd across the way. "The fish," she prompted. "And the oxygen in the water."

When he didn't respond, Myna motioned to the newspaper in Linnet's hand. "Did you read the article?" she asked.

"You got lucky," Linnet said. "It's not so bad. But I wish they would've chosen a different photo."

The image was of the picketers standing outside the diner holding up their signs. It wasn't the picture Myna had wanted for the piece, but if people read the article underneath they would understand their father had refuted the end-of-the-world claims.

Pop suddenly continued as though he'd never been interrupted. "Winterkill occurs in shallow lakes where there is an abundance of vegetation. We had a lot of snow and ice this winter, and it prevented sunlight from getting through, forcing the plants to cut back on the oxygen they produce. Not to mention the amount of decaying plants, lowering the oxygen levels even more. And when the oxygen depletion is severe enough, the fish die."

Linnet nodded. "The snow geese were supposed to take care of thinning out the vegetation."

"Right." Myna jumped in. "But it's only been a few days without the geese. How could the plants have taken over so quickly?"

"The total number of geese that passed through this winter was down. We didn't see the thousands of birds we typically see," Linnet explained to Myna in a voice not unkind. But what Myna heard was something different, another way of pointing out her absence in their life here.

"When you combine the cold weather, the shallow water freezing over, the thick vegetation, and the decrease in the number of geese, it was enough to upset the balance of things."

More people showed up across the dam. The picketers arrived one by one, jumping out of their tired-looking minibuses, waving their signs, shouting propaganda. The local news reporters piled out of vans. It was only a matter of time before the bigger news stations learned about another sign of the apocalypse. Within hours CNN would return, and their little town would make the national news for the second time in a week.

"I don't suppose they're going to listen to reason," Linnet said about the crowd.

"No," Pop said. "Probably not."

Charlie's police cruiser flashed its blue lights as it drove into the lot, forcing the doomsayers out of the way.

Linnet's hand shot out and clutched Pop's. "We have to go. Now," she said.

Myna understood the urgency to get him out of Charlie's sight. "Come on, Pop."

They got up, Linnet in the lead, followed by their father in soggy, mud-caked pants, the dirt running all the way up the back of his shirt. Myna walked behind him in her own muddy pajamas, feeling Charlie's eyes on them as they hurried down the path.

CHAPTER TWENTY-SIX

Linnet paused in the backyard. The sun's rays warmed her chilled skin; the goose bumps that had traveled up and down her arms and legs from sitting underneath the shade of the trees by the water disappeared. Her father and Myna stood next to her. They looked up at the sky, where a flock of geese called for their attention, the cacophony of honking a welcoming sound.

"Hello, my friends," Myna said with a childlike expression on her face. She looked so much like the old Myna, the little sister who had been attached to Linnet's side. Linnet had an urge to throw an arm around her shoulder and pull her into an embrace for old time's sake. But it was as though her arms had forgotten how to move. When was the last time they'd hugged? And not just the quick pat on the back, good-to-see-you kind of hug, but an affectionate, I love you, you're-my-sister kind of hug. It had been too many years for her to remember.

"They won't stop," Pop said about the geese. "It might be some time until they do." He continued walking toward the guesthouse.

Linnet's focus drifted to Pop, the back of his pants and shirt covered in mud. She didn't want to think about what would happen to him if the geese stayed away, what would happen to him if he'd done what Charlie had suspected. Her mind jumped to the conversation she'd had with Ian about Professor Coyle and an alleged affair. What if it was true, and it had something to do with what had happened to him? How could she find out for Pop's sake?

"I'll go make sure Pop has some clean clothes," Myna said. "I'll bring him up for breakfast in a few minutes."

"You don't have to do that," she said. "I'll take care of it." She set off after him.

Myna rushed to catch up and tapped her on the arm. "I know you will," she said. "But I'm only here for a few days. I don't mind. Let me help."

"Right," Linnet said. "You're only here for a few days." *The rest of the year our father is my responsibility*, she thought. She was about to tell her sister this, but instead she said, "Fine." She crumpled the newspaper in her fist and headed toward the main house, crushing Jake's article and the interview. So he'd kept his word. *Big deal*. All it meant was that they'd dodged one bullet today. She wondered if Jake had any say on which photo they'd used. As much as she wanted to hang on to her anger toward him, she found herself hoping he hadn't had anything to do with the picture at all.

Ian was putting his coffee cup in the sink when she stepped into the kitchen. The sight of his tie thrown over his shoulder was comforting, signifying their family routine was the same despite so many changes taking place around them.

"I found Pop at the dam with Myna," she said, and put the paper on the counter. She'd hollered up to Ian earlier that she was going to get her father to bring him up for breakfast, and she'd be back before he'd left for work. "You'll never guess what's happened now." She explained about the fish. Ian stared at her with an expression of disbelief and awe.

"That's going to hurt a lot more businesses in the area," he said. "Including ours."

"Have you thought about what you're going to tell Walter and Lyle?" he asked.

"No, I completely forgot." Walter and Lyle had stayed at the B&B every weekend for the last ten years on opening day of fishing season. "I'm going to have to tell them what happened. I don't see there's any other way."

"Do you think they'll cancel?"

"I'm not sure there are any fish left for them to catch, so yeah, I think it's a good possibility I'm going to lose my last two guests this weekend." She feared hundreds of the fish were dead. "The town's going to have to pay someone to clean them up." Imagine what the place would smell like otherwise.

Hank bounded into the kitchen with his backpack. "Ready, Dad?"

Ian whispered in her ear, "I'll tell him what happened to the fish in the car."

She leaned into him, and he put his arm around her shoulder. "Hang in there," he said.

"Daaad," Hank said.

She pulled Hank's lunch bag from the refrigerator and handed it to him.

"Text me," was the last thing Ian said as he walked out the door. Hank had already raced ahead to the car.

Linnet was left alone in the kitchen. She picked up the phone.

"Mom!" Linnet called through the closed door. It had been five long days since her mother had left her bedroom. The smell of dirty sheets and unwashed skin seeped underneath the crack between the door and the hardwood floor. She stepped back, hesitant to knock. She was afraid of what she'd find if she forced the door open. She was afraid of what could happen if she didn't.

All the doors in the B&B had locks, but every room had a spare key so guests couldn't lock themselves out. Pop had set it up this way when he'd had the house *reimagined*. When he'd originally purchased the property, he'd had visions of filling the rooms with five or six children or more, his own personal flock, he'd teased. "So why was there only Myna and me?" a young Linnet had asked. He hadn't answered, but she hadn't needed him to. Just like she hadn't needed to ask why he'd had a spare key made for the master bedroom, the bedroom he'd shared with her mother.

Myna leaned against the wall, insisting they try to coax her out. Myna was wearing cutoff shorts and a tank top. Her curls were matted to her head. Linnet wondered when her sister had last brushed her hair. In the weeks following that horrible night, she'd felt Myna slipping away from her. She was more troubled about what was happening between the two of them than she was about their mother. What she'd figured out, and Myna hadn't, was that their mother had been long gone by then. She'd left them anyway.

"Mom!" She knocked hard. She'd do this for her sister. "If you don't answer, you're leaving me no choice but to force my way in."

Myna's eyes grew wide. Linnet showed her the spare key.

"Maybe we should get Pop," Myna said.

"And tell him what?" Linnet asked. She refused to feel responsible for their mother's sudden relapse. Their mother had brought it on herself by getting involved with that awful man.

Myna looked at her feet.

Linnet continued. "Pop's busy. He has classes to teach. And

don't forget about the grant money he's been working so hard to get. Someone's got to take responsibility around here. I've already booked two rooms for the weekend."

"You didn't!" Myna pushed off the wall. "Mom is in no shape to entertain guests."

"Who said she has to do anything?"

"Then who's going to do it?" Myna asked.

Linnet could always tell which family member was weighing on Myna's mind. Right now, the worried eyes and pouty lips said she was concerned for her sister. Linnet knocked harder. "Mom, can I come in?"

"Leave me alone. Would you, please?" she said from behind the closed door. "Just leave me be."

"How do you expect to feed them?" Myna asked, ignoring their mother's plea. "What are you going to do with them?"

"Don't worry," Linnet said. "I can handle it. How hard can it be to cook breakfast? And I know more about the geese and what there is to do around here, much more than Mom ever did."

But Linnet had been wrong, disastrously so. The French toast had been runny, the coffee too strong. The linens and towels hadn't been washed. The guests had complained, insisting on speaking with an adult. When her mother had appeared, the couple had gasped at the sight of her, driving her back inside the bedroom and deeper into despair.

Her mother had stayed locked inside the room for three more days until Pop had forced her out, carrying her in his arms, putting her in the tub and bathing her.

And all the while, Linnet had blamed herself.

Linnet spent the next ten minutes talking with Walter. He'd heard about the fish on the news. He had every intention of calling. They'd already made arrangements at another lake in the Poconos.

She hung up with Walter and was about to call the lawyer when there was a knock at the door. "It's you," she said to Charlie.

He removed his chief's hat. He couldn't meet her eyes. She knew straightaway it was more bad news.

"What now?" she asked, and stepped aside to let him in.

"I'm here for your dad."

"I don't understand."

He put his hat on the counter. He'd stood in this kitchen so many times before in his uniform, in his regular clothes, as a friend. It was hard to think of him as the enemy. But that's what he was, wasn't he?

"The footprint," he said. "It's the same shoe size your dad wears."

Her heart ricocheted inside her chest. She should've called the lawyer first, prioritized better. What was wrong with her? "Come on, Charlie. I told you before, Pop's footprints are all over the yard."

"Yes, and so are yours and Hank's and Ian's. But the three of you have alibis. And your prints weren't found next to the body," he said, and picked up his hat. "I'm going to have to take him in for questioning."

"You know he couldn't have had anything to do with that man's death." Should she tell Charlie about the professor's alleged affair? Or was she just desperate to point the finger at anyone other than Pop? "What if someone else was in the yard, maybe someone you didn't identify, someone who doesn't live here?"

"We didn't find any evidence of another party." Charlie kept his expression neutral. She couldn't read him. "Now, I assume he's at the guesthouse?"

"Please," she said. "Can't it wait a few minutes? Let him eat breakfast first. I promise I'll bring him to the station once he's done." She pictured Pop scared, childlike, lashing out. She didn't want Charlie or any cop near him. Not without a lawyer present.

Charlie scratched his chin, where a considerable amount of stubble had accumulated. She couldn't remember the last time she'd seen him any other way but clean-shaven.

"Okay," he said, finally. "Under one condition. I want you to give me his shoes, the loafers he always wears." He didn't wait for her to answer and kept talking. "The guy's family is really breathing down my neck. And I don't have to tell you about all the news reporters sniffing around here lately. Hell, even the mayor is pushing for an arrest."

"Don't you need some kind of warrant to take someone's personal property?"

"I have a warrant," he said, straightening his shoulders. "And I can get an arrest warrant if I need it. Do I need it?"

She touched her neck, her throat. "Damn it, Charlie."

"I know," he said, and squeezed her arm, the first sign of compassion he'd shown since walking through her door. "It's killing me, too."

Linnet ran to the guesthouse and flung open the door. Myna was standing in the small living room next to the old armchair, a pile of muddy clothes in her arms.

"Where are Pop's shoes?" she asked.

"By the door," Myna said.

Linnet heard the shower running.

Myna continued. "I left clean clothes out on the bed for him. You didn't have to come down here and check up on us."

"I wish that's what I was doing." She picked up the mud-caked loafers.

"Then what are you doing?"

"Charlie's up at the main house. He has another search warrant. Do me a favor and keep Pop here for another twenty minutes or so until I can get rid of him." She turned to go. "And tell Pop I'm going to clean his shoes for him if he asks. He'll have to wear something else for now."

She hurried out the door to find Charlie on the side of the main house near the driveway and his patrol car. His hat was on his head. He was standing erect, official looking.

She was about to shove the shoes into his hands, but he quickly opened a plastic bag and had her drop them in. "I'm calling a lawyer. You're not questioning him without a lawyer present," she said, and marched toward the house.

"Linnet," he called after her.

She stopped and turned around.

"I just got word there's a town meeting in thirty minutes. It's about the dam and what to do about the fish. I figure all the local business owners will be there, including you."

"What about Pop?" She couldn't be in two places at once.

"Bring him around when you get back." He got in his patrol car.

She had a feeling she'd made a terrible mistake by handing over the evidence he'd needed without ever seeing that warrant.

CHAPTER TWENTY-SEVEN

Jake hopped in his car and headed for the mountain road, making a quick detour before driving to Easton. He rolled the windows down for some fresh air, the radio set to a rock-and-roll station playing Kid Rock's "All Summer Long." Under ordinary circumstances he might've sang along. But today he was on his way to the county coroner's office to pick up a copy of the autopsy report on his father. They wouldn't send him the information until Jake provided identification, proof he was next of kin.

He made his way on the windy road, the arched branches of trees overhead forming a dense green tunnel that blocked much of the sunlight. Shadows crossed the pavement, making odd shapes and forms. It wasn't until he approached the sharp turn, first going left and then veering right, that he pressed the brake and slowed. The tires crackled on the gravel as the car rolled to a stop on the shoulder in the exact spot where he'd broken down, and where he'd sat on the trunk waiting for someone to find him. He couldn't imagine what it must've been like for his father, injured and all alone, wondering if help would come along. Was he conscious, waiting to be found? Or was he unconscious the entire time, never knowing the end was near?

There was only one way to find out. He'd put it off long enough.

He turned the car around and pulled back onto the road, continuing over the mountain the way he came, the little four-cylinder engine chug, chug, chugging up the steep incline, teetering at the top as though he were on a roller coaster before soaring down the hill only to rise up again.

Once in Easton, he located the county coroner's office and parked, slipping his bag with his wallet and laptop around his neck and shoulder. He ran his fingers through his windblown hair, although the bangs fell across his forehead in waves no matter how many times he'd tried to keep them in place. His hands were clammy.

He pulled open the door and stepped inside. A woman sat behind a glass partition. She slid the window open as he approached, as though he were a patient checking in to see a doctor.

"Can I help you?" She gave him a pinched smile.

"I'm here to pick up a copy of a report." He handed her a printed copy of his original request and his driver's license.

"I'll check if it was authorized for release," she said. "You can take a seat." She started closing the glass window, but he held up his pointer finger for her to wait a second.

"Can I get a copy of the toxicology report if there was one?" He assumed there was, since his father had been involved in a single-car accident of unknown cause. "I'll pay whatever the additional cost may be."

"I'll look."

Jake took a seat. His leg bounced up and down. He checked his phone repeatedly. Dennis had sent him an e-mail, something to the tune of, Stop avoiding my phone calls and texts. *One more day*, Jake thought. *Give me one more day.* If he didn't hear from Kim after today, he'd pack up his gear and drive home. Dennis was a friend, but he was also his editor. He didn't want to test Dennis's patience any longer than necessary. It wasn't worth losing his only steady paying gig over.

Or was it?

Probably not.

Or maybe it was.

He'd written freelance articles for local magazines and even made some of the national magazines. It wasn't much money, but he'd managed to pay the bills. His mother had left him a large amount in a life insurance policy he'd never expected. He'd be okay for a while.

He drummed his fingers on his thigh. Waiting. Waiting. Waiting.

Finally, after twenty minutes or more, the secretary returned to her desk and opened the sliding window again. She motioned for him to approach. He crossed the small waiting room in two strides. His pulse spiked.

"The autopsy and toxicology reports," she said in a matter-of-fact tone.

He paid the fee and she passed him the file. He looked at the manila folder in his hand. "Thanks," he said, and slowly turned toward the door. He waited to open the file until he was in the privacy of his car.

The first thing he confirmed was that his father had not been drinking. No drugs or alcohol had been found in his father's system at the time of the autopsy. Jake was relieved. He didn't want to believe his dad could've been so careless. He put the toxicology report aside.

The autopsy report was tough to read through; the precise medical terminology was written to sound technical, clinical, *legal*, as though his father were a criminal or the victim of a crime, an object rather than a human being, a thing rather than a person who had loved ones waiting for him to come home. Jake gleaned from the report that his dad had died from blunt chest trauma. His heart had been compressed between the sternum and spine, his lungs had been punctured. He'd bled internally.

Jake shuffled through the pages. Where did it say what the hell he was doing on the mountain road in the first place? Why couldn't he have just stayed home for once? Why did he have to travel all the time? Why? Why weren't the answers he was seeking in the stupid, blasted medical-jargon-filled file?

He tossed the papers on the passenger seat and wiped his eyes. This was what his mother had avoided all those years, asking the questions that had no answers. Maybe she'd been right all along in her refusal to talk about the accident. It could've driven her crazy, the late nights, turning over all of the unknowns in her mind, but she hadn't let it. She'd insisted on remembering the man he'd been, the good husband. The good father. She'd been lucky to have him for as long as she had. His death had been nothing more than an unfortunate accident.

Jake put the key in the ignition and was about to start the engine when his phone pinged. He pulled the phone from his bag and wasn't surprised when Kim's name appeared. He'd given her number a distinct chime so he'd know immediately when she texted him.

Found it! The phone number belonged to a Henry Jenkins of Mountain Springs. It was a bugger to find. I had to call in a favor or two. You owe me big-time. Ha!

Jake read the text several times. He replied. *Are you absolutely, positively certain you have the right name?*

Of course! What kind of hacker do you take me for?

Moisture collected underneath his arms. He had to wipe his sweaty palms on his jeans. *The best kind. Thanks, Kim.*

Isn't this the guy you interviewed for your article in today's paper?

It appears to be. I'll explain later. Thanks again. He shot off that last text and started the engine. He couldn't believe he'd been sitting across from Henry Jenkins—Dr. Henry Jenkins—just yesterday morning. Questions flooded his mind. They piled up so high inside of him he thought he might choke.

He punched the steering wheel before pulling from the parking lot, making his way toward the mountain road. One thing was certain. Jake was going to track down the old doc and finish what he'd started.

CHAPTER TWENTY-EIGHT

Linnet plopped onto an uncomfortable metal chair in the back of the crowded hall. The mayor and town council sat in cushioned leather chairs behind a long table in the front of the room. Betty Shulman, the town clerk, was situated in the corner ready to record the meeting. A man Linnet didn't recognize talked with the mayor. Most everyone else was familiar. Leo and several of the local fishermen were seated in the front row. Chicky was in the two rows behind them.

She turned to the sound of the door slamming behind her. Al held up his hand in apology. She motioned for him to sit in one of the empty seats next to her. He made his way over, shy and sheepish, taking his place on her right. He sat so close to her they bumped elbows and thighs.

"I stopped by your place earlier to do some trimming," he said. "And I saw Charlie's cruiser in your driveway again."

"I know," she said. "It's all right. With everything going on, I completely forgot about the trees." She'd left Myna and Pop at the kitchen table with bacon and eggs on their plates, their coffee mugs full. She'd pulled Myna aside and made her promise to keep Pop at the house until she got back. "No one's allowed to talk with him. No reporters or cops," she'd said. "And definitely not that journalist."

"Okay," Myna had said.

Linnet had given her a stern look. "I mean it."

"Okay," Myna had said again, and Linnet could've sworn her sister had rolled her eyes.

She had to trust Myna would listen. But she hadn't listened before, and now Linnet wondered if coming to the meeting was a mistake.

The mayor turned his chair toward the table, preparing to address the crowd. The moderator banged the gavel.

"This is going to be an informal meeting." He looked at his constituents. He was young, early forties, only a few years older than Linnet. He was polished in his pinstriped suit, his shined shoes. Despite his slick clothes, his face had a boyish look to it, a face you could trust—or rather, as Linnet saw it, a face for politics.

He continued. "I'd like to hear from the fish and game commission first."

The man Linnet hadn't recognized reached for the microphone positioned in front of him. He explained that the lack of water-control devices in the dam had led to an excess of aquatic weed growth. "And if you account for the decreasing numbers of snow geese in recent years . . ." he paused, possibly for effect, "all these conditions breed an unhealthy and, in this case, fatal, habitat for fish."

His comment created chatter among the crowd. "Is he blaming us?" a woman asked. "So it's our fault?" someone said. The moderator let it continue for a minute before banging the gavel again.

"What do you recommend we do?" the mayor asked.

"Dredge the dam," the representative said.

The crowd exploded, with everyone talking out of turn. The

moderator banged the gavel several times, trying to regain control. Al leaned over and spoke in Linnet's ear. "That's going to cost quite a bit of money," he said.

"Yes," she said, thinking about her local taxes and wondering how much they would go up. And of course, this was what the other small business owners were worried about.

"Who's going to pay for this?" one of the men shouted.

"We are," one of the fishermen said. "Every single one of us. But what other choice do we have?"

"You feel that way because your livelihood depends on that dam," Chicky said. "But what about me? Why do I have to pay for it?"

The moderator stood, banging the gavel, and finally got the crowd to calm down.

"How much are we talking about here?" the mayor asked.

"The first step would be to contact two or three contractors who specialize in dredging and secure bids," he said. "Also, you'll probably want to dispose of the dead fish."

"What if we dredged the dam ourselves?" Leo asked.

"Just tell us how much it's going to cost," a woman hollered.

The conversation went round and round for the next twenty minutes, with most of the discussion focused on money. The bottom line, in Linnet's mind, was that they'd dredge what they could and pay for what they couldn't. Either way, it was going to cost them.

She picked up her purse. "I've heard enough," she said to Al, and stood. He got up and followed her to the door. She felt people's eyes on her back as she slipped out with Al close behind her. Most of the local reporters were in the meeting. Outside, television crews were standing around their vans. They looked up, eying them for a moment before going back to whatever it was they were doing.

"Do you want me to follow you home?" Al asked. "I don't trust all these reporters hanging around."

She smiled. "No, I don't think that's necessary."

He nodded and looked at the ground, mumbling something into his chest.

She touched his arm, thinking he was upset about the town's troubles of late. "It's no one's fault."

He nodded again, shrugging.

"Why don't you come over tomorrow, and we'll take a look at those trees."

"Yeah, okay."

"Let's get out of here."

Al strode to his pickup. She was about to get in her car when she noticed Terry rushing out of the building. He was big and round and moved quickly for his size. She didn't know what made her do it. She was acting on impulse, something she almost never did, but the next thing she knew, she was jogging to catch up with him. She wasn't prepared for what she'd say once she reached him, but she had to say, *to do*, something. Desperation forced her to take action. *For Pop.* She grabbed Terry's arm.

"What the? . . ." He spun around.

"What do you know about Professor Coyle?" she blurted.

"Who?" His face was red and puffy. He looked angry. But if the rumors were true, and his wife had been cheating on him, Linnet supposed he had every right to stomp around town in a huff.

"You know. Professor Coyle." She said the name slow, enunciating each syllable. And then she added, "Donna's friend."

He ripped his arm away. He looked as if he were an animal about to charge. "What do you know about it?" he shouted.

She took a step back, alarmed. "I . . ."

"Stay the hell away from me," he hollered, spit flying. Then he turned and raced down the street. She didn't move for a full two minutes, thinking maybe he did have something to hide.

Linnet and Myna sat side by side on a cold hard bench inside the police station. Myna sat hunched over with her elbows on top of her thighs and her chin in her hands. Linnet sat erect, her eyes on the door through which Charlie had taken Pop along with his lawyer some forty minutes ago.

"What do I need you for?" Pop had asked when Greg Lyons had introduced himself.

"I was hired to represent you." Mr. Lyons was small and thin with soft brown eyes. He wasn't attractive by normal standards, but there was something about him, a calm confidence that drew you to him.

"What do I need you for?" Pop had asked him again.

Linnet had answered. "Charlie has a few questions for you, and I thought it would be best to have someone with you who can help."

Pop had been agitated and confused. Myna had stepped in and rubbed his arm, comforting him. Linnet had slipped her hand in his. But it wasn't until Mr. Lyons had taken his place by Pop's side that Linnet had breathed a little easier. She'd spoken to Mr. Lyons briefly on the phone before meeting him, but she'd felt his competence immediately.

Charlie had escorted the pair into the interrogation room, motioning for Linnet and Myna to wait outside. She'd watched enough television shows about law enforcement to know all about such rooms without ever having to be inside one.

Neither sister had said a word to each other since the door closed behind them. But Linnet wanted to know what was on her sister's mind. She'd been unusually quiet on the ride to the station when Pop asked why they were going to see Charlie, and what it had to do with the dead fish, which led to a discussion about the town hall meeting and dredging the dam.

"You're not thinking about giving Jake another exclusive interview with Pop, are you?" she asked now, keeping her eyes straight ahead on the beige metal door.

"No," Myna said without looking up. "But if I did, I'd make sure it was only to ask him questions about the fish and the dam."

"He's being questioned by the police about *a murder* at this very moment, and you still think it's a good idea to let him talk to a journalist? Don't you care about what happens to him at all?" She was picking a fight, taking out her frustration on her sister. It was a dumb thing to do, a sisterly thing to do.

"Of course I care. But I don't see how helping Jake hurts Pop. And besides, you brought it up. I didn't."

Linnet was about to lay into her sister when the beige metal door swung open and Pop and Mr. Lyons walked out. Charlie emerged behind them. Linnet met Charlie's gaze.

"Let's go," Mr. Lyons said, taking Pop by the elbow and leading him outside. Linnet and Myna followed.

The media was waiting for them in the parking lot. Hugh Huntley rushed toward them, pushing past Linnet and shoving the microphone into Pop's face. "What do you know about the murder of Professor Coyle?"

Mr. Lyons stepped between them, smooth as silk, and said to Hugh in a calm voice, "My client isn't answering any questions at this time."

"Is he a suspect?" Hugh asked. "Is he being charged with murder?"

"No comment," Mr. Lyons said.

They continued to their car, the media falling in step beside them. Linnet and Myna took up the rear. Mr. Lyons opened the front passenger door and helped Pop inside. Myna opened the rear door, looking over her shoulder across the parking lot. Linnet followed her gaze. Jake was headed their way.

"Get in," Linnet said in a harsher tone than she'd intended. Myna did as she was told.

Mr. Lyons slipped his hand under Linnet's arm and guided her to the driver's side door. By this time, the media was dispersing. Someone stopped to talk to Jake. Mr. Lyons whispered into her ear. "I want an IME done on your dad."

"What's an IME?"

"An independent medical exam. He hasn't been charged with anything, but I think we should be prepared."

"He couldn't remember anything, could he?" she asked.

"Your dad couldn't answer one question," he said.

Ian was waiting in the kitchen when they got home. She sensed he was anxious, although based on his body language—leaning against the counter, leisurely holding a coffee mug, his feet crossed in front of him—you would think he hadn't a care in the world. But Linnet knew her husband, felt the tension inside of him despite his casual appearance.

Myna and Pop walked to the table and sat. Perhaps Myna also felt the stress in the room because she purposely kept her head down and avoided making eye contact with anyone.

"Can I get you anything, Pop?" Linnet asked, and poured a glass of cold lemonade from a pitcher and set it in front of him. "Where's Hank?" she asked Ian.

"At the dam," Ian said.

"By himself?" she asked, putting the pitcher down.

"He wanted to be alone," he said. "But now that you're home, you might want to talk with him."

She left through the side door and made her way to the dam. The smell of rotten fish stained the air, the warmth of the sun speeding up the decomposing process. She found Hank lying on the dock, his feet dangling over the side but not touching the water where the fish floated belly-up. It had only been a few days since the geese had been in the same position as the fish.

"Hey," she said. "Do you mind if I join you?"

He didn't answer, but he scooted to his left to make room for her. His bangs fell away from his forehead. The four o'clock sun cast shadows across his freckled nose. They stared at the blue sky and the fluffy cumulus clouds drifting over the mountaintop. Across the dam she could make out one of the old buses that had been carting around the End-of-the-Worlders. The group was quiet at the moment, sitting on blankets in the grass next to the parking lot.

"Are you sure you want to be here?" Hank asked. "It kind of smells."

"I've smelled worse," she said.

"The geese smelled after a few days, too."

"Yes, they did."

He was quiet and then he said, "It's not fair what happened to them."

"No, it's not fair. But that's life, kiddo. And sometimes life isn't fair."

"I guess," he said, and turned his head away.

She leaned on her elbow and gazed at his face, at the seriousness of his expression for someone so young. "I know you're worried about Pop. I'm not going to lie to you. I am, too."

"Did he hurt that man?" Hank asked, and for the first time she saw real fear in her son's eyes.

"I don't know," she said, trying to be as honest as she could.

"But what I do know is that your grandfather would never hurt anyone on purpose."

He nodded, but she wasn't sure he believed her.

"Kids at school say he's crazy."

She pulled him to her, and to her surprise, he didn't push her away. Instead, they lay on the dock, her arm around him, his head on her shoulder. He smelled familiar, his typical boy smell, salty and sweet, and something else she recognized as testosterone, a sign of the changes coming. *Remember this*, she thought. *Remember this moment*. It may be the last she saw of his boyhood.

She placed a hand on her stomach, touching the scar on her abdomen. She hadn't been able to give him a sibling, someone close to his age who he could've counted on, someone who would've always had his back, been his best friend like she'd had with Myna at one time. She and Ian had tried to have another child the first few years after Hank had been born. But all of their attempts had failed, miserably so. After more time had passed, a year, two, then three, it had become an unspoken agreement that it was time to move on.

"They're wrong," Hank said.

"Who's wrong?"

"The kids at school," he said. "Pop's not crazy. He's just different."

She looked at him. "There's nothing wrong with being different." She kissed his forehead without worrying he'd pull away, and he didn't.

The sound of an engine drifted across the water. They sat up to find a news van had pulled into the parking lot. The picketers were no longer sitting but standing, holding their signs in the air. A cameraman fiddled with his equipment while the reporter talked with the small crowd that had gathered around her. She was positioning them in front of the dam, trying to get the shot she wanted for the five o'clock news. Two more news vans pulled into the lot.

"Come on," she said to Hank. "Let's get out of here."

They walked the path through the woods. The wet earth had dried some throughout the day. They stepped over a tree root. Squirrels scampered in the limbs above. She ducked under a low branch of cherry blossoms as they headed up the yard to the side door. A car she didn't recognize pulled into their driveway. Two other vehicles were stopped on the street in front of the house, more reporters looking to cover the latest news. She imagined what the five o'clock news would look like, a shot of the dam first, and then—Now over to you—another reporter standing on the street in front of the B&B discussing the murder of the young professor.

"Go in the house," she said to Hank, and then she strode to the vehicle in the driveway.

Jake got out of the car.

Adrenalin shot through her chest and limbs. She was struck again by his good looks. *My God.* She'd been blind to how much he looked like his father. She felt sick. She lifted her chin. "What do you want?"

He stood by the driver's side door, talking over the roof of the car. "I need to talk to your dad."

She snorted. "Is that so?"

"It's important," he said.

She shot a look to the street where the reporters had gathered. Jake glanced over his shoulder at the commotion behind him.

"You want to talk with my dad," she said. "Well, get in line." She turned away in time to catch Myna flinging open the door and rushing outside.

CHAPTER TWENTY-NINE

Myna stumbled on the steps, finding her footing at the last second, and avoided tumbling to the ground. Hank had said the newspaper guy was back, and he was in their driveway.

Ian followed her outside, joining Linnet at the edge of the yard. Linnet's long lean body was so stiff she could've been mistaken for a pole. A hard cold metal pole. She glared at Myna. Myna glared right back.

"Go back in the house," Linnet said. Ian was already reaching out to put his hand on her shoulder as if to hold her steady.

"No, I will not go in the house," she said, and headed toward the driveway where Jake stood helpless, looking back and forth between them.

Linnet grabbed her by the arm as she passed by. "Yes, you will," she said. There was a look of desperation in her eyes. This was more than Linnet's concern that Myna would say something to harm Pop's case. This was about protecting all of them. Ian didn't know about the connection the sisters had with Jake. No one knew.

Not even Jake.

"I need to talk to your dad," Jake said, addressing Myna specifically.

Myna pulled her arm out of Linnet's grasp and took the last few steps to the edge of the drive. "About the fish?" she asked, hoping he'd say, yes, he wanted Pop's thoughts on the dead fish.

He shook his head. His face was pasty, sweaty. Something was wrong.

"We have no comment," Linnet said, and walked up behind Myna. "Get off my property," she said to Jake, and grabbed Myna's arm again, pulling her away, marching her toward the door. This time Myna didn't resist. Ian was two steps ahead of them.

"I have questions for him," Jake shouted.

Somewhere behind Jake a woman on the street called, "There's the family now. Hello, can we ask you a few questions?"

Myna was almost to the door, Linnet's hand gripped tightly on her arm.

"Dr. Jenkins!" Jake yelled. "Are you in there?"

Ian pulled the door open, motioning them to hurry inside.

"Can you please come out and talk with me?" Jake shouted. "It's about my dad! Warren Mann."

Myna's steps faltered again. Linnet caught her and pulled her through the door. They retreated to opposite sides of the kitchen and avoided looking at each other. *What had Jake meant? Why did he want to talk to Pop about his dad?* Linnet stood at the sink with her back to the room. Pop was alert, watching them.

"What was that about?" Ian asked, leaning against the counter next to Linnet.

Linnet picked up a dirty mug from the sink, dropped it, and picked it up again. "I have no idea what his problem is," she said, and put the mug in the dishwasher.

Hank walked into the kitchen. He was wearing his baseball hat and holding his glove. "Ready, Dad?"

"I forgot about practice," Ian said.

Myna slipped into a chair at the table. She held her head in her hands.

"You need to eat something first," Linnet said to Hank.

While Linnet was distracted, fixing Hank a hot dog and spooning applesauce into a bowl, Pop leaned in close and whispered into Myna's ear, "Does that journalist want to talk to me again?"

She dropped her hands to her lap. So he was aware Jake had been outside calling for him. His whispering meant he was also aware Linnet didn't want him speaking with him. "Yes, he does," she said. "Do you want to talk to him?"

"I can only tell him about the fish. I'm not allowed to talk about anything else."

She searched his face, the gray bushy eyebrows, the skin sagging around his sensitive eyes. How much did her father know about the present? How much did he remember about the past? For the first time, she wondered if his memory loss was intentional, if he'd used it to his advantage when it was convenient.

He reached out and touched her forearm, covering the birthmark. It was then Myna remembered something her mother had once said about him.

Myna returned home after taking her last exam before spring break during her junior year at the university. She'd dumped her backpack onto the kitchen table and grabbed an apple from the refrigerator, biting into it without washing it first. Linnet would have scolded her for her lack of good judgment, for not washing the chemicals from the skin of the fruit before putting it into her mouth. *Too late.* She rubbed the apple on her shirt, shining it up, and took another bite.

Linnet had gotten worse in the last few months, bossing Myna around, telling her to pick up her clothes off their bedroom floor, stomping through the house complaining she was the only one in their family doing all of the cleaning. She'd watched her sister during these tantrums, thinking she'd brought them on herself. She'd never worried about cleaning their bedroom before, the one they'd shared since they were toddlers. But that was then, when her sister had been her best friend. Myna wasn't sure what they were now.

She bit into the apple again. A loud thump came from somewhere in the back of the house. She stopped chewing and put the apple on the countertop. She didn't think Linnet was home. Lately, her sister had been spending all of her free time with her boyfriend, Ian. Myna followed the creaky wooden floor in the hallway, pausing outside of her mother's bedroom door. Pop had stopped sleeping in the main house when she was still in high school, around the same time Linnet had stopped being her friend.

"Mom," Myna said, and opened the door a crack, peeking inside. Her mother sat on the end of the bed, facing the mirror, a hairbrush in her hand.

"Come in," she said.

Myna pushed the door open and stepped inside. The room smelled stale, the air stagnant.

"He tricked me, you know," her mother said, combing the ends of her hair over and over again. She licked her dry lips. "He was my professor. And I was just a kid." She gazed at Myna in the mirror, unblinking as she spoke. "He knew better. I didn't."

She'd been only one year older than Myna was now when she'd married Pop. Myna wondered how she might've reacted if one of her professors had pursued her. There was one teacher in particular in her sophomore year that she'd daydreamed about, fantasized about. It had been a schoolgirl crush.

She imagined herself in her mother's place, sitting in the

canoe on the dam, surrounded by the snow geese, the handsome professor from her sophomore year standing, falling into the water, his clothes wet, searching for the ring, proposing. It was the kind of scene every girl dreamed about, complete with romance and charm. What girl could resist?

But what Myna wanted to know was when her mother had realized she'd made a mistake. Was it before or after the wedding, before or after she and Linnet had been born? Or had it happened around the time her dark days had taken over? She'd never been afraid to ask her mother questions when she was a child and had been naive. But she *was* afraid to ask this woman on the bed, the one who'd been absent much of Myna's life for reasons she hadn't always been able to control. For once, Myna was too scared to hear the answer.

"I shouldn't have told you that. I don't know why I have these thoughts. I don't know why I say these things." Her mother brushed her hair, slowly and methodically, over and over again.

Myna was unsure what to say, so she didn't say anything. Instead, she stood there in the silence, helpless, waiting to be dismissed.

When it became practically unbearable, she left quietly and gently pulled the door closed behind her. She turned and jumped at the sight of Linnet standing in the hallway.

"You startled me," Myna said.

"Sorry," Linnet mumbled, and hurried by.

Myna made her way back to the kitchen and out the side door. She promised herself she'd never be fooled into marrying someone the way her mother had been, wooed by romance, lured to a place she didn't want to be by a man as sweet and smart and charming as Pop. She wouldn't allow her life to be wasted that way. She *wouldn't*. She kicked a stone in the yard, sending it sailing into the woods. She wiped her eyes with the back of her arm.

It was during that same week that Pop had found Myna's mother unconscious in bed. She was rushed to the hospital. Pop, Linnet, and Myna had sat in the emergency waiting room, holding hands. Hours later a doctor emerged from behind the closed doors marked Personnel Only. He'd explained she'd taken pills, mixed prescriptions. It was ruled an accidental overdose.

It wasn't until after the funeral that Myna had found herself walking the path to the dam alone. Pop had retreated to his study, his journals, to mourn. Linnet and Ian had shown the last of the remaining guests, most of whom were Pop's colleagues, out the door. A thin flock of snow geese, stragglers really, milled around. The majority of the birds had already come and gone, making their way north to Canada for the mating season.

She picked up a feather from the ground. It was a contour feather, a wing feather, responsible for supporting the bird during flight. The tip was black, the rest as white as snow. She turned it with her fingertips. If ever she needed a sign, this was it. She'd do the very thing her mother had been incapable of.

She'd leave Mountain Springs, The Snow Goose. And fly away.

"Myna," Linnet said, her jaw set, her features pulled tight. "Can I talk with you alone, please? Now."

Pop removed his hand from Myna's forearm. "I'll just go to my study if you don't mind. It's been a long day," he said.

"Why don't you wait, and I'll walk you down in a few minutes," Linnet said.

He rose from the table. "I'm more than capable of walking myself home."

Home, Myna thought. He'd stopped thinking of the main house as home long before her mother had died. Surely, she knew the reason why. The three of them knew the reason why.

Ian had taken Hank to baseball practice, and Pop left for his study, leaving Linnet and Myna alone.

"What the hell did you say to Jake?" Linnet spat. "What did he mean he wants to talk to Pop about that, that *man*?"

"I didn't say anything to him," she said. "I swear I have no idea where that came from."

"He knows something," Linnet said.

"Whatever he knows, it didn't come from me."

"Maybe not. But you invited him into our lives. You let him talk to Pop. I told you it was a bad idea." Her voice faltered. She turned away.

Myna couldn't recall the last time she'd seen her sister so shaken. She got up from the chair and crossed the room, standing close but unable to reach out and comfort her. "I can find out what he wants."

Linnet's head snapped up. "No," she said. "No way. We have to avoid him. We have to stay as far away from him as possible." She grabbed Myna's hand. "Please, stay away from him."

"Okay," Myna said without much conviction.

"Promise me," Linnet said.

She didn't want to promise Linnet anything until she found out what Jake wanted. It was more than just guilt, regret. It was always that. But Jake was like a burr that stuck to her clothes when she strayed too far from the path to the dam. She couldn't shake him off easily, not when he was a connection, a missing piece to her mother she'd never been able to let go of.

"Promise me you'll stay away from him," Linnet said again, giving her hand a squeeze.

"I promise," she said.

CHAPTER THIRTY

Jake pulled open the door of the Loose Goose and stepped inside. Several men and women were seated at the bar. A few others were scattered around tables. Every single patron turned to see who had walked in.

He eased the door closed behind him. He tried to ignore their staring as he made his way across the room. He found an empty stool in a corner of the bar. It was a good seat, out of the regulars' way, and yet he could see every one of their faces.

Rodney set a cold beer in front of him. "Don't mind them," he said. "It's been a long few days around here, and they're a little skittish with all these reporters around. Don't take it personally."

"Thanks," he said, appreciating Rodney's attempt at a few kind words even though they didn't help much. He couldn't shake the way Linnet had looked at him as though he were the enemy. *But not Myna.* She had wanted to talk with him. He'd learned from years in the newspaper business, from interviewing all sorts of people, who would or wouldn't cooperate. Myna might be his only way to get close enough to the doc to be able to talk with him again.

His phone rang. He recognized the chime and picked it up. "What's going on, Jake?" Kim asked. "Did you see the news?"

"It's about to come on now." The small television at the other end of the bar was turned on, the volume low. The five o'clock news had ended some time ago. An ad for dish detergent played on the screen. The few people scattered around tables had come to stand near the TV, gearing up for the six o'clock news that would replay what everyone had already heard at five and Jake had missed.

"The guy, Henry Jenkins, was questioned by the police today," Kim said. "He's a suspect in a murder investigation." She paused. "Are you involved in some way? It's kind of a huge coincidence you were asking me to find out about a phone number, and then it turns out to be this guy's."

"I can't talk about it right now." He glanced around. "I'm not involved, not directly."

"Are you in trouble?"

"No, at least I don't think so. If I could just talk with him again . . . but the sisters won't let me near him." He said the last part under his breath.

"The who?"

"He has two daughters. They're very protective of him."

Myna had told Jake that her father had trouble remembering things. He'd sensed there had been something off with the doc when he'd been talking with him about the birds. At the time Jake had felt sorry for him. But what if he had something to do with the professor's murder? What if he'd been involved in some way with Jake's father's accident?

"Maybe you should go to the police," Kim said. "I can send the documents verifying who the phone number belongs to.

But you'll have to protect me and my . . ." she coughed, "source, so to speak."

Jake had never questioned how she hacked into computer files, nor had he ever asked who helped her when she couldn't come up with answers on her own. "You have my word."

"So you're doing it? You're going to the police?"

"I think so." He'd take one more shot with Myna and try to get to the doc one last time. The justice system was slow, and once the police and lawyers were involved, Jake may never get the answers he was seeking.

"Please be careful," Kim said.

He liked that she was worried about him. "I'll keep you posted."

After he hung up the phone with Kim, he directed his attention to the TV. The room had grown quiet as the crowd listened to a female reporter broadcasting from the parking lot near the boat launch, the dam in the background. The camera panned out for a full view of the water as well as the stream of picketers chanting and waving signs. Then it zoomed in on the fish, belly-up, the current pushing their bloated bodies against the shoreline. So this was what Myna had been talking about. The place and time for volunteers to meet for the dredging of the dam and disposing of the fish flashed at the bottom of the screen. Jake jotted the information down not only for his article for the paper but also to search for the sisters and the doc among the volunteers.

The camera cut away to another reporter, this one standing on the street in front of The Snow Goose. "Dr. Henry Jenkins was questioned by police today concerning the death of Professor James Coyle." He went on to explain that the investigation was ongoing. The police hadn't released an official statement.

Jake's phone pinged. He looked at the text message. He couldn't believe his luck.

It's Myna. If you still want to talk, text me.

Jake rubbed his hands together, pacing the length of the small, rented room above the LG. Downstairs in the bar he could hear the clinking of glasses, the hum of conversation, the scraping of barstools. He checked his face in the bathroom mirror one last time: clean-shaven, a little puffy around the eyes, otherwise he looked like himself, but the permanent scowl had to go. He shook his shoulders and arms, clearing his face of all expression. *Play it cool, man. Don't scare her off.*

Footsteps sounded on the metal steps of the fire escape. He greeted her at the door.

"Thanks for coming," he said. Their arrangement to meet in his room felt indecent now that she was here. It wasn't anything like that, but if someone saw her coming, if someone saw her leaving, it would look suspicious to an outsider, maybe even scandalous.

Screw it. He didn't care. It wouldn't hurt his reputation. It would only make him look good, proof he was going straight to the source.

He motioned for her to sit, but where? There wasn't a chair in his room, only a bed with an ugly orange bedcover. She sat on the edge of the mattress, tucking her hands between her knees. The collar of her sweatshirt was stretched and worn and hung off one shoulder. He met her gaze, forgetting himself for a moment in her big brown eyes.

"My sister doesn't want me to talk to you," she said. "And, to tell you the truth, I'm not really sure I should. So whatever it is you want, you better ask quick before I change my mind."

"I need to talk with your dad."

She was shaking her head before he'd finished. "No, I can't set that up for you."

"Can't or won't?"

"Won't." She stared at the floor.

Jake noticed her flip-flops, her pink toenails. "I was very young when I lost my dad," he said. "I was barely nine years old." He sat on the edge of the mattress next to her, aware his shoulders slumped. "I'm trying to hold on to the few memories I have of him, but most are bits and pieces of stories my mom told me. I don't know which ones are mine anymore and which ones are hers. And now I don't even have her memories of him." He swallowed the rock in his throat. He hadn't meant to share such private thoughts.

"I'm sorry." She put her hand on his thigh. "But I'm not sure how I can help."

"I think your dad knew him. I'd like to talk to him about how he knew him."

She removed her hand, dropping her gaze to her lap.

"I just want to talk to him. That's all," Jake said.

"I don't see how he could've known your dad. He doesn't have many friends outside of Mountain Springs. The ones he does have are his colleagues. And I'm not even sure you could count those anymore." She touched her forearm, and then pulled the sleeve of her sweatshirt down.

"I didn't say they were friends." Something in Jake's voice shifted, making his words sound more like a growl rather than empathetic. He sensed her body tense up, stiffen, but he couldn't stop himself from continuing in the same gruff tone. "I'm not sure how they knew each other. But they must have. You have to let me talk to him."

"No, I don't." She stood.

"Please," he said, and got up, taking a step toward her.

She backed away from him.

"Then tell me why your father's number is the only one on my dad's phone?" He pulled the scraped, black Nokia from his pocket and showed it to her. "I found it with his personal effects from the night of his car accident."

Recognition registered in her eyes. Fear flickered across her face. She touched her lips, and for a moment she looked as though she were going to scream.

"You've seen this before?" he asked, and took a step closer.

She backed up.

"What do you know about it?"

She blinked. For every step he took toward her, she took one step back until she was against the wall, and there was nowhere else to go.

"What does your dad know about it? Why was his phone number the only contact listed?" He was scaring her, he could see it in her face, but he couldn't stop himself from pushing. "Tell me what you know."

Her phone pinged. She pulled it out. "It's Linnet. I have to go."

Before he knew what was happening, she was racing out the door and down the fire escape stairs.

"Wait!" he called. "What are you hiding?" he shouted.

CHAPTER THIRTY-ONE

Myna ran to her car. The text message had been from Ben, not her sister. He'd saved her, although he hadn't known it. Ben had seen the news about the fish and then, later, the report about her father. He'd been concerned about her. He wanted her to call him.

Her heart flapped as though a thousand snow geese had taken off inside her chest. She gripped the steering wheel, checking once, twice, three times in the rearview mirror that Jake hadn't followed her.

She'd thought she'd been clever, leaving the house only after Linnet had left to check on Pop one last time before bed. Ian had been in Hank's bedroom helping him with his algebra homework. And then there had been the phone calls. How many phone calls had Linnet taken after the news had aired about Pop? It had to have been at least ten, all cancellations for the upcoming weekends at the B&B. No one wanted to rent a room where a suspected murderer lived. The Snow Goose would be empty the next few months. Linnet hadn't shown any emotion about the cancellations one way or the other.

She punched the steering wheel with her palm. She checked the rearview again, seeing a blanket of darkness behind her.

The road dipped and swayed. The full moon shined down from above, but it did little to light the way under the branches of trees. She moved through the black tunnel, guided by the two small headlights of her rental car. She started to sweat.

When she reached the B&B, she pulled into the driveway, parking under the cover of an old maple tree. She cut the headlights and turned off the engine. She breathed deeply and rubbed her eyes, trying to settle down. She needed to collect herself before confronting her sister.

"Linnet," Myna whispered, and tapped on her sister's bedroom door. "Are you up?" She couldn't keep her hands from shaking. She knocked again.

"Hold on." There was the sound of sheets, the creak of the box spring. In the next second, Linnet pulled the door open, wrapping a robe around her.

Myna couldn't remember the last time she'd seen her sister naked, probably not since they were teenagers. Her sister was still muscular, lean.

"What is it?" Linnet asked. "Is it Pop?"

"No."

"What's going on?" Ian asked from somewhere behind Linnet. He made no attempt to get out of bed.

"I just need to talk to Linnet about something," Myna said. "It won't take long." She motioned for her to follow.

Linnet looked over her shoulder and said to Ian, "I'll be right back." She closed the bedroom door behind her. "What's happened?" she asked once they were a few steps down the hall. "You look like you've seen a ghost."

She grabbed Linnet's wrist and led her to the guest bedroom where she'd been sleeping since she'd arrived. There weren't any other guests besides Myna, no one to overhear their conversation on the third floor. Once they were inside her room, she shut the door and put her back against it. "Don't be mad," she said.

"What did you do?"

"It's bad, Linny," she said, her legs starting to tremble. "You were right. And now I have to tell him the truth. He has to know. It's the only way." She couldn't stop from blubbering. "Please don't hate me." She covered her face with her hands.

"What are you talking about? Why would I hate you?" She stepped toward her. "Tell me what you did."

"I saw Jake."

"You did what?" She crossed her arms. "After I specifically told you not to go near him? You couldn't listen to me. You're like a spoiled, rebellious child, you know that? Always doing what you want to do and never thinking about how it might affect other people."

"Me? What about you?" she asked. "You made the decision not to tell." Her voice rose higher. "And I listened to you. That time, I listened to you, and I shouldn't have." Her hands balled into fists at her sides. "He deserves to know the truth."

Linnet was breathing deeply, clearly trying to control her anger. "What did you tell him?"

"I didn't tell him anything." She paused. "I got scared." She stared at her sister. "I wanted to talk with you first."

"What scared you?"

"He has the phone, Linny."

"What are you talking about?"

"The *phone*," she said, and paced around in circles as she talked. "The cell phone. You know." She pulled at her fingers.

"That old Nokia?"

"Ding, ding, ding," Myna said.

"That's not possible. It doesn't make sense. How?"

"He found it with his father's personal effects or belongings or whatever." She stopped pacing and grabbed Linnet's biceps. "Our phone number is on it. Do you understand me now? He thinks Pop had something to do with the car accident."

Linnet covered her mouth and slowly sat on the edge of the bed, the quilt flattening around her.

"Don't you see? We have to tell him the truth," Myna said.

They were silent. The window was open, and a breeze blew into the room. Outside, the crickets chirped. The lightning bugs blinked on and off in the backyard. Birds rustled in the trees. But the geese were absent. There would be no honking to lull them to sleep, no comforting sounds from their childhood, only the memory of one horrible night invading their dreams.

"It's your fault," Linnet said, breaking the silence. "It's all your fault. You let him talk to Pop. And now this happened."

"No, you're wrong." She shook her head. "It's not my fault." She hesitated. "Maybe it is, a little." She knelt on the floor at her sister's feet. She placed her hands on her sister's thighs, the robe silky underneath her fingers. "We have to tell Jake the truth. We owe it to him. We owe it to Mom."

Something dark moved across Linnet's face. Her features turned cold, hard. "I don't owe Mom anything."

Myna removed her hands from her sister's legs. She sat back on her heels. There was so much hatred in her sister's words, so much pain. "Don't you see what this has done to us? This lie. Look what it has done to you and me."

"To you, maybe. Not to me. What did you lose, anyway? *I* became your mother. I was the one who took care of you better than she ever had even on her best days."

"You're right. You *were* a better mother to me." Linnet had taken care of her, had been there every day, all through high school and college, cooking dinners, helping with homework, washing her laundry, doing all the things a mother would do, all the things their mother hadn't been capable of doing. "But I lost something, too, and it was more than losing Mom," she said. "It's something you've never understood."

"What are you talking about?"

"You, Linny. I lost you," she said. "I lost my *sister.*"

CHAPTER THIRTY-TWO

Linnet closed the master bedroom door at the same time Ian turned on the small light on the nightstand. He was sitting up in bed.

"Everything okay?" he asked, and pulled the covers aside to welcome her back in.

She slipped off the robe, letting it fall to the floor, and crawled into his open arms. They spooned. Her back pressed against his bare chest, his legs tucked neatly into the folds behind hers. His arm dangled around her waist. They'd finished having sex minutes before Myna had knocked on their door, disrupting their quiet time in each other's arms. Linnet had reached for him like she'd always done whenever she'd been troubled about something, seeking his love, wanting him close.

"Hold me," she said, needing him now maybe more than she ever had.

He pulled her closer, wrapping his arms firmly around her waist, his breath warm on the back of her neck.

"Tell me what I can do," he said softly into her ear. She linked her fingers through his and closed her eyes. How could she explain to him without admitting what she'd done?

"Whatever happens," he said, "I'll be by your side. We'll get through this together." He kissed the back of her head. "I do love him," he said about Pop.

She nodded. They stayed this way, curled around each other, for some time. Her last thoughts as her eyelids grew heavy were on her sister and the night Jake had lost his father.

Linnet had taken her time on her hair, trying to straighten the tangles of curls. Straight hair was in. She'd seen it in all the magazines, sleek and shiny and sophisticated. She wanted to look older. She had to pass for a college student if they were going to pull this off.

Myna, on the other hand, was lying on her back on the bed staring up at the ceiling, curly hair splayed all around her head. She'd run her fingers through the long, kinky locks earlier. "There," she'd said. "All done. Ready when you are."

Linnet had scoffed, but secretly she'd admired her sister's cavalier attitude about her appearance. Myna had been comfortable in her own skin since they'd been kids, and it hadn't changed even now that her sister was fifteen. The more Linnet fussed over her hair, the less Myna cared about her own.

Linnet put the flatiron down. Myna clasped her hands behind her head. She was singing the words to one of her favorite songs, "All I Wanna Do." Linnet turned the volume up on the CD player and sang along with her, the words perfect for the occasion.

Myna reached across the bed and turned the volume down. "We don't want to wake up Mom," she said.

"Oh, please," Linnet said. "Like I care."

Myna sat up and reached across the bed a second time. She turned off the music. She put her finger to her lips. "Listen," she said before Linnet could protest.

There were sounds coming from their mother's bedroom. It almost sounded like . . . but no, it couldn't be. Was their mother singing? She heard the spraying of an aerosol can, hairspray or maybe perfume. There was more singing, or rather it was more like humming—happy, joyful humming.

"What's she doing?" Myna asked, her eyes wide, worried. "Is she going somewhere?"

"I don't know," Linnet said. "I doubt she's going anywhere. Don't worry." She picked up her blue rattan bag and slung it over her shoulder. *Was* their mother going somewhere? No, *no*, she couldn't be. Since when did she leave the house? Somewhere in the back of her mind she remembered the phone conversation she'd listened in on between her mother and that man, but that had been weeks ago.

She refused to think about it any further. She wasn't going to let it ruin their plans.

If ever there was a night to get out of Dodge, it was tonight, now more than ever. The small town, the petty girls in her class, *her mother*, it was all getting to her. She suspected it was also getting to her sister. Myna had been rubbing her forearm more and more lately, scratching at the birthmark on her arm, a habit she had whenever she was agitated or stressed.

When Myna started picking at her skin, Linnet's decision to go to the college party, the spring fling, was cemented.

"Let's go." She grabbed the car keys from the top of the dresser.

Myna slid off the bed and followed Linnet out of the bedroom.

They were halfway down the hallway when she stopped. "Wait here," she said. "I forgot the phone Pop gave us." She rushed back into the bedroom, plucked the black Nokia from the nightstand, and tossed it into her bag.

CHAPTER THIRTY-THREE

Jake parked his car in the public lot at the dam. The place was nearly filled with pickup trucks, minibuses, and news vans. A light rain made everything wet and muddy. Fog lifted from the water, a white haze amidst the gray. All around him the mountains stood tall, the trees' new green leaves slick from the spring shower.

Several men congregated around the dock and shoreline dressed in rain jackets and waders, holding masks to their mouths and noses to block the stink of rotting fish. Three men who appeared to be in charge pointed toward the dam. A large dredger machine had entered the water at the boat launch. The machine would drag along the bottom, removing the plant life that had choked the fish.

Jake had done his research late last night after returning to the bar after his conversation with Myna. He'd needed a drink. The crowd had loosened up after a few beers. A couple fishermen had even talked with him about their concerns, about what the dredging would cost them. But it hadn't been until the mayor showed up that Jake had gotten his break. The mayor had loosened his collar, had talked to the men and women as though they were pals. Yes, he'd told them, paying to have the dam dredged was going to set the town's finances back. But he'd had no other choice but to contract an outside source to handle the matter. The town's survival had depended on it. How else were they supposed to compete with the other tourist towns if their main attraction—the birds and the fishing—had all gone belly-up?

The taxpayers had voiced their complaints late into the night. By the time the bar closed at 2 A.M., however, most of them had come around to the side of the mayor's decision. It had been damn good politicking on the mayor's part.

Jake gathered enough material to write a decent article, and he'd sent it to Dennis two minutes before deadline. Dennis had texted him immediately afterward. *Okay. But keep in contact.* It had been Dennis's way of saying Jake could stay in Mountain Springs on assignment for at least another day.

Jake wove his way through the crowd of picketers. This time the doomsayers were joined by environmental activists. One of the women holding a sign grabbed his arm as he walked by. He shook her off. "Member of the press," he said, his mood sour.

He passed a carton of masks on the ground and bent down to pick one up. The smell was bad, and he put the mask to his mouth and nose as he made his way over to the men on the dock. When he got closer, he recognized the placard on one man's jacket: EPA, Emergency Management Personnel.

They were discussing the best method to remove the aquatic life, to dispose of the dead fish, safely. The contractor hired by the town—or, rather, by the mayor—assured the EPA he would not be using any chemicals to kill the weeds. He motioned to the dredging equipment, which he argued was an acceptable, environmentally safe option. He also pointed to several men in waders. "These men will remove the weeds by hand in the areas around overhanging trees, where harvesting is difficult."

Papers were exchanged—permits and licenses, perhaps. Jake wasn't close enough to get a good look. But from where he stood, he could see into the crowd. He searched for the doc and his two daughters. Specifically, Myna. He was certain she wasn't telling him everything she knew. She'd been shocked at seeing the old cell phone. He'd go as far as to say she'd been frightened.

But why?

He scanned the crowd again. One of the other journalists waved a friendly hello. She wrote for the paper that covered Monroe County exclusively. He'd shared a drink or two with her on occasion when he'd been on assignment during the winter ski season. What was her name? He couldn't remember. She made her way over to him.

"What do you make of all this the last few days?" she asked.

"It's quite a busy little town."

"Yes," she said, eying a shot of the newest picketers. She was wearing jeans and a windbreaker. Rain splattered her head and shoulders. She pulled up her hood. "Where did you get the mask?" she asked. "It certainly does stink, doesn't it?"

Jake happened to peer across the dam. Emerging from a path in the woods was Myna and the doc. "I gotta go," he said to the woman with the forgotten name, and he took off running for his car.

"Hey," she called after him. "Where are you going? What about the mask?"

Once in his car, he dropped the mask on the passenger seat and started the engine. He beeped his horn several times to get the picketers to move out of his way. He remembered the road around the dam was windy and narrow. He'd have to be careful, but his adrenalin had kicked in. If he could get to the other side in time, he could confront them together. But even as his blood rushed to his head and he pressed on the gas, somewhere in the back of his mind a voice was telling him to go easy on the old doc—and his pretty younger daughter.

Jake prided himself on being a good judge of character, and they didn't seem as though they were bad people. But they were hiding something.

Sometimes the people you least suspected harbored the darkest secrets.

CHAPTER THIRTY-FOUR

Linnet was standing in front of the kitchen sink with a cup of coffee, thinking about what Myna had said to her the night before about losing a sister. How dare she feel as though she'd lost her after everything Linnet had done for her, after everything she'd done to keep their family together? And now, even after sleeping on it, Linnet couldn't shake the indignation of it. Resentment wriggled its way around her heart. It was a terrible feeling, but it was there nonetheless.

She watched the spring shower become nothing more than a drizzle. The gray day was getting brighter as the sun worked to break through the cloudy haze. She sipped from the cup. How did she and Myna get to this place where she was unable to share even the simplest of thoughts, let alone the ones that needed to be said the most?

The back door swung open, and Cora stepped inside. She slipped off her raincoat, hanging it on the hook in the small mudroom. "I saw the local news." She crossed the kitchen and grabbed an apron from the drawer. "I don't believe a word of it. I told my husband it's all a big mistake. I've known your dad for how many years?" She tied the apron behind her back.

Linnet put the coffee cup in the sink and touched her brow. She thought she'd called Cora and told her not to come to work. "It's nonsense," she said.

The little voice in the back of her mind asked, *But what if it isn't?* What if Pop really did have something to do with the young professor's death?

Stop it, she scolded herself. Greg Lyons had said Pop hadn't been charged with anything, that they needed to take things one step at a time and not get ahead of themselves.

"I have some more bad news," she said to Cora. "More guests have canceled. In fact, all of the guests for the next two months have canceled." Saying it out loud sounded so much worse than keeping inside.

Cora wasn't moving. A look of confusion crossed her face and then one of understanding. She started to untie the apron.

"Once all this is behind us, I will get people back here and into the rooms," Linnet said. "And I will need you again. Please say you'll come back."

Cora retied the apron again. "Let me fix you a couple of meals while I'm here. Don't worry about paying me." She waved her hand. "You and your family are going through hard times. It's the least I can do." She put her hand on Linnet's arm. "Let me do this little thing for you. And when this all blows over, you call me."

Linnet closed her hand around Cora's. "Thank you," she said.

They both turned to look out the garden window when they heard voices. Al was in the yard with Pop.

"Excuse me," she said to Cora, and raced outside. "Hey," she called as she approached them.

Al turned around. He twisted the work gloves he was carry-ing in his hands.

"What's going on?" she asked.

"I was trying to talk your dad out of going to the dam. They're going to start dredging, and there are all kinds of reporters around."

"Al has a point, Pop," she said. "Why don't you come up to the house? Cora's fixing some breakfast."

"Would you two stop treating me like a child?" Pop said, and started walking toward the path through the woods.

"Pop!" she called, and rushed to catch up to him. She grabbed his arm so he had no choice but to stop. This time more firmly, she said, "This is not a good idea."

Myna walked outside. Her hair was curlier than usual in the damp air. The rain had stopped finally, but the moisture hung on. She was wearing the same ripped jeans. She leaned in and kissed Pop on the cheek. "Morning," she said, and waved to Al, who stood a few feet away.

Linnet didn't like the tiny seed of jealousy that had sprouted in her stomach watching her sister and father interact so casually in the midst of their troubles. She stood a little taller and touched the side of her head where the hair was pulled tight into a ponytail. "They're dredging the dam this morning, and I was trying to convince Pop not to go," she said.

"Your sister and her lawyer want to keep me locked up in the house."

"He's *your* lawyer, Pop," Linnet said.

"Mine? What do I need a lawyer for?" he asked.

"Come on, Pop," Myna said. "I'll go with you. I'll keep an eye on him," she promised Linnet, and took his arm.

It was a bad idea. And still Linnet let them walk away, watching the two of them take the path until they disappeared from view. Al came up and stood next to her.

"There's no rush on the trees, Al," she said. "There won't be anyone staying in The Snow Goose for a while to pay for the view." She turned and headed back toward the main house. Flashing red-and-blue lights cut across the white siding of the B&B and the cherry blossom trees. The panic she'd been pushing down since the first bird dropped from the sky began to rise inside her chest. She imagined herself walking to the front of the house, screaming, sending the police car away with the sheer volume of her voice. But there she stood, silent, unable to move.

And she waited.

Charlie turned the flashing lights off and got out of the cruiser. He spotted Linnet in the yard on his way to the side door.

"Maybe I should go," Al said in a low voice from behind her.

"Wait," she said. She needed someone by her side. Ian was still in the house getting ready for work. *Hank, my god*, Hank was still home. He was in his room getting dressed for school.

Charlie approached, taking his time making his way over to them, or it felt that way to Linnet, as though time moved in slow motion. He nodded to Al, who dropped one of the work gloves he'd been twisting in his hands. Charlie reached down and picked it up.

"I'll just be going then," Al said, and disappeared around the opposite side of the house where the rose bushes were located, the same bushes he'd trimmed a few short days ago.

"Were the lights necessary?" she asked Charlie.

"I flashed them to warn you," he said, and removed his chief's hat. "I'm here to arrest your dad."

The muscles coiled along her spine. "You're arresting him?"

"I'm afraid I don't have a choice," Charlie said. "Is he in the guesthouse?"

Ian emerged from the main house. He was carrying his brief-case.

"Did you know Professor Coyle had a mistress in town?" she blurted, glancing as Ian approached, the words coming out in a rush. She'd meant to have a conversation with Ian last night about bumping into Terry and how oddly he'd behaved. But then Myna had knocked on their bedroom door, and she'd been so distracted by the conversation with her sister that she'd never gotten around to talking with him about it. She hated having to break his confidence. But she had to throw something at Charlie, force him to see there were other possibilities, other suspects. "And that the professor didn't come straight to the dam that day?" She remembered now. He'd mentioned going somewhere else first, and she'd thought it strange at the time. She continued. "What if he stopped at her house? You'd have to check into it, wouldn't you?"

"Where did you hear this?" Charlie asked, narrowing his eyes.

She shook her head, signaling they'd talk about it later. Ian was two steps away.

"I saw the lights," Ian said.

"He's here for Pop."

Hank came out of the house wearing his backpack.

She said to Charlie, "Please, don't do anything in front of Hank." She turned to Ian. "Take Hank to school. Go to work. I'll text you later."

"I should be here. I'm sure I can find a sub."

"I know, but what I really need is for you to get Hank out of here. I don't want him to see his grandfather getting arrested."

Ian stared at Linnet. "Are you sure?"

"Go," she said to him.

"Text me as soon as you can," Ian said. "I love you."

"I love you, too."

Ian met Hank at the car. She waved and watched them leave. Once they were out of view, she turned back to Charlie.

"Do you have the name of this mistress?" he asked.

"Donna Cowell." Her tongue was thick, swollen with gossip. "She's one of the teachers who works with Ian at the high school. She took a continuing education course at the university recently, and that's how they met. That's all I know."

Charlie nodded and pointed toward the guesthouse. "I'll go and get him now."

"Wait." She was panicking. "There's something else you should know. Yesterday, I ran into Donna's husband, Terry. He looked angry. When I brought up the professor and his wife, he told me to stay the hell away from him. That has to mean something, doesn't it?"

He seemed to consider what she'd said, taking a moment before replying. "I'll look into it. But I've got a witness, one of the reporters from out of town." He hesitated as though he wasn't sure if he should say anything more, and then he added, "He saw your dad with Professor Coyle at the dam not thirty minutes before . . ." He glanced in the direction of the guesthouse.

"He's not there. He's with Myna. They're watching them dredge the dam." Charlie couldn't arrest Pop at the dam, not with all the locals and the reporters across the way. "Let me go and get him," she said.

"I'll go with you."

"No, please, wait here." How many times had she said *please* in the last few days? More times than she'd ever had to before. "He's not going anywhere, and there are so many people around."

He nodded, and she turned to go.

"Linnet," Charlie called.

Her steps faltered, but she didn't respond. She refused to look

back at him. Her strides were long and purposeful and somehow clumsy. There were voices coming from the dam. Two she
recognized. The third had her racing down the path, tripping
on the uneven terrain.

It couldn't be.

But it was.

She stopped short of the water, her feet sinking into the
mud on the embankment. Jake was standing next to the bench
where her sister and Pop were sitting. What the hell was *he*
doing here? The anger in her chest lodged in her windpipe,
white and hot. Dead fish were all around her. Their scales were
shiny, their eyes vacant. She picked one up, feeling its heft,
smelling the horrible scent, the winterkill. It hit Jake in the
shoulder before she realized she'd thrown it.

"What the? . . ." Jake whipped around.

"Get away from them!" she shouted. "Leave them alone."

Myna and Pop both looked stricken. Myna shot up from the
bench first. "What do you think you're doing?" she yelled.

Linnet reached down and threw another fish. This one struck
Jake on the hip. He held up his arms to protect himself.

"Please!" Myna shouted. "Stop it!"

But Linnet had no intention of stopping until she ran Jake off
their property. "Stay away from my family!" she shrieked. She
was vaguely aware of voices bouncing off the water, people
hollering from the other side of the dam. Flashes went off, but
she wasn't registering the light as flash from the expensive news
cameras. She picked up another fish and was about to chuck it
when someone grabbed her arm.

"No, you don't," Charlie said, and pinned her arm behind her
back. He pulled her close, his breath hot in her ear. "You're
making matters worse."

She struggled to get away from him, but his grip on her arm tightened. "Ow," she said.

"Listen to me," Charlie said. "The reporters are taking pictures. You're going to be all over the front page if you don't knock it off right now."

She looked at the crowd across the water. Picketers and reporters and fishermen all stood in silence watching the scene unfold. Charlie relaxed his grip on her forearm, but when she tried to wrestle herself free, he wouldn't release her entirely.

"Do you mind telling me what this is all about?" Charlie asked the four of them.

"I'm glad you're here, Chief," Jake said, and wiped his shoulder where one of the fish had struck him. "I need to have a word with you." He pulled an old, black cell phone from his pocket.

CHAPTER THIRTY-FIVE

Myna rushed to Jake's side and slipped her hand over his, hiding the phone from Charlie's view. "Please, Jake," she said quietly. "Put the phone away."

Pop was up from the bench and walking toward Charlie. "Take your hands off my daughter," he said. And then he said to Linnet, "What in the world has come over you?"

While Pop and Charlie and Linnet argued, Myna seized her opportunity to talk with Jake. "Please leave Charlie out of this."

"Why should I?" Jake asked.

"Do it for me. And I promise I'll tell you everything I know about . . ." She closed her eyes and released a slow breath. "I promise I'll tell you what I know about the phone and your father. But not now. Not here."

"Then when?"

"Meet me tonight. I'll text you the details later. Just promise me you won't talk to Charlie, at least until after you hear me out. I'm begging you."

He stared at her long and hard, as though he were trying to decide if she was pulling one over on him. "Fine," he said. "But you better tell me what the hell is going on. This is your last chance to be straight with me, or I'm going to the police."

"I promise," she said, wondering how in the world she was going to convince Linnet this was the right thing to do, that it was the only option.

"Your sister's crazy," Jake said, and put the old cell phone back in his pocket.

"Yes," she said, and couldn't help but smile a little. In a screwed-up way, it had been good to see Linnet pummel Jake with fish. It reminded Myna of the kind of sister Linnet used to be. Spunky. Fun.

Jake wiped his hip where it was wet and slimy and then swiped his hands down his jeans. He smelled. The whole place smelled.

"What is it you need from me?" Charlie asked, turning his attention away from Linnet and onto Jake.

"It's not important." Jake shook his head. "It can wait."

Linnet glared at both Myna and Jake.

"We're all going to walk back to the B&B nice and civilized," Charlie said. "Does everyone understand?"

Myna nodded and stepped away from Jake, shooing him away. He'd told her and Pop earlier that he'd parked his car up the street from The Snow Goose and had picked his way through the woods to the dam. Myna didn't have to ask why he hadn't taken the path. He'd been trying to avoid Linnet this entire time. "Go," she said to him now. Somewhat reluctantly, he retreated through the woods back the way he came.

"Where's he going?" Charlie asked.

"Let him go," Linnet said. "He's just a troublemaker looking for an inside scoop."

"All right," Charlie said. "Come on." He corralled them

together and ushered them back onto the path. Once they were in their driveway, he read Pop his rights and cuffed him.

"Is that really necessary?" Myna asked.

"It's standard procedure," Charlie said. "I wish I didn't have to do it, but I have to go by the book. I've got a lot of eyes on me right now."

"I'll call your lawyer, and we'll meet you at the station," Linnet said to Pop.

His eyes had clouded over as though he were somewhere else. His spectacles dangled on the edge of his nose. He didn't have a free hand to push them up. Myna did it for him right before Charlie put him in the back of the patrol car.

Myna sat across from Linnet at the kitchen table. They'd spent the afternoon at the police station. Mr. Lyons had advised Pop not to give Charlie a statement, putting an end to any attempt at discovering whether or not he'd been able to remember anything new about the night in question.

The clock on the wall ticked off the seconds, fraying Myna's nerves. Ian and Hank had returned home and walked down to the dam. Hank had wanted to see the dredging equipment. He was taking the news about Pop hard.

"I don't understand," he'd cried, and rubbed his eyes over and over again. "They don't arrest innocent people. And Pop is innocent. Isn't he?"

"Of course he is." Linnet had put her arm around him. "They made a mistake, and his lawyer will prove it."

"But why does he have to stay in jail?"

"The arraignment is set for tomorrow morning," Ian said, and then explained what an arraignment was. "My guess is that Pop will be home in time for lunch."

Myna could tell her nephew was trying hard to fight the tears that kept rolling down his cheeks. She wanted to hold him, wrap her arms around him, comfort him. Linnet and Ian had beaten her to it.

Now, Ian had taken Hank to the dam, and the sisters were left alone together.

Myna pulled the sleeve of her sweatshirt down to cover her arm. She played with the cuff, waiting for Linnet to say something. While she waited, her mind drifted to Ben. He'd been empathetic if a bit careful with his words when she'd spoken to him on the phone. She'd spent most of the time convincing him, or maybe she'd been convincing herself, of Pop's innocence. And now she'd have to tell him Pop had been arrested. None of it felt real.

"Well?" Linnet asked. "Are you going to tell me what the hell that was about with Jake?" She kept her voice down.

Myna put her elbow on the table and rested her forehead in the palm of her hand. "I told you. He wants to know why Pop's number was on what he thinks is his father's phone. And if I don't tell him why, if I don't tell him the truth, he's going to go straight to Charlie." She dropped her hand to the table.

"Well, why the hell was the phone with his father's stuff anyway?"

"I don't know," she said. "I've been trying to figure that out. But I don't think it really matters at this point. Does it?"

Linnet pushed away from the table and stood. She walked over to the garden window and looked out. After a long moment she said, "I'm worried about Pop."

"How do you think he's doing?" Myna asked.

"I don't know." Linnet shook her head. "Charlie promised he'd stay with him overnight. But if Pop gets confused, he'll be scared."

"What if he's having one of his good days, or moments? Would that be worse?"

"Knowing is better than not knowing."

"That's exactly it," Myna said. "Knowing is better than not knowing." But she wasn't talking about Pop any longer. She was talking about Jake.

Linnet turned her head slightly in Myna's direction. "You're going to tell him what we did no matter what I say, aren't you?"

Myna wasn't aware she was picking at her forearm. "We can't let him think it was Pop's fault. Pop's in enough trouble." She paused. "Pop doesn't know Mom was going to leave him. He doesn't know about the affair. If he found out now after all this time, it would destroy him."

Linnet didn't respond for a longtime. Myna watched her sister carefully, checking for signs of anger, bracing for an argument. But her sister's shoulders slumped, her head bowed.

When the silence continued, Myna said the one thing she'd felt all along, the thing she'd believed in her heart. "It was never our decision to make, Linny," she said softly.

Linnet turned around. There was so much anguish in her sister's eyes, Myna could do nothing but look away.

"Okay," Linnet said finally.

"You agree I should tell Jake?" she asked.

"No," she said. "I'm going to tell him."

CHAPTER THIRTY-SIX

Jake paced back and forth in the parking lot of the Laundromat. He'd gone to the LG to change out of his fish-slimed clothes only to find he hadn't any clean ones left. His phone went off. Dennis had already left him half a dozen text messages. This last one was meant to serve as a warning. Dennis expected one last article from Jake about the dredging and another short piece on the recent arrest of the old doc, and then he wanted Jake back covering the Lehigh Valley. Dennis was pissed they'd used the doc as an expert on a previous article about the snow geese. Jake had never known Dennis to use so many exclamation points in one text message before. *It hurts the paper's credibility!!! It hurts your credibility as a journalist!!!*

Kim had sent two text messages. *They arrested the old geezer! Now what are you going to do?* He debated whether or not to get back to her. He didn't have anything new to tell her other than he might've blown his chance to find out the truth from the doc when he'd had the police chief standing right there next to him at the dam.

But Myna had convinced him with her big brown eyes to hear her out first. Had he been suckered by a pretty woman? He hadn't thought so. If there was a woman who had made his heart pound and his palms clammy, it was Kim. So what the hell had he been thinking?

He'd been thinking he could trust her.

Or maybe there was a small part of him, a deeper part, that didn't want to know the answer to the questions he'd been asking— Who was his father outside of the wonderful man his mother had painted him to be?

A cloud had moved in front of the sun, turning the day gray once again. The scent of rain from the morning shower lingered in the air. There was a good chance they'd see more rain before the day ended. April showers bring May flowers and all that crap. A minibus pulled into the lot followed by two smaller vehicles Jake recognized as belonging to the doomsday picketers. Two women piled out of the bus. One of the women carried a large duffel bag similar to Jake's.

"Hi," he said as they approached. Even activists needed clean clothes. But there was something about the group that was different. Whatever spark they'd had earlier in the week had been extinguished.

As if sensing what was on Jake's mind, the woman said, "We're moving on. But, mark my words, this is just the beginning. You'd do best to prepare yourself for Judgment Day." She pulled a pamphlet from her back pocket. "Keep this," she said. "In case you lost the other one."

So she remembered him.

They stopped and watched as a couple of news vans drove past. Everyone was heading out of town now that the drama had ended. The fish were being cleaned up, the dam dredged. An argument could be made that even the young professor's murder had been wrapped up, suspect arrested, nothing new to report. It was time to move on and search for the next big story.

She heaved the duffel bag over her shoulder. He followed her inside the Laundromat to see if the dryer full of his clothes had stopped. It had. He pulled his clean clothes out and tossed them into the bag, then he made his way back to the LG. The place was deserted. Rodney stood behind the bar drying a glass with a dish towel.

"Where is everybody?" Jake asked, checking his phone for messages and the time. It was late afternoon. There were usually a few regulars at the bar getting a head start on happy hour.

"They're all at the dam. I think the whole town is there pulling up weeds and cleaning up the fish. The birds were one thing, but the guys around here won't have anything disrupt their fishing season."

Jake nodded. So it had become a town effort to salvage the fishing season. He told Rodney he'd see him later, and he made his way to the door that led upstairs to his room. Once inside, he changed into a clean pair of jeans and a long-sleeve shirt. Then he sat on the bed—back against the headboard, legs crossed, his cell phone placed directly in front of him—waiting for a text from Myna.

CHAPTER THIRTY-SEVEN

Linnet parked two blocks away from the Loose Goose. She got out of the car. Myna got out with her, and the two of them walked shoulder to shoulder to the bar. The phrase *dead man walking* crossed her mind, but in their case it was *dead sisters walking*.

"Are you sure Jake said the LG was deserted?" she asked.

"Yes," Myna said. "He said we'd be able to talk in private. Rodney told him everyone was at the dam and would be until the sun goes down."

She nodded. She'd heard the men's voices cutting across the water in between the sounds of the dredging equipment. She hadn't dared to return to the dam to do her part in the community's cleanup effort, not since she'd thrown the fish at Jake earlier that morning, and definitely not since Pop had been arrested.

A flock of snow geese honked overhead. Both she and Myna stopped and looked to the sky. They watched the geese fly by and disappear behind the mountain. Only when the birds were out of sight did they continue walking again.

Linnet pulled the door open and held it for her sister to walk through first. She stepped in behind her. Jake was sitting at a table in the corner of the bar. He stood upon seeing them, or rather, he shot up out of his chair upon seeing *her*.

"I gather you didn't tell him I was coming," she said to Myna.

"I thought it was best he didn't know up front," Myna said as they made their way over to him.

Jake pulled his shoulders back. He gazed at Myna, giving her a look that Linnet interpreted as asking what the heck she was doing here. "You're not planning on throwing any more fish at me, are you?" he asked her.

She snorted. "You're getting off easy this time," she said, and laid her purse on the table. "But don't tempt me."

"Let's sit," Myna said. "And please, no more talk about throwing fish." She directed this last statement at Linnet.

Rodney cleared his throat from behind the bar. He flipped the dish towel onto his shoulder. "What can I get you, ladies?"

"Club soda," she said at the same time Myna said, "A pitcher of beer."

Rodney's eyebrows shot up. Then he poured a pitcher of beer and a single glass of club soda.

Linnet pulled out a chair and plopped down on it. Myna and Jake followed her lead. They waited to say anything more until Rodney brought over their drinks.

"Thanks," Jake said to him.

Rodney hesitated a beat or two, eying them up before returning behind the bar. He turned on the small television and continued drying glasses while he stared at the screen. The low hum of the news coming from the tiny speakers was the only sound filling the room.

Jake pulled the old black cell phone from his pocket and tossed it on the table between them. Linnet concentrated on keeping her face neutral. Myna had already started rubbing her forearm. Linnet wondered if her sister was even aware she was doing it.

"May I?" Linnet asked, and pointed to the phone.

"Go ahead," Jake said.

She picked it up and turned it over. The back was full of scratches. She ran her finger over the grooves, the jagged lines rough on her skin. The memory of that night on the mountain road had always been in the dark corners of her mind. Sometimes she'd dream about it, waking up sweaty and frantic. Other times it was as though none of it had been real, the memories more like remnants, broken pieces of a long-forgotten childhood nightmare.

She laid the Nokia down. "It was our phone," she said to Jake. "Mine and Myna's when we were teenagers."

Underneath the table, Myna reached for Linnet's hand.

"Your phone?" Jake asked. "Then how did my father end up with it?"

"I'm not sure exactly," she said. "But I have an idea."

"Go on," Jake said.

She glimpsed at the ring on Jake's pinky. She turned to her sister and looked into her eyes, a look that she hoped said, *I'm doing this for you as much as I am for Pop.* By telling the truth, maybe, just maybe, she and Myna could find their way back to each other. "Let me start at the beginning," she said.

Linnet viewed the mountain road through the headlights, two small orbs piercing a thick curtain of darkness. The hills grew taller, bulkier as the road narrowed, the mountain swallowing her with each tick of the odometer. The tree branches, full with new spring leaves, created a lush green tunnel over the road that was breathtaking in daylight, but now felt ominous and monster-like. Pop had warned about driving over the mountain, how it was treacherous in daytime at best and impossible to navigate at night.

She'd dismissed his concerns, thinking him a worrywart, an apprehensive father with the kind of overdeveloped sense of caution that came with age. He was older than most of the other kids' fathers by at least a decade. *My god, he was in his fifties. Ancient.*

And Linnet, the teenager, wasn't anything like him. She was afraid of nothing. Well, that wasn't altogether true. She was afraid of one thing, more frightened than even Myna knew— Myna, who knew everything there was to know about her. But Linnet wouldn't think about that right now. She wouldn't think about their mother, wouldn't think about where she might be going or whether she would be coming back.

She soared over the winding road, the wind of freedom blowing through her hair. There were boys over the mountain, and not just any boys, but college boys. Excitement fluttered like a thousand butterflies in her stomach. She glanced in the rear-view mirror. Nothing behind her but a stream of darkness. She resisted the urge to check her makeup in the visor mirror, keeping her hands firmly on the wheel. She didn't need to check her face, she decided. Her makeup had come out perfect, not a clump in her black mascara. Her hair was washed and sleek. She'd taken her time on it with the flatiron, sectioning off pieces one at a time until it lay smooth and straight. The low humidity on this particular spring night had kept the frizz away.

She looked over at her sister, taking her eyes off of the road for a second. Myna had stuck her head out the window as if she were a dog, her curly hair blowing in a mess of tangles. Normally, Linnet would've made her sister stick her head back inside the car; beg for her to fix herself up, make herself presentable. But she was in too good of a mood to let Myna's wild appearance bother her. She had a feeling something big was about to happen. She'd felt it in her bones as soon as she climbed into the car, and she still felt it now as they sped down a small hill and crested another, TLC blaring from the tiny speakers, warning their listeners about the dangers of chasing waterfalls.

She braked around a bend, her whole body leaning into the sharp turn. The headlights cut across the woods, lighting the trunks of trees as though cutting them off at the knees. The road straightened for a stretch, then bent to the left before winding its way to the right again. Her stomach dipped and swayed with the back-and-forth motion.

Myna pulled her head back into the car. "Do you have your high beams on?" she asked at the same time Linnet saw something in the road. She slammed on the brake, swerving into the oncoming lane. Myna flew into the dashboard, knocking hard against the plastic interior. The car skidded before coming to a stop. Linnet's first thought was, What was that? and then, Why wasn't Myna wearing her seat belt?

"What the hell?" Myna held her right cheek.

"Are you hurt?" She would never forgive herself if she'd harmed her baby sister.

"I'm okay I think," she said, checking her cheek in the visor mirror. "What happened?"

"I thought I saw something in the road." Linnet was hesitant to look over her shoulder, hoping there was something there and at the same time hoping there wasn't. It could've been the shadows, her eyes playing tricks on her.

Myna looked back for her. "What is that?" she asked.

So there *was* something there. "I'm not sure. Hang on." She put the car in reverse, then back in drive, and in reverse again, making a K-turn like she'd learned to do in driver's education class last summer. Once the car was turned around and they were facing the direction of home, the headlights settled in the opposite lane. "It's a car," she said. It was flipped over on its roof.

"Holy shit," Myna said. "Do you see anyone?"

"No," Linnet said, and pulled on the door handle. "We'd better go check."

Myna grabbed her arm. "Maybe we shouldn't get out."

She hesitated, staring through the windshield, trying to see through the small beams of light.

"I only see one car," Myna said. "What happened?"

"I don't know."

Linnet looked at the road behind her. A few more miles and they would've made it over the mountain to where the college boys and partying awaited. It felt like a test, a turning point in her short life: keep going and be the fun, free-spirited girl she longed to be, or stay and do what she knew was right. "We should get out and see if we can help," she said. She reached across Myna and opened the glove box, grabbing the flashlight Pop had put there for emergencies.

They stepped out of the car, meeting by the front bumper of their Honda coupe. They reached for each other like they always had, linking arms. The light from the Honda's headlights bounced through their legs as they walked closer to the overturned car. Myna pushed against Linnet's side, gripping her tightly. Her sister's breath touched her cheek. Fear emanated from her body. The smell of burning rubber stung the air, or maybe it was the scent of a hot engine or leaking antifreeze. It was darker than pitch, and the small flashlight coupled with their car's high beams weren't enough to pierce it.

"Do you see anyone?" Myna asked.

"Hello!" Linnet called. "Is anybody there? Can you hear me? Do you need help?"

Rustling sounds came from the woods on their right. Linnet swung the flashlight in the direction of the noise, lighting up the trees and brush. Her heart pounded in her ears. "It must've been an animal."

"What if it's a bear?" Myna asked.

"It's not a bear. It was probably just a squirrel or raccoon or something."

"What if it's a skunk?"

"Would you stop? You're not helping."

Something fluttered behind them.

Linnet whipped around. "It's just a goose," she said, relieved, clutching her chest. "Come on." She shined the flashlight back onto the overturned car. Myna squeezed her arm more firmly. They inched closer. Glass crackled underneath their sneakers. A cool breeze blew.

"Hello," she said again. "We're here to help if you need it."

"I'm scared," Myna said as they got closer to the driver's side door.

Linnet shined the light in the front seat. Blood was splattered on the window. They stepped closer and peered in as best they could, but they didn't see anyone inside. Linnet noticed more blood smeared across the blacktop at her feet. She traced the stain with the small beam of light.

Someone moaned.

"There." Myna pointed a few feet away from them. Linnet followed with the light. Not far from the front of the car a man lay on his stomach. Neither sister moved for several long seconds, so frightened by what they saw.

"Are you hurt?" Linnet asked, knowing it was a stupid question. Of course he was hurt. "Is anyone with you?" She shined the light back on the car, looking for signs of a passenger. She didn't see anyone else.

"I'm going to get the phone," Myna said, and unraveled her arm from Linnet's. Pop had given them a cell phone for emergencies. The cost had set him back, but he'd said he'd never get any sleep knowing they were out there somewhere without any way to contact him if they needed to.

While Myna made her way back to the car, Linnet stared at the man on the ground. She shined the light on his legs. He was wearing jeans. His feet were bare. His white T-shirt was smudged with dirt. A puddle of blood pulled around his mouth and neck. His brown hair was stained black from a cut by his temple. He moaned again, the sound gurgling from somewhere deep inside his throat. She took a small step closer, leaning forward to get a better look, to offer comforting words, to tell him that her sister went to get their phone. They'd call for help. But something stopped her. She'd seen him before, recognized the gold ring on his left pinky finger.

She stood up straight, her spine rigid. Her breathing came in rapid bursts.

Myna rushed back with the phone. "My hands are shaking too much. You do it," she said, and shoved the phone at Linnet.

Linnet ignored her sister as she tried to push the phone into her hand. Her nostrils flared, and despite the cool air, the gentle breeze rustling the leaves, she was sweating.

"Here, take it," Myna said about the phone.

The man continued to moan.

When Linnet still didn't take it, Myna said, "Fine, I'll do it myself."

"Does he look familiar to you?"

"What?" Myna asked.

"Do you recognize him?"

Myna leaned in, clinging to her sister's arm for support as though she were afraid of falling on top of him.

"Well?"

"Oh, my god." Myna turned toward her.

Linnet's insides burned. If he wasn't on the side of the road bleeding, she might've spit on him.

"What are we going to do?" Myna whispered.

Linnet knew what she wanted to do, and it wasn't anywhere close to doing what was right.

Myna pushed the phone at her again. "We have to," she said. "Take it."

"No," Linnet said, batting her sister's hand away, knocking the phone to the ground, sending it skidding across the road.

"Now look what you've done!" Myna dropped to her knees, her hands frantically searching the macadam.

CHAPTER THIRTY-EIGHT

Myna focused on Linnet's face the entire time her sister talked. Her sister's monotone voice belied the trembling of her lips, the remorse reflecting in her eyes; all the while she told Jake the events as she remembered them. When Linnet's gaze drifted to her lap, Myna understood her sister had taken it as far as she could. It was up to Myna to finish it.

"You didn't call for help?" Jake asked. His face was pale. He remained still, unmoving, as though he were frozen to his seat.

"We didn't call for help," she said.

"What did you do then?" Jake asked. "You had to have done something. You couldn't have just left him there." His tone was weighted with disbelief, his face contorted into something like incredulity.

Myna clung to her sister's hand. "We fought," she said.

"Why did you do that?" Myna's palms scraped the macadam, unable to see the little black phone in the dark. "Help me find it. We have to call someone." She pulled herself up and yanked the small flashlight from Linnet's hand. Her sister didn't resist, just stood there, motionless, staring where the man lay on the side of the road. He'd stopped moving, or moaning, or whatever it was he'd been doing when they'd first found him.

"We have to go," Linnet said.

"What? No." She shined the light all around, knowing it was futile. How could she find something so small and dark on the blackest of nights?

Linnet grabbed Myna's forearm and squeezed, her nails digging into Myna's skin at the exact spot of her birthmark.

"We have to go," Linnet said again. There was something frightening about her voice. "We have to go *now*," she said, but there were so many more words she'd spoken in their private sister language. *If they leave now, he won't be able to take Mom away.*

Linnet raced to their car. Myna hesitated. Maybe it was too late to save him anyway. But no. *No.* She could've sworn she heard him breathing, a faint feathery sound. *He was breathing.*

"Let's go," Linnet hollered.

Myna took two steps backward. "I'm sorry," she whispered. "I'm so sorry." She turned and joined her sister.

Linnet started the engine and pulled away from the overturned vehicle. While Linnet concentrated on driving, navigating the windy road toward home, Myna held her stomach and rocked. Time became a hazy thing, thick, permeable, the cracks in her sister's logic already filling with doubt.

Finally, *finally*, they arrived home. Linnet pulled into the driveway, and they got out of the car. Their mother ran down the steps of the front porch. She was halfway across the yard when she stopped suddenly. Myna noticed a suitcase in her hand.

"Oh," their mother said. It was clear who she was expecting, and it wasn't them. "Oh."

Silence fell between them. It buzzed in Myna's ears, filling her head, absorbing her thoughts, extinguishing all words.

A strange noise erupted from their mother's lips. It started softly, a hiccup kind of laughing sound growing gradually in volume. She started pulling bobby pins from her updo, the curls falling and bouncing, half up and half down, all around her head. Her laughter became harder, unpleasant. She turned then and slowly made her way back inside the house, leaving the awful din echoing in the night air.

Myna's breathing was heavy, her underarms damp. She clung to Linnet, needing to anchor herself from the sinking feeling of hopelessness pressing on her shoulders.

She wasn't aware of how long she stood clinging to her sister in the driveway. She didn't remember walking to the side door. The lights in the guesthouse were turned on. Pop was busy working in his study, unaware of the events unfolding around him.

They crept through the kitchen and down the hall, pausing outside the master bedroom where they heard sobbing coming from inside.

"Come on," Linnet said, and held Myna's hand, leading her to their bedroom.

They lay on the bed, side by side in the dark room, their hips and elbows touching, their hands firmly clasped together. Myna smelled the sweat on her sister's skin, the scent of nervous odor underneath her own arms.

"So it was true," she whispered. "She was going to run away with him tonight. She was leaving us."

After a long pause, Linnet said, "Well, she can't now, can she?"

Myna let go of Linnet's hand. She reached across the table to touch Jake's arm to offer some kind of comfort. "I know this isn't easy to hear," she said.

"No, it's not." He pulled his arm away.

"I understand you're angry," Myna said. *Why wasn't Linnet saying anything?* Her sister sat rigid in her seat, her spine straight.

"I don't know what I am," he said. His eyebrows knotted together. He seemed to be trying to reconcile everything they'd just told him.

"What do you plan on doing now that you know the truth?" Linnet asked. There was something hard in her tone.

"I don't know," he said. "I just don't know what to make of all of this."

"We understand," Myna said. If she showed him some compassion, maybe he'd understand why they had done what they had. They'd been two scared kids who had made a terrible, awful mistake. If she could go back in time, she'd call 911, she'd stay until help had arrived. She had never been so sorry about anything than she was about this.

"Do you really understand?" he asked. "Do you really get what you both just told me?" His hands were in fists on top of the table. The vein in his neck bulged.

"I think you need some time," Myna said. "Maybe we should go." She stood.

Linnet hadn't moved. "I want to know what you're planning to do."

Myna slipped her hand underneath Linnet's arm. "Come on." She attempted to pull her up. "Let's give him some space."

"What are you going to do, Jake?" Linnet asked, allowing Myna to lift her out of the chair. "We didn't break any laws!" she hollered as Myna continued to pull her across the room and out the door.

CHAPTER THIRTY-NINE

Linnet tossed her purse and car keys onto the kitchen counter. She rubbed the back of her neck where a tension knot had formed. Ian's car was in the driveway. Either he'd decided Hank should miss baseball practice or the rain had decided for him. She imagined Hank was in his room studying, although she doubted he could concentrate.

Myna came to stand beside her. Rain struck the garden window, pattered against the siding.

"We didn't do anything illegal," she said.

"Maybe not," Myna said. "But what we did was still wrong."

Linnet nodded.

They were quiet after that, listening to the rumble of thunder. Finally, Linnet gathered a deep breath and said, "I'm going to tell Ian. He has to hear it from me. I don't want him to hear it from anyone else."

"Do you want me to come with you?"

"No," she said. "I have to tell him myself."

"Tell me what?" Ian asked, stepping into the kitchen with a dour look on his face. His normal relaxed posture gone, the ropy muscles in his arms, in his entire body, were taut. Linnet rarely saw this side of her husband. She turned to confront him.

"I'm going to go to my room," Myna said, and scurried out of the kitchen.

Ian shoved his hands in his pockets. "Why did you tell Charlie about Donna Cowell? I told you it was a rumor. Gossip. You don't know whether it was true."

"It just came out when he showed up to arrest Pop. I panicked. I had to do something."

"Well, while you were off with your sister doing who knows what, I had a little visit from Donna."

"She came here?"

"Yes."

"Where was Hank?"

"I sent him to his room."

"What did she say?"

"First, she said she hated me. And then she said I ruined her marriage."

"Her marriage was already ruined if she was having an affair."

"Maybe, but apparently, she'd broken it off with Professor Coyle that same day."

She'd guessed right that the professor had stopped in town to see his mistress.

Ian continued. "But wait until you hear the best part. Both Donna and her husband were out of town that night for a family wedding. They have alibis." He took his hands out of his pockets and tossed them in the air. "I have to work with her, Lin!"

"I was only trying to help Pop."

"I get why you did it," he said, and lowered his voice. "But why didn't you come to me first? I mean, shit, I was ambushed."

She went to him, put her hands on his chest, and rested her

head on his beating heart. "You're right. I shouldn't have said anything without talking it over with you first."

He stood motionless, unwilling to give in so easily.

She slipped her arms around his waist, clinging to him. "I didn't mean to break your trust in me. I was just so scared for Pop." Pop needed an alibi, and she'd pointed Charlie in a direction that she had no idea would lead to a dead end. What was she supposed to have done? She was trying to keep her family from falling apart.

He sighed heavily. "It's okay," he said. "It's been a stressful few days." He wrapped his arms around her. "But please don't do it again."

"I won't, I promise." She stayed tucked in his arms, his warmth, savoring it for as long as she could.

The rain continued tapping on the house like sticks on a drum. She pinched her eyes closed. She had to tell him the truth. It was now or never. "There's something else you need to know."

CHAPTER FORTY

"Thanks for calling me," Myna said to Rodney. The LG wasn't exactly crowded late at night, but some of the regulars hung around the bar, not willing to leave until last call. Jake was hunched over in a chair at the table in the corner of the room.

"He's been sitting there all night since you left, not talking to anyone, drinking pitcher after pitcher. When I thought he'd had enough and refused to serve him anymore, he got up in my face about it." He motioned to a few tables and chairs that were overturned. "A couple of the guys got a little protective and knocked him around a bit. He's lucky I didn't call the police."

At the mention of the guys, some of them eyeballed her, sizing her up. They had to have recognized her as one of the doc's daughters.

"I'll take care of it," she said about Jake, picking up a chair that had fallen on the floor next to him and setting it upright.

Jake knocked it back over. "Leave it," he said.

She set the chair upright again.

"I said leave it!" Jake yelled.

A couple of the guys from the bar turned around to stare at them.

"Get his things and get him out of here," Rodney said.

One of the guys said, "How about we toss him out for you?"

Myna held up her hand. "That won't be necessary. We're leaving. Right, Jake?" She bent over, trying to get him to look at her. His head was buried in his arm. She placed her hand on his back. "Hey, Jake," she said. "It's time to go. Do you think you can walk?"

He lifted his head. He smelled of booze. His eyes were bloodshot, his left cheekbone red and swollen. It wouldn't be long until it turned black-and-blue. Someone had hit him good. *How dare they?*

"It's time to go," she said again. It took all her strength not to confront the men at the bar who had roughed him up.

He tried to stand, holding his left shoulder where he might've taken another hit, or perhaps he'd fallen.

"I've got you," she said, and helped him walk to the door that led upstairs to his room.

"Pack up his things," Rodney said. "You can settle his bill later. Just get him out of here."

She nodded and helped Jake up the stairs. She had a feeling Rodney was on their side, and his bravado was just for show in front of his regulars. Otherwise, he would've demanded payment for his room right then and there.

Jake leaned on her heavily, his sour breath hitting her in the face.

"You stink," she said.

"Thank you."

She laughed, imagining how ridiculous they must look trying to walk up the narrow staircase together. Once inside his room, he dropped onto the bed, folding his arms over his chest, as still as if he were in a coffin.

She smacked his shin. "Don't you dare pass out on me. We

have to get out of here, and I can't carry you. Now, where's all your stuff?"

"Just leave me alone."

There was a small desk in the corner of the room where his laptop sat beside a manila folder. A duffel bag was on the floor in front of the bed. She went over to the desk to pack up his computer. She picked up the folder and peeked inside, finding the coroner's report on his father, but she didn't read it. She didn't want to know the details of his death. She couldn't bear the thought of Jake's father lying on the road, all the pain and suffering he'd had to endure because of her, because of Linnet. They'd been so young and selfish. They'd been cowards. She wanted to cry out to her mother and tell her how sorry she was, how the child in her hadn't understood the ramifications of her decision, but the adult in her understood her mother's need for help even if it had meant leaving them. She wiped her cheeks.

Jake was leaning up on his elbows watching her.

"My mother was depressed," she said. "And I hated your father for being the person who made her happy." She jammed her finger into her chest. "Why couldn't I make her happy? Or my sister? Or my father? What was wrong with us?" She swiped a tear from her chin.

"I don't know." He got up and stumbled, grabbing the manila folder and shoving it into the duffle bag. "I think I'm going to be sick." He raced to the bathroom, bumping into the wall before dropping to his knees and emptying the contents of his stomach into the toilet.

Voices from the bar traveled upstairs. One of the men shouted profanity. They had to get out of here. She stuffed the laptop into Jake's bag. She picked up a few more of his personal items scattered about the room: a pair of socks, a belt, his car keys. He wasn't driving anywhere tonight. She shoved the keys into the pocket of her jeans. They'd pick up his car tomorrow. She poked her head inside the bathroom. He sat on the dirty tile floor, slumped against the wall.

"Do you think you can make it to my car?"

He nodded. She closed the lid and flushed. Then she reached for his hands and helped him up. They used the fire escape rather than going through the bar. She carried his computer bag and duffel bag. He concentrated on walking, trying not to slip on the wet metal stairs. The thunderstorm that had lit up the sky had eased, but the air was charged. The storm wasn't over. It had just paused to take a breath. The sticky sweet scent of cherry blossoms filled Myna's nose, the pink petals now clumped into wet soggy piles underneath their feet. They reached her rental car. She tossed the duffel bag into the back, laying the bag with his laptop down more gently.

"Where are you taking me?" he asked, resting his head against the back of the seat. His eye was nearly swollen shut from the punch he took on his cheek.

"The Snow Goose," she said.

CHAPTER FORTY-ONE

Linnet lay awake, watching the shadows move across the walls. Outside, the rain had stopped and then started again, pounding the roof for another round. Thunder marched across the night sky. Next to her, Ian snored softly. He'd dozed off some time ago, but only after she'd told him what she and Myna had done.

"I get that you were scared," he'd said, rubbing her back, comforting her. "But *Jesus*, to just leave him there?"

"I know," she'd said, curling her body around his, wanting to disappear in his arms. They were quiet for a longtime until she'd summoned the courage to ask the question to which she'd always feared the answer. "Does this change how you feel about me?"

"What? No, nothing could change how I feel about you."

"Not even this?" she'd asked.

"Not even this," he'd said.

She looked at his face, his fair skin like a halo in the dark. The thing she loved most about him—his acceptance of her faults, *his goodness*—couldn't touch her tonight. What should've brought her closer to him had the opposite effect. His kindness only magnified her shame, as though he'd smeared it on a slide and put it under a microscope.

Shame either belonged to you or it didn't. It couldn't be shared, unless the person had taken part in whatever had caused it in the first place. Ian couldn't understand this, but her sister could. They were feathers of the same bird.

Linnet slipped from underneath the covers as quietly as she could, reached for her robe, and crept into the hall. She paused outside of Hank's bedroom and peeked inside. His arm was flung over his head, his mouth open. If it wasn't for the thunderstorm, she'd hear the same breathy snoring of his father. *I love you*, she said, and pulled his door closed, then pushed it open a crack. She couldn't bear the thought of having him sealed off from her, not completely anyway, for even a second.

She busied herself in the kitchen by making two cups of hot tea. She'd offer her sister something warm to drink. It could be her excuse for going to her room. She could say *I couldn't sleep. I thought maybe you couldn't either*, and hand her a steaming cup of herbal blend. Myna would take it, and they would talk, and maybe somehow, someway, they could start to find their way back to each other.

Linnet grabbed the tea kettle from the stove. She turned toward the counter. Lightning lit up the sky.

A man's face appeared on the other side of the garden window, startling her.

The kettle fell from her hand with a clatter. The boiling water splattered the front of her robe, nearly scorching her skin. She plucked the kettle from the counter and placed it in the sink. She was shaking, straining to listen for any sounds, waiting for the next lightning strike. She didn't have to wait long. Thunder cracked and lightning illuminated the yard. The man was there again. Her hand flew to her chest. She recognized the high cheekbones, the strong jaw. Al.

She hurried to the door and yanked it open. "Al," she called. "Get in here." He appeared from around the corner, a black mass inching his way toward her. When he was close she said, "What in the world are you doing out there?" and grabbed his arm, pulling him inside and out of the storm. "You scared me half to death."

He dripped water onto the floor. His boots were muddy. "I didn't mean to frighten you."

"I was just about to make some tea." She walked back to the sink. She refilled the kettle with water and set it on the stove, wondering whether she should wake up Ian. Maybe he'd heard the commotion and he was already getting out of bed to investigate.

Al sat at the table dripping fresh water onto the wooden floor. She grabbed a couple hand towels from the drawer and dropped them by his feet. She sat across from him.

"It's past midnight, Al. What are you doing here?" The hallway that led to her bedroom and Hank's was quiet. The entire house was silent. No one had woken up. She secured the robe around her waist.

He scratched the stubble on his chin.

She blinked. *Did he hear her?* "Al, what were you doing in the backyard?"

The phone rang. They both started. She got up from the table, clutching her robe at the collar, and picked up the receiver.

"I'm sorry to call so late, but I need to talk with you," Charlie said. He continued before she could ask if this had to do with Pop. "When was the last time you saw Al?"

She put her back to Al and lowered her voice. "What is this about?"

"I'll tell you everything once I find him."

"He's here," she whispered.

"He's there? With you? Now?"

"Yes." She felt Al watching her.

"Don't let him leave. I'm on my way," he said, and hung up.

She put the phone back in the charger. Her movements were slow and deliberate. Her heart thudded against her rib cage. What could Charlie want with Al? She turned around and pointed to the hallway. "I should get Ian."

"No," Al said much too quickly, making her jump. He removed his baseball cap and twisted it in his hands, ringing the water out and onto the table.

She didn't move.

"You're afraid of me," he said. "I can see it in your face."

"Yes," she said, and swallowed. "I am a little. I'm not sure what's going on here."

"I'd never hurt you," he said.

"Then tell me what's going on. I don't understand why you're here in the middle of the night, but if you don't tell me soon, I'm going to get Ian." *And then what?* She didn't know. She glanced at the entrance to the hallway and bedroom where her husband lay sleeping, where Hank's door was ajar.

"I should go," he said, and stood, pushing the chair back and nearly knocking it over.

"No," she said, and reached for him. She had to keep him here, and yet she wanted nothing more than for him to leave. She squeezed his arm, feeling his muscle underneath her palm. "Not yet."

His eyes searched her body through the thin, silky robe.

The side door flew open.

She cried out in relief at the sight of her sister. *But no, not Jake, too.* What was he doing here? Why was Myna propping him up?

Myna froze, clearly not expecting to see Linnet with Al. A thousand questions moved across Myna's face. Linnet was about to say it wasn't what it looked like when Ian walked into the kitchen.

"What's going on?" he asked, wearing only pajama bottoms, his chest and feet bare. There was something accusatory in his tone.

"I . . ." Linnet said.

Al stared at her, twisting his hat in his hands.

"Can I get some help here?" Myna asked, cutting her off, struggling to keep Jake upright.

Ian scooted around the table, past Linnet and Al, and slipped his arm around Jake's waist.

"Let's put him in the guest room next to mine," Myna said. "I should keep an eye on him so he doesn't pass out and get sick and choke or something."

"Someone really did a number on you," Ian said to Jake.

Jake reached up and touched his face. He winced.

"I should go," Al said, and took a step forward.

"Wait," Linnet said just as there was a knock on the door. "That must be Charlie." She rushed to let him in.

Charlie was dressed in uniform. He stepped inside, eying the five of them. Water dripped from the rim of his police chief's hat. Thunder rumbled. The wind blew the rain sideways against the house. Linnet rubbed her arms against the chill prickling her skin. They all seemed to be waiting for someone to speak.

"Why don't you take Jake upstairs," Linnet said to Myna.

"Our friend had one too many," Ian said to Charlie. "He needs to sleep it off."

There was a moment when Jake met Linnet's gaze. She pulled in a sharp breath, fearing he was going to lash out at her and make a scene. But he didn't say or do anything. Instead, he allowed himself to be helped out of the room and upstairs to one of the guest rooms to be dealt with later.

"Al," Charlie said. "I need you to come with me."

Al nodded and wiped his brow.

"What has he done?" she asked.

"Do you want to tell her?" Charlie asked.

Al shook his head.

"Maybe you want to meet us down at the station," Charlie said to Linnet. "I think you'll want to see your dad."

CHAPTER FORTY-TWO

Myna and Ian helped Jake into one of the guest rooms with a little more urgency now that Charlie was downstairs. Neither one admitted to rushing Jake along, but there was an unspoken understanding, a catch of an eye, that said there was no need for Charlie to know what Linnet and Myna had done. It was clear Ian knew everything. The blaming way he'd looked at her as though it had been her fault. Of course he'd feel that way, wanting to believe his wife had had as little as possible to do with the decisions made that night.

"Lie down," Myna said to Jake. "I'll get your bags from the car."

"You might want to grab him an ice pack for that cheek," Ian said.

Jake lay down on the bed, keeping one foot on the floor to stop the room from spinning.

"I'll be right back," she said.

Ian followed her out and closed the door behind him. She opened her mouth to explain her side of the story.

"Stop right there," he said. "You don't have to say another word. It was wrong what you did. I don't like it. I don't like to think about my wife being capable of something so cruel."

"But . . ."

He cut her off. "But I think I understand. At least, I'm trying to." They started walking. "So what's he doing here?" He hitched his thumb, indicating Jake sleeping it off in the guest room.

"He had nowhere else to go."

Ian snorted. "You're going to need to come up with a better reason than that for your sister."

Back in the kitchen, Charlie and Al had gone. Linnet was dressed. She grabbed her purse and car keys. "I'm going down to the station," she said. "It has something to do with Pop, but I'm not sure what. I already called Greg Lyons and told him to meet me there."

"I'll go get dressed," Ian said. "I'm coming with you."

"I'd feel better if I knew you were here in case Hank wakes up." She turned to Myna. "You're not off the hook. You're going to tell me why in the hell you brought Jake back here and your reason had better be good." She left before Myna had a chance to reply.

"What did I tell you?" Ian said, and went to check on Hank, leaving Myna alone.

Myna opened the freezer and pulled out a couple of ice cubes, dropping them in the center of a tea towel. Then she headed outside for Jake's duffel bag and computer. She returned to Jake's room with his bags and the ice. He opened the one eye he could when she walked in.

"Here," she said putting the ice on his swollen cheek. He raised his hand to hold it against his face, and she noticed the ring once again.

"Thanks." His voice was hoarse.

She lay on the bed next to him. It seemed like the right thing to do, to not leave him alone just yet. Two geese sculptures hung on the wall, the male slightly larger, wings spread in flight, flying inches ahead of the female. She thought of Ben. They'd exchanged several texts and one phone call earlier before she'd gotten the message from Rodney to come and pick up Jake. Ben had been supportive, kind, showing his concern for her father. His love for her was in the words he hadn't spoken, and it touched her deeply.

"Did you know that snow geese mate for life?" she asked.

Jake didn't answer. She checked to see if he was asleep. His eyes were closed, the towel full of ice covering his cheek. She reached and turned off the light on the nightstand. She was about to get up and go back to her room when he said, "I think she knew about the affair."

She turned toward him, seeing only the profile of his face in the shadows. "Who? Your mom?"

He removed the ice from his cheek and turned his head on the pillow. They were face-to-face, but they couldn't see each other. Maybe some things were better left said in the dark.

"I think she was trying to protect me from the truth."

She didn't know what to say, but she sensed that he didn't want her to say anything. He put the ice pack back on his swollen cheek.

A few seconds passed. He cleared his throat. "I guess she wanted me to believe my father was a good man. Or maybe that's just what *she* needed to believe." He turned his head away, talking into the empty space in the room. "I guess I'll never really know."

CHAPTER FORTY-THREE

Linnet sat across the table from Charlie in a room that had no windows and was the color of pea soup. Al sat next to her, wringing his baseball cap in his hands. He smelled wet. The muscles in his chest and arms bulged underneath the soggy clothes clinging to his skin. Water dripped from his chin. He'd admitted to standing outside in the B&B's backyard since the thunderstorm had started, lurking, trying to get up the courage to talk with her.

Now he asked her to stay with him. He wanted her to hear it from him first before word got out around town.

Linnet sat motionless, waiting for what was coming next. On the outside, she appeared calm, in control. On the inside, she was screaming, *What's happening here?* She wanted to see Pop.

"I'll get right to the point," Charlie said, finally. "We found fibers from a glove on the pole that struck Professor Coyle. The fibers match your gloves, Al."

Al lowered his head.

Linnet knew Al had always worn work gloves whenever he'd worked at the B&B. They were either on his hands or he was twisting them out of a nervous habit. But this was the first she'd heard about the fibers. "If you knew about the gloves, why did you arrest Pop?"

"I just got the report a couple of hours ago." Charlie rubbed his eye. "All the evidence pointed to your dad at first look. But that's not the case now."

"What about this witness you mentioned who saw Pop and Professor Coyle together?"

"He saw them at the dam. I was hoping Al, here, could fill in the details about what happened afterward."

"He wasn't supposed to be messing with the birds," Al said. "No one was supposed to touch them."

Charlie held up his hand. "Hang on," he said, and slid a sheet of paper across the desk. "This is a written Miranda warning. Read it and then sign here." He pointed to where Al should sign his name.

Al scanned it before signing. Then he started talking fast, as though he couldn't hold the truth inside any longer. "We were arguing. He wouldn't listen to me. He was just so belligerent and cocky. I'm not sure who pushed who first, but the next thing I knew I was wrestling the pole away from him. And then I, I . . ." He faltered.

"And then you what?" Charlie asked.

Al hesitated. "I didn't know he was from the university. Everything happened so fast."

"Did you hit him with the pole, Al?"

Al nodded. He turned to Linnet. "I never meant for your dad to be arrested. I couldn't live with myself knowing I hurt you."

"But what were you doing there at night? Why would you be in the yard?" she asked.

"I wanted to knock down the beehive in one of the maple trees before I set to trimming the branches like you wanted. It's best to knock it down at night when all the bees are inside and less active." He looked at Charlie. "But I didn't get around to it that night because of that guy." He turned to Linnet. "I did come back later though and knock it down for you. Your sister saw me. So you don't have to worry about the bees."

"Al, I'm not worried about some bees."

The door behind them opened and Greg Lyons breezed into the room as if it were the middle of the day and not two thirty in the morning. He set his briefcase down. "I hope you have a very good reason for getting me out of bed in the middle of the night," he said to Charlie.

"I'm releasing Dr. Jenkins," Charlie said.

Linnet cried out in relief. Al sunk down in the chair. Something inside of her broke for him, and it was more than just compassion. She knew all about poor decisions, mistakes, how they could cost you the most important people in your life. "Mr. Lyons," she said. "I'd like for you to represent Al in this matter."

Mr. Lyons looked toward the ceiling as if he were asking some higher power how he'd gotten himself tangled up in this mess. Then he ran his hand down his face. "Okay, let me get this straight," he said to Charlie. "You're releasing Dr. Jenkins, and charging this man, Al, for the same crime?"

"That's right," Charlie said.

"It was an accident," Al said.

"Don't say another word," Mr. Lyons warned, and then he said to Charlie, "I'd like to speak with my client alone."

Charlie stood and motioned for Linnet to follow. "Let's go spring the doc."

Linnet pulled into the driveway of The Snow Goose. She turned toward Pop. He'd remained quiet ever since leaving the police station. "We're home," she said.

"Yes," he said, and slowly got out of the car.

She walked alongside him through the wet grass to the stone path that led to the guesthouse. The rain had stopped. The storm had ended. They took their time, picking their way through the shadows. His steps were stiff and labored. In a few hours, the sun would be coming up.

She opened the front door and flipped on the light. Magazines and papers were strewn about the place. The cushion on his favorite chair was askew. The drawer on the end table had been left open. Signs the police had been rummaging through his things. She'd meant to straighten up after they'd left, but so much had happened between then and now that she'd forgotten.

He walked straight through the bedroom and into the bathroom, closing the door behind him.

While she waited, she picked up magazines and journals, pushed in opened drawers, fluffed the cushion on his favorite chair, and searched his bedroom for his slippers. They were under the bed, and she picked them up and put them where he'd find them in the morning. Next, she laid out his pajamas.

When he came out of the bathroom, she said, "I'll let you get dressed," and stepped out of the room. She was tired. Her neck and back were stiff. But she was so relieved Pop was home, safe inside the guesthouse. She waited until she heard the familiar squeak of the box spring before she went back in to turn out the light. She bent to pull the string on the lamp on the nightstand. He touched her arm and stopped her from turning it off. His eyelids were heavy with sleep.

"Don't be hard on Charlie," he said.

"For arresting you?"

"Yes. He did the best he could with what he had. It's not like the police department is used to these kinds of things, and for that we should be thankful."

She frowned. "I imagine he'll retire after this."

"I imagine so."

"Get some sleep," she said, and was about to turn off the light when he stopped her a second time.

"I didn't mean to scare you. I was just trying to help Al."

"What are saying? You knew he was responsible this whole time?"

"I know that everyone makes mistakes, but it doesn't make them a bad person."

She pulled in a slow breath. "You're not talking about Al, are you?" *No, of course he wasn't.* He was talking about her, about the three of them, wanting love so desperately from a woman who had been incapable of loving them back.

"If I could," he said, "I'd do things differently."

She moved a lock of white hair from his forehead. "Me, too, Pop." *Me, too.*

"And Al," he said.

"Al's going to be okay. He'll get through this. He has a very good lawyer."

"Mmm," he said, and closed his eyes.

She removed his spectacles and set them on the nightstand. Then she kissed his forehead and turned out the light. Her heart was so full of love for this silly old man. "Sweet dreams," she whispered, knowing he may not remember their conversation in the morning, knowing it didn't matter because she would.

Linnet walked back to the main house. The dark clouds had been replaced by the gray haze of morning. She found Myna sitting at the kitchen table. She'd texted her and Ian earlier explaining that Al had been arrested for Professor Coyle's murder, and she was bringing Pop home.

"How is he?" Myna asked about Pop.

"He's sleeping in his own bed, so I'd say he's pretty good."

"No, I mean, how *is* he?"

"Oh." She took a minute to think while she put a pot of coffee on. She smoothed her hair, the ends frizzy from the dampness in the air. Myna's hair was bigger than ever, the curls springing in every direction as if she'd had a wild night. Linnet supposed in ways she had. "Right now, I can manage him. Tomorrow? A week from now, a month, I don't know. I'm taking it one day at a time."

"Will you let me know when it does get bad? *If* it gets bad? Will you keep me updated on how he's doing?"

"Sure." She looked at the floor, noticing the muddy puddle of water under the chair, the towels, where Al had sat a few hours ago. Her week with Myna was coming to an end. An ache swarmed her chest at the thought of her sister leaving.

"So," she said. "Are you going to tell me what Jake's doing here?"

"Rodney called me. I guess he figured we were friends since he saw us with Jake earlier. Anyway, Jake got drunk and stirred up some trouble. You saw his face. Rodney asked me to pick up Jake and get him out of there."

"And you thought it was a good idea to bring him here?"

"It didn't feel right taking him someplace else. Not after everything. I couldn't just dump him off somewhere."

"I can't believe he agreed to it."

"Well, he didn't really have a choice," Myna said, and smiled.

They sat in silence after that, the bond between them twisted and bent, but perhaps not broken, not completely anyway. And somewhere in the quiet, the first rays of sunshine streamed through the garden window, dancing on the floor at their feet. As the light spread across the wooden boards, Linnet felt something opening inside her chest, something that felt an awful lot like hope. It was distant, but it was there.

They continued sitting across from each other quietly. Linnet's thoughts turned to Ian and Hank. They would be waking up soon. She couldn't wait to tell Hank the good news. Pop was home, sleeping in the guesthouse. He'd be so relieved. She'd cook breakfast, and the day would start as though it were any other day, her family together again. Her mind was already working out how to get people back into the B&B, how to get her business back on track.

She was thinking about the snow geese when Jake walked into the kitchen. His clothes were rumpled as though he'd slept in them, and she guessed he probably had. He looked like shit. The bruise under his eye had morphed into something black and purple and ugly.

Linnet stood. Jake stepped back and raised his arms as though he were afraid she was going to strike him.

"Sit," she said.

"I called a cab," he said. "I'll just wait outside." He walked out the side door with the duffel bag and computer bag hanging off his shoulder.

Linnet made a fresh pot of coffee. At the sink, she looked out the garden window. The robins were busy searching for worms. The squirrels raced up and down the trees. Branches were scattered across the lawn, the result of the thunderstorm. Al wouldn't be coming to clean up the yard, and the thought made her sad, but she had no doubt Ian and Hank would pitch in with outside chores until she found a new groundskeeper.

Behind her, Myna said, "Maybe I should go talk to Jake."

Linnet shook her head. When the coffee finished brewing, she poured three cups. "I'll go." She brought one to Jake. He looked at her, surprised.

She shrugged. "It's the least I can do," she said.

"The very least." He was about to say something more, but he was interrupted by the sound of honking.

"The snow geese," Linnet said. "I think they're on the dam." Myna burst outside.

Jake put the coffee down, and the three of them raced through the yard, slipping on the wet grass, weaving their way through the path in the woods, only stopping when they reached the dock. There on the water were the geese—two dozen or more. The flock was landing, breaking to rest before heading farther north, foraging the vegetation that had been thinned by the result of the community's dredging efforts.

Linnet reached for Myna and hugged her tight, joy reaching to the far corners of her heart and beyond. They hugged and laughed as more snow geese arrived, the sound of their wings like a thousand thunderclaps, the honking filling every space of silence.

When most of the flock had settled down, Linnet stepped onto the dock. Several kilometers away, the dredging equipment sat silent. It looked a lot like a piece of farm equipment, half in and half out of the water. There was still work to be done, but as far as Linnet could tell, the fish had been cleaned up. The sun peaked over the mountain. Its warm rays touched her face.

Myna came to stand next to her. Jake lingered somewhere off to their side.

"Look." Myna pointed to the sky. "An eagle."

The geese took flight, a hundred or more flapping wings, the sound like the thunder of beating drums, their honking like a chorus, warning of a predator in their midst. The birds surrounded the sisters and Jake in a blizzard of white. Jake spun around, head tilted toward the sky, an expression of awe on his face. The flock circled back and landed once again for a brief pause of silence, only to rise like a crescendo when the eagle returned.

When the threat disappeared and the geese settled down and the quiet was restored, Linnet said to Jake, "That's what we call the snow globe effect. People pay money to come here in hopes of experiencing what you just did."

"I can see why," Jake said. "That's amazing."

"Yes," Linnet said. "It is."

A man stepped from the path. "Did someone call for a cab?"

Jake raised his arm. "That would be me." He reached into his pocket and pulled out the old black Nokia. He gripped it in his hand, and after some hesitation, he said, "This is yours," and tossed the phone to Linnet.

Linnet turned it over, gazing at the scratches on the back from where it had skidded across the road. Although it wasn't easy, and she was having a hard time swallowing, she said to Jake, "Thank you."

"It doesn't mean I forgive you."

"No, of course not," she said.

He nodded at Myna.

The sisters watched him walk away at the same time Ian, Hank, and Pop emerged from the path. They'd heard the honking and had come to see the birds.

CHAPTER FORTY-FOUR

Myna was in the guest room packing her bags. She needed to be at the airport to catch her flight in two hours. Her cell phone rang. She grabbed it from the dresser, finding a text from Ben. He'd gotten her message about the snow geese returning to the dam, the news of Pop's release. She'd known in her heart Pop was innocent. She'd been so sure of it, sure of him her whole life, so certain of the kind of man he was. But she realized even he had faults, made mistakes. There were no guarantees the person you loved wouldn't come with their own set of flaws and scars. Maybe that was what she hadn't understood. Loving someone was simply about taking a chance and hoping for the best.

I'm coming home, she texted.

Okay, Ben replied. *I'll be here waiting.*

She set the phone down. When she finished putting the last pair of jeans into the suitcase, she zipped it up and set it on the floor. She lifted her chest, feeling a little lighter, freer, now that she'd come to a decision. She wasn't ready to give Ben the commitment he wanted. She needed more time. But maybe, *maybe,* one day she'd take that chance on happily ever after.

Hank was lying on the bed sideways. He was playing a game on the iPad, asking Myna for pointers to help him get to the next level. She wished she would've spent more time with him while she was here. It had been a crazy week, but she needed to return to Florida.

"You'll still Skype me, right?" she asked Hank.

"Duh," he said, and she smiled.

"Maybe when you do, you can ask your mom to join you?"

"Sure."

"Okay, I'm heading down."

"I'll be there in a minute when this game is over."

She wheeled her suitcase down the hall and stairs, stopping when she reached the kitchen. Linnet and Ian were standing at the counter. They stopped talking when they saw her with her suitcase. Pop was sitting at the table, the newspaper spread in front of him. She put her hand on his shoulder. He smelled like the outdoors, fresh from the dam where he'd spent the day watching the geese.

"Did you see this?" he asked. "The test results on the fallen geese are inconclusive." He peered at her over his spectacles. "I stand by my theory. I think it had something to do with the turbulence of that particular thunderstorm that night."

"I don't doubt you," she said, and kissed the top of his head. "I'll see you soon, Pop. I love you."

He covered her hand. "I love you, too, Myna-bird."

"I'll put your suitcase in the car for you," Ian said, and hugged her. "Don't be a stranger," he said, exchanging a glance with Linnet on his way out.

Linnet leaned against the counter, arms folded, wearing her typical khakis and oxford shirt, her hair in another slick ponytail. "I guess you have to get back to Florida," she said.

"Classes start again on Monday." She wanted nothing more than to cross the room and throw herself into Linnet's arms, tell her she was sorry for the distance between them all these years, tell her she wanted them to be the way they used to be with each other when they were kids, best friends, confidantes. Sisters.

"Okay," Linnet said. "Have a safe trip, and let us know you arrived safely."

"I will," she said, and started walking to the door, thinking maybe they just needed more time, hopeful they'd find their way back to each other in the weeks, months, years ahead.

"Wait," Linnet said.

Myna stopped, more of that hope rising inside of her as she waited for whatever her sister would say or do next.

Linnet pulled open a drawer and took out the feather. "I remembered this morning it was here. I didn't mean to take it from you. I don't know what I was thinking." She handed it to her.

"Thank you," Myna said, running her fingers up the soft barbs.

"I'm sorry I went through your things. It was just . . . I was just . . ." She paused. "I was mad at you for shutting me out. I know that's no excuse, but I was hurt, and I'm sorry."

"It's okay," she said, wanting to say so much more—how much she was going to miss her, how much she wanted her sister in her life.

"Do me a favor," Linnet said, and touched the feather in Myna's hand. "And migrate home once in a while."

Myna's words, her love, backed up in her throat. She threw her arms around her sister and finally was able to choke out the words she'd longed to say. "I love you, Linny."

They embraced as though they were ten years old again and nothing had come between them. They held each other with more love and understanding because of all that had.